Sweet Constance

Jane Carlsen

SWEET CONSTANCE
Copyright © 2025 Jane Carlsen
All Rights Reserved.
Published by Unsolicited Press.
Printed in the United States of America.
First Edition.

Attention schools and businesses: for discounted copies on large orders, please contact the publisher directly.

For information contact:
Unsolicited Press
Portland, Oregon
www.unsolicitedpress.com
orders@unsolicitedpress.com
619-354-8005

Book Design: Kathryn Gerhardt
Editor: Kristen Marckmann
ISBN: 978-1-963115-44-4

For Anina and Sam and the farm we called home.

Sweet Constance

1

Connie Sweet lay with her head in the weeds and her ear to the ground. Damp spread like a rumor: from the sleeping bag she was wrapped in all the way to her bones. Cold. But her head didn't hurt as long as she didn't move. She pressed her ear into the rotting mulch of leaves and straw. Beneath the ground, a constant susurration indicated small, secret movement, but when she slapped the earth, sudden effervescence followed. Then silence for a moment before the mysterious static began again, creeping upwards. She dug her hand into the cold soil and clawed out a fistful of worms. Pink and intricately plaited, they entwined one another, moving slowly, exuding a glistening goo that carried eggs and sperm.

Or they would have if Connie had not disturbed them. Now in her palm, they writhed at the shock of sunlight and the fearsome nothingness of air. They moved into her unyielding fingers, finding their way to the dark crevices between but stuck there, still tethered to one another.

"Sweet Constance!"

She was startled to see shiny work boots three feet from her nose. Dew beaded their oiled surface. They were strangely clean, considering the season, and no one called her Constance. She closed her eyes and curled her fist around the handful of dirt. Strong fingers grasped her shoulder and shook her. She remembered she was too thin. She shrugged the hand away and sat up quickly.

"Ms. Sweet. Are you alright?"

"Everyone calls me Connie." Her body awoke when the sleeping bag fell away. She was cold. Her head hurt. She hugged herself.

"I thought you'd fainted."

Connie's eyes were level with the large man's thighs. His jeans were stiff and midnight blue and she did not look beyond them. "People don't faint wrapped in a blanket."

"As long as you're okay." He squatted and peered at her with blue eyes, his tanned face very near her own.

She stared back to demonstrate her level gaze. He was assessing her, going through some medical checklist in his mind. She didn't wipe the mud from her cheeks; she concentrated on the moving soil in her grasp. As she waited, the man's kind expression shifted from concern to humor, but still she wouldn't look away. Not first. The fine wrinkles around his eyes gathered as he began to smile, but the flesh of his brow remained heavy. Connie's forehead contracted too, instinctively mirroring. Caught in his gaze, she felt a sudden panic, and she blinked to come back to herself.

"I was listening to worms." She spoke with exaggerated authority to demonstrate her coherent speech. He rocked back on his heels and stood.

"You can hear worms?"

"Not anymore." She had to squint into the sky now that he was standing. He shifted to block the sun. Connie scrambled to her feet. One worm oozed from between her knuckles and plopped to the ground. "You scared them away."

"Well, I'm sorry." He took a step back. "But I was really afraid there was something wrong."

"Nothing that won't be fixed by you leaving." She returned the teeming fistful of dirt to the earth and pulled the mulch over like a blanket. When she stood up, the man was already walking away.

She watched him grow smaller as he trudged up the grassy hill. Now the worms could relax, and she imagined them traveling down the length of each other, skin to skin, the goo drying slowly, rolling from their bodies like a silk stocking from a leg, becoming, once the worms had finally reached the end of one another, a tiny pearl, translucent and golden. An egg.

2

That morning, in the middle of a reluctant spring, sunlight finally poured from the sky, drenching the oaks right down to the ground. Connie Sweet had laid in bed trying to recall a myth, some story of sacrifice in pursuit of honey. The problem was the honey could not come into the world until the world turned upside down. Well, now the world had turned upside down. Outside Connie's window, honeyed light made the turgid pillows of moss blaze. Sunlight poured down and plants ate it up. Appetite. It was disgusting. Entitled. She had rolled out of bed in pieces: first her feet then her legs. When her hips were almost falling off the edge of the mattress, she heaved herself to standing. The lifeforce was a dreadful, importunate thing. It fueled cancer and made the headless chicken run. It ate its mate.

She clung to the railing as she went downstairs, her ankles and knees stiff in the mornings. Since Cary's death, Connie's friend Ellen had come almost every morning, bringing blocks of cheese and bags of apples, frozen casseroles, and outrageous stories. Ellen would watch Connie eat before herding her outside to walk the roads around their rural neighborhood. But that morning, Ellen's fierce ministrations were claimed by a wayward nephew, arriving later in the day from some unsuitable home in Seattle. Connie had not paid attention to the details.

Sunlight filtered through the trees and flooded Connie's kitchen with hallucinatory effect heightened by the wine she had drunk the night before as she sat on her porch, watching the moon cross a tattered sky. Now the clouds were gone, the sun triumphant, and steam rose from the damp ground. Pressure built. Seeds cracked, buds broke, and insects split cocoons. The grass was now ankle high, and the Indian plum leaned into the house, heavy with fine white blossoms weighted with rain.

Without Ellen there to manage her, Connie felt like a truant. She had her coffee standing up, and then she had dragged the old sleeping bag all the way out to the neglected vegetable garden where she lay down to listen to the unimaginable population of worms. A million bodies mated, a million mouths consumed. But the constant, permeating sound they made probably came from transit, like the oceanic roar of the distant freeway.

Neither freeway nor worms had been audible when Connie and her ex-husband Mike bought their little farm twenty-five years earlier. Then, the small mountain homes of her neighborhood had little value. The place was too steep and rocky for crops and required a slow winding drive to stores. Hermits, survivalists, and back-to-the-landers found common ground sharing tractors and posthole diggers. They thought they could keep it that way. Land-use laws passed in 1973 had established rural zones to protect the agricultural and forest lands. But at the foot of the mountain, where the soil was rich and deep, houses sprouted from oat fields, and mall parking lots crusted over the wetlands near the freeway. That was the lifeforce again, and people were pushed up the mountain seeking nature or solitude or the sense of dominance that comes from a big house with a hundred-mile view. Connie and some neighbors had made a pamphlet for the newcomers. They illustrated poison oak and listed the benefits of nettles; they described watersheds and aquifers and the dangers of large manure piles. A literary neighbor wrote an oddly sexy poem about the soil as a living skin, but no one had the heart to exclude it. Connie still had some of those pamphlets around somewhere, and they shamed her. That effort had also been fueled by the lifeforce, like the cars they drove, the orchards they planted, and the children they had.

Summers got hotter. Vineyards crept up the mountainside, and California vintners began to buy land in Oregon. People started moving to Connie's neighborhood from Palo Alto or Chicago or Beaverton. These new people could purchase all the equipment they needed. There was no reason to visit or receive. They bulldozed the ferns and the thimble berry, the nettles and the red flowering current. Homesteads became estates. Tennis courts. Equestrian arenas. Connie's newest neighbors arrived from France and South Africa, Minnesota and Texas. There was no point in giving them a pamphlet about the forest because they were going to raze it with a team of professionals and a viticulturist from Napa. Not only would they drive heavy equipment over the earth's tender flesh, they would dynamite the rocks beneath. No one could make a pamphlet now; the poems would be violent and pornographic.

3

"I hear you've been alienating the neighbors." Ellen set a bag on the counter and a couple apples rolled out. "Cheese." She waved a large block of cheddar at Connie. It looked appropriate in Ellen's big hand, but Connie knew it would harden and mold in the refrigerator until she threw it away. "Some almond butter too. This is healthy food that you don't have to prepare."

"Thanks."

"I had to go to the store anyway, to stock up for Dylan." Ellen served them each a cup of tea and sat down. "Look at me! Taking care of everyone!" She shook her head and her coarse dark hair, frosted with silver, bounced against the restraint of the red knit cap she wore all winter.

"That man called me Sweet Constance."

"Ha." Ellen blew on her tea. "He thought that bothered you. Your name's listed that way on all the paperwork. He felt bad."

"You two are best friends?"

"He's my nearest neighbor." Ellen polished one of the apples she'd brought and bit into it. "And he's got a Ford pick-up from the sixties. I always wanted an old pick-up."

"He's from Texas."

"Nice people can come from Texas."

But Connie didn't think so.

Connie had sold thirty acres of steep forest and pasture to Otto Walter, who came from Texas although he didn't have a Texan accent so maybe he came from somewhere else first. Her timing was lucky, people said. The sale of the forest allowed Connie to be independent, a status she considered with bitter irony along with the luck of her timing. In the last year, life itself had been relentless in establishing Connie's independence, beginning with her daughter Cary's death of leukemia. Twenty-five years old. Through the horror of the illness, Connie and her husband Mike found they could not face one another, as though in having and losing Cary they were complicit in a crime. The divorce was quickly finished; neither had much to say beyond *I'm sorry.*

Ellen sighed dramatically and let her long-suffering gaze rest on Connie who still slumped over her empty coffee cup. Connie could swear the gaze had actual weight, and she turned away.

"Come on." Ellen pushed the teacup away and stood near the door.

"There's no place to walk." Despite herself, Connie's eyes filled with tears. "The forest is gone."

"It's not gone. You could still walk there if you were nice and made friends with Otto."

The man's face had been too close to her own. She had smelled coffee on his breath. "Aren't you supposed to be taking care of your nephew?"

"He sleeps until noon. Anyway, you're going to take charge of him. We have to talk about that. Put on your shoes."

Ellen charged ahead until Connie's breath became fast and forceful. Heat rose to her cheeks. When they had crested the hill, they settled into a rhythm, and Ellen finally spoke.

"Helping with Dylan is a brilliant plan." Ellen sounded defensive, and Connie knew all at once that no good could come from this. "Only it's not my plan. It's God's plan. If I believed in God. Providence."

Connie came to a complete halt. Ellen never worried about God's plans; her own plans were hard enough to manage. Connie had taught high school science for twenty-five years, but the idea that she might now help with the boy was impossible, improper even, and Ellen ought to know that. Connie understood that cancer was one of life's random tragedies; theoretically, it could happen to anyone, but it didn't happen to anyone. It happened to Cary and such a failure marked you. It wasn't like Connie thought she was cursed, but she was done with children.

"Come on," Ellen urged, turning to walk backward so she could face Connie. "It's the aerobic exercise that helps mood. It's not going to work if you mope along like that."

A cold wind from the west pulled at their hair and jackets. "It feels like February." Connie jogged to catch up, and Ellen turned to walk shoulder to shoulder.

"You know I can't take care of a child," Ellen said more reasonably. In all the time Connie had known her, Ellen had never even cared for a pet. "I already told him he'd be paid fifteen dollars an hour as your farm and environmental assistant. It's the only way I got him to agree to come. I'll pay him, and you'll work him so hard he'll come home and fall right to sleep. We all win."

"He's what? Around eight? That's too young."

"He's fifteen, Connie. You forget how fast other people's kids grow up. I'm going to pay him. You just have to make him to fill out those plant surveys you have the kids do. Keep him busy in the healthful outdoors."

"I quit. I don't teach anymore."

"My sister has gone off the rails." Ellen was stern. "If Dylan doesn't come here, he'll end up in the streets or the foster system. We don't really have a choice."

"We?" Connie felt a rising panic. "What about school? You're going to drive him to town every morning? Pick him up in the afternoon?"

Ellen had her own insurance brokerage and she worked hard, but strictly on her own schedule. She discarded Connie's concern with a wave of her hand. "He hasn't been to school regularly for years. They moved too often for anyone to keep track of him. You can figure out where he is with his education, maybe tutor him a little. Next fall we'll get him enrolled somewhere."

"Ellen."

"He won't give you any trouble," Ellen interrupted. "There, look. A pileated woodpecker."

They stopped at the base of a rotting oak. The top had been whittled to an improbable splinter and the woodpecker drilled like crazy, sifting a cloud of sawdust over the women's heads and shoulders. Connie looked up as directed. For twenty-five years, the natural world had been a bottomless source of inspiration. Now, she couldn't remember why she had ever been interested.

"You and Dylan will get on fine," Ellen said walking on, "and now that's settled, I can tell you the gossip."

"Can we slow down?"

"No. The exercise is good for depression. Just listen: The new guy is kind of appealing."

"I don't want to know anything about him." But Connie was curious; Ellen hardly ever found people appealing.

Ellen dismissed Connie's objection with a shake of her head. "Otto came down to your place because he wanted to invite you to a little gathering he hosted to meet the neighbors."

"Then I'm glad I sent him away."

"We told him you were grieving. He doesn't hold it against you. It was a funny party. He was all prepared to give us a presentation on viticulture if we'd let him. He had charts and soil tests tacked up on the walls. He's sort of cute and innocent." She turned and frowned at Connie. "I'm afraid your rudeness scarred him. But Annabelle is ready to offer comfort."

Ellen placed her hands on her broad hips and tossed her head. The beat-up cap bounced right off, and she picked it up and twirled it. "She was trussed up in tight jeans and cowboy boots," Ellen said over her shoulder. "Otto's sparing no expense, which excited Annabelle, and she started unbuttoning her blouse one sneaky button at a time." Ellen smashed her hat back on and undid the buttons of her own plaid shirt, revealing an ancient AC/DC tee shirt splashed with bleach. She looked down at herself in mock disappointment.

"Are you making that up?" Connie stuffed her hands in her pockets. "Are you trying to distract me with local color?"

"I'm not even exaggerating. But you should have seen it yourself." Ellen rebuttoned her shirt. "Then you wouldn't have to rely on me. By the time the party ended, you could see right down her blouse to her perfect breasts barely contained by her leopard-print, fuchsia-laced bra."

"You're definitely making that up."

"Annabelle is going to help him with his landscaping."

"What's there to landscape?"

Zoning laws did not allow a dwelling on the land. That had been Connie's consolation when she sold. She couldn't really have a neighbor up there.

"Oh," Ellen waved her hand vaguely. "You know how it is when folks move in. Lots of unrealistic plans. Annabelle will help him sort it out."

4

Connie returned from their walk and made lunch, wondering how she could get out of tutoring Dylan. She knew Ellen worried, but Connie's lack of engagement was not the accidental result of depression. Her lack of engagement was deliberate and studied, and Connie did not intend to change course. But if she managed to *look* busy, Ellen might leave her alone and get some other plan from Providence. The problem was looking busy without building on or adding to or shaping the over-burdened world.

All around her, Connie's farmhouse had been worn and softened by generations. The dents and scratches in the woodwork caught the light and made the house glow, and Connie treasured these marks of time. But the house itself was filled with stuff—bright canisters, pretentious serving bowls, souvenir tea towels. Worse than useless, these dust-catching, attention-stealing things. She boxed them up, then she went after the hand-carved spoons, the juicers and graters. While the soup heated, she gathered everything off the counter and piled it near the door to take to Goodwill.

By late afternoon, she had cleaned out all the drawers. At the donation center, she waited in a line of cars, watching the industrious homeowners ahead of her unload their pots and pans and toys and clothes. When her turn came, an attendant met her with a large, wheeled cart, and before the automatic doors slid shut, Connie glimpsed all the full carts inside, as crowded as barnacles. She had taken on the project for Ellen's benefit, and this was a saving grace.

If she had any personal investment, the sight of that room crowded with castoffs might have broken her heart. Stuff changed location. The only thing that really disappeared was life itself.

The next morning, she still felt sour. Her house was immaculate, and Ellen would notice her industry, but then what? She watched hot water filter through the coffee grounds, and its essential morning aroma rattled her. Mornings were dangerous, a time of plans and ambition. Better to be tethered to Ellen and pulled like a kite around the mountain. If Ellen took this nephew on, what would become of Connie?

Outside Connie's kitchen window, the forest she had sold to Otto Walter looked the same as always. A redtail hawk perched at the top of an old fir and surveyed the shallow valley for voles. If Connie had gone to Otto's party, could she have been friendly? To see his maps—free of trees. His soil analyses—free of life. To see Annabelle, avid. Otto, ambitious. Annabelle thought madrones were messy. If she helped him with landscaping, she would have him remove the trees at the head of his drive to make room for an electric gate. They'd grow English ivy over everything to make it look old. Maybe they'd keep the biggest oaks, but Annabelle was fond of outdoor lighting, and it would end by looking like the landscaping around the parking lot of an expensive resort. Someone ought to stop them, and if Ellen thought Connie needed a job, this was something Connie might take on. Alienating neighbors came naturally to her. She finished her coffee and the too-sweet granola that Ellen had included in her bag of rations, then she found the old pamphlets. If she hurried, she might be able to leave a welcome basket before Otto arrived at the work site.

Outside, mist crouched in the low places so the black tree trunks rose from air to air, revealing their earthly origins only when Connie was close enough to smell the funk of their wet bark. Above, the hillside shone in the sun, and beyond its greening pasture, a pale ridge of oak trees deepened to fir forest to the north. She had once owned all she could see (it was a narrow view), but now the hill belonged to Otto. She followed the farm lane south through the shallow upland valley that now comprised her farm. While the drive from Connie's house to Otto's worksite skirted the valley for about two miles, she could reach him in ten minutes on foot by heading south past the wetland and cutting straight up the hill.

She stopped at the barn to throw hay to her flock of sheep. They clamored when they saw her, tripping on their dainty hooves and jostling one another for space at the feeder. They were her last remaining responsibility, but a dwindling one. She hadn't even bred them this year. She dug her fingers into the greasy fleece of the nearest ewe, and as she walked into the thicker fog near the wetland, she kept her hand by her nose to smell the lanolin. When she reached the fence that separated the wetland from Annabelle's backyard, she veered uphill into the steep sunny pasture Otto had purchased. It would easily be converted to vineyard, but the oak grove that crowned the hill would give him some trouble. Most of the trees were too large for the local mills. For all she knew, they would go to firewood. She tried not to think about it. She followed the ridge into the darker forest of Douglas fir. She had walked this path nearly daily for twenty-five years, and the forest floor was still plush with leaves and needles. Mushrooms ruptured the soil as they did every spring. But when she crested the ridge, she spotted the bare swath of Otto's new driveway. She aimed toward that and arrived at a clearing on a knoll facing southeast.

The clearing was wholly unfamiliar. Mount Hood dominated a horizon she had never seen before. Fresh with spring snow and lit by sun, it gleamed like a fancy logo and Connie slowed, feeling alien and uncertain. She looked for landmarks to try to understand what part of the forest Otto had taken to make the clearing, to remember which trees had grown where, but she couldn't orient herself. To the north, Mount St. Helens and Mount Adams were both newly visible and to the south, Mount Jefferson peeked above the distant foothills. Past the raw new shed and the parked equipment, at the end of the narrowing lane, she spotted Otto himself, in white pajamas that dazzled as brightly as the iconic mountain. He moved with slow fluid constancy in front of a large tipi that rose from a deck so new Connie could smell the wood. She stopped in the shadow of a bushy young fir, confused by the pantomime and reluctant to interrupt the movement. Each gesture flowed from the previous gesture as though it were the only possible recourse. It took Connie a moment to realize he must be practicing Tai Chi.

She should have left then. But the strange fluidity kept her spellbound. He rose and then squatted, his arms lifting and falling like waves on the ocean. At the apogee of each gesture he paused, just for a heartbeat, a brief culmination before the completed gesture dissolved into the next gesture. With his white pajamas and strange choreography, he looked like a wizard, the clockwork of his movements conjuring the money, the vineyard, the vintage pickup, and the neighborhood admirers. Bitterness rose in Connie's throat. She felt an impulse to shriek, something loud and disruptive like the scream of a hawk, but she only watched, rapt, until the moment he stepped his feet together and dropped his hands to his sides. Then he walked to the edge of the deck and peed.

If she brought her basket then, he would know she'd been watching. She was embarrassed by her voyeurism and strangely disturbed by the Tai Chi. Her basket of homemade treats, her pamphlet, and knowledge were worse than irrelevant; they were pathetic. Otto's camp was neat and functional, and he had everything he needed. He disappeared into the tipi and returned with an electric tea kettle which he plugged in to an outlet at the edge of the deck. He would sit in the sun, lord of that wide vista, and plan his new farm, his new friends, and his new life. He thought he was on top of the world, but the world was always turning upside down. As he made tea, Connie slipped back into the woods.

5

Connie walked home slowly, reluctant to unpack the basket and refile the pamphlet. On the edge of the oak grove, she lay down near an old yew tree. Its branches draped around it like a skirt, and a blackberry vine grew high in the tree where some accident had sheared the top. When the tree was a seedling, the fur trappers hadn't arrived in the west, and it would be another hundred years before the European settlers came to the Willamette Valley. The yew lived through homesteading, grazing livestock, and acid rain. It had survived at least two loggings, and it wasn't even very old for a yew. The future is unknowable, too strange to imagine, but Connie knew this: the yew would not survive Otto's vineyard.

Acorn woodpeckers percolated among the oak branches, calling garrulously. When Cary had been about twelve, She and Connie were rear-ended at a yellow light. The driver had charged out to yell at them, his white shirt blotched with coffee. Connie and Cary were still stunned by the impact, and Cary's eyes had widened with fear at the man's anger. Connie rose to meet him, ready to fight, but as she left the car, she was distracted by a large flock of passing geese. She and Cary both turned to look, leaving the man isolated with his fury. When they looked away from the sky, the man appeared small and beleaguered, and Connie heard his peevish complaint without comment as she copied his insurance information. She had listened, nodding until he was spent. Once home, Connie took Cary up the hill to sit beneath these oaks.

"Listen," she had told her. "See if you can hear a moment with no birdsong near or far."

It wasn't easy to let the sound pour in without discriminating. When they thought they'd found a moment of silence, they'd hear a crow in the distance or warbling so constant they had discounted it. They listened for fifteen minutes. When they were done, the crash was all but forgotten. They had strolled home trying to whistle the robin's song. After that day, Cary became a dedicated birder, eventually working at the Bird Sanctuary. Not that she gave Connie credit; she said she didn't remember the crash or their meditation on the hill. Even so, Connie had thought she was a good mother, and her hubris still filled the grove. Hubris haunted every part of her little farm. Each project trumpeted pride and righteousness, but still Cary was gone and when the woodpeckers quieted, minutes would pass in silence. And yet she had come with a neighbor basket and a pamphlet.

Suddenly the birds sprayed from the branches like shattering glass, and fat drops fell from the shaken trees. The birds regrouped in the air above the tree canopy and with an arabesque settled on a branch only for a moment before rising again, bickering and posturing. She shouldn't feel responsible; not for anything. That was more hubris. She was just another animal in the scrim of survival, and life was messy, extravagantly sensitive to circumstances. Everything was contingent, wobbly and surprising, not like the kind of science you explored on a whiteboard with pens and equations. That was Otto. Some kind of mathematician or software engineer, making plans and carrying them out. Living in a tipi, Connie thought with irritation. He wasn't supposed to be living there at all.

She could turn him in. She wouldn't even have to identify herself. She could call the county planning department. They were generally in favor of development and the wealth it brought, but if she tipped them off, they would have to enforce the law. Connie opened the zucchini bread and broke off a large chunk. She ate half and threw the other half out into the grass where jays descended to stalk it with cautious excitement. As she headed home, she imagined Otto packing up his ridiculous tipi. He'd have to move to one of the many apartments that had been sprouting in the village, and it was a safe bet that someone who lived in a tipi would chafe at a tacky suburban apartment. Otto might move all the way to Portland.

But when Connie called, the planning director wasn't interested. It's perfectly legal, he told her, for Otto to camp on his property. The tipi didn't qualify as a dwelling since it had neither a kitchen nor indoor plumbing. *But he's living there*, Connie insisted. *A dwelling is the place you live.* No, a dwelling is a place with both a kitchen and a bathroom, the director said as though he were reading the definition from a book. He wouldn't even make the trip to see for himself. When Connie pressed him, his tone changed.

"Who am I speaking with?" he asked, and Connie, ashamed, hung up without responding.

6

"Move it! Move it! Move it!" Ellen chanted as Connie dawdled on their walk the next morning.

Connie ignored her and continued wading the weedy margin of the road where the grasses brushed her ankles and wet them. Water soaked through her shoes, cold at first but warming gradually. Each footstep squelched, giving Connie something to think about. Ellen circled around and poked her hard in the back.

"You may have all day, but I have work to do."

"I'm not stopping you," Connie said. "Go for it."

Ellen closed her eyes for a moment. Her patience was easily tested. "Just a little faster for your circulation." Ellen waited until Connie caught up, and then she fell in, shoulder to shoulder. "I LEFT my wife in New Orleans, with TWO fat kids and a bottle of beans. LEFT. LEFT. Left, right, left." On each beat, Ellen bumped Connie.

"For God's sake," Connie said, shoving Ellen away. "Go on without me."

"Never. We're going to walk every day until you're fit and healthy."

"I'm fine."

"I'm not doing it for you. You're one of those people who's bound to go somewhere. I'm going to help you get back on track and then I'll ride your coattails. Adventure. Success. Love." At each word, Ellen threw her hands up like she was scattering confetti.

The lane followed the creek and the hills rose steeply from the side of the road. Connie looked up to the narrow sliver of grey sky. It was still too cold for insects. The plants were growing but slowly, knotted and arthritic. In any other year, she might have been impatient with the frigid spring, but this year she was glad for the abeyance. "I don't care about that stuff."

"Which is why you'll attract it. I'm going to tag along and feed at your trough."

Connie had always been athletic, and her bright dark eyes and luxurious brown hair had probably conferred advantages. Ellen, who had never been pretty, claimed it did. But Connie's pretty face had not been a ticket to fortune. Maybe success came easier, but when trouble finally came, she had been wholly unprepared. She stepped up the pace. The more she walked, the easier walking became. Anyway, it filled the mornings.

"I put Dylan right to work." Ellen spoke loudly to pull Connie out of her reverie.

Connie waited several long moments before responding. "Doing what?" She felt a queasy dread.

"Exploring the neighborhood. Looking at plants. Noticing wildlife, although that kid's going to need help. I don't think he even knows what a robin is."

"Great."

"I think he enjoyed being outside. As much as he enjoys anything. He was gone for hours. Anyway, he'll be a good project for you. I thought I'd have him come by your place tomorrow morning. That work?"

"I'm not up to this, Ellen."

"It won't be hard, Connie. Dylan's very responsible in his way. He had to take care of his mother from an early age. Now he needs something wholesome to do, and I'd like to get him back on track for school. I'll send him by tomorrow. We can stop if it doesn't work."

"Ellen, I'm not wholesome."

"Ha!" Ellen's voice cracked the soft spring air and a small wren flew as though from gunshot. "But you're wholesome for other people. You create wholesome conditions."

Wholesome conditions. Her daughter was *dead*. And Cary hadn't died like those young people you sometimes read about, wise beyond their years, full of love and tender sympathy in the face of mortality. No, Cary had been angry, bitter and petulant, and her last months were not only freighted with the sorrow of impending death but were miserable with complaint. *That* had been the result of Connie's conditions.

7

Dylan didn't arrive the next day until after eleven. By that time, Connie had finished feeding the sheep and clearing the manure from the barn. She had just sat down to a cup of tea when she heard sounds on the stairs. She peeked out the window and saw a long-legged spider of a boy, crumpled and cringing on the edge of her porch. His face was mostly hidden in a big black hoodie, but the skin that showed beneath was dewy as a child's. He chewed on his thumbnail as he looked off toward the sheep pasture, and Connie thought he might sneak away. Instead, she heard a quiet knock on the door.

"My Aunt Ellen?" He stood on the edge of the porch near the stairs as though he was sure he'd made a mistake and might have to leave in a hurry. She waited for him to say more, but he didn't speak. His mouth was dull, almost sullen, but the fine muscles around his eyes tightened.

"You must be Dylan." Connie turned and walked back to the kitchen. He might have responded, but she couldn't hear anything beyond the shuffling of his feet as he followed her. She slumped into a chair and traced her finger over the stains that spangled the old table. "Sit down." Connie waved her hand at the opposite chair and closed her eyes a moment.

Dylan pulled the chair away from the table and its legs shrieked on the floor. Connie's eyes flew open. "Sorry." He sat down quickly, as though to subdue it, and slouched deeply into his jacket.

"Ellen says you want to learn about field biology."

"What?" He looked startled, as though she had accused him of something.

"She thinks you should do wildlife surveys."

"I don't even know what those are."

The boy was skinny, but he had the pasty puffy look of someone who didn't eat well and spent all his time indoors. "What do *you* want?"

"Does it matter?"

"To me, yes."

"I want to go back to Seattle."

His nostrils flared slightly, though his face remained mask-like. He reminded Connie of a loose calf, stupid with fear and fixed on escape. One wrong move and he'd bolt, and maybe that would be easiest. She sighed loudly. "I can't help you with that. You have to talk to your Aunt Ellen."

"Aunt Ellen just yells."

Connie didn't want to know the details. "Let's assume you're not going back to Seattle for a while. Do you want to learn about ecosystems?"

He looked at her through his long, childish lashes. They both knew he didn't have a choice. "I don't have anything else to do," he said at last.

"Right." Connie didn't have anything else to do either. She went to the mudroom and rummaged around until she found an old pair of Mike's rubber boots. "What size are your feet?"

"I don't know." He followed her into the little room. It was one of the few places she hadn't yet cleaned. Work clothes moldered on the bench mixed up with clippers and seed packets and small hard dirt clods that dried and fell from the muddy gloves like little nuts. She handed him one of Mike's old jackets, and Dylan dangled the red plaid fleece from the ends of his fingers. "I don't need this."

Connie looked up. "Your hoodie's not warm enough."

"This is plaid," he said at last.

"So what?"

"I don't wear plaid."

"Ha." Connie stood up. "Look at me." She swept her hand from shoulder to knee, showing off her baggy jeans and the sweatshirt stained with motor oil, the sleeves shot with small tears. She had gathered her brown hair into a ponytail to keep it out of her way, but she no longer considered how she appeared to others. When she brushed her teeth, she didn't stand in front of the mirror but wandered from room to room. "We don't have an audience. Put on the jacket. No one will see you, but if they do, I can promise they won't think twice about the plaid."

"The boots are too big."

They looked like stovepipes on his skinny legs, cartoonish, but Connie didn't even smile. "You can walk?"

"I guess."

"Fine." She opened the back door and led him out to the porch. "See that lane?" She pointed to the gravel drive that led past the sheep barn, past the pasture and straight on to the wetland. "If you follow that to the end, it comes to a wetland area that we're restoring. That's your teacher. Go out there. Look and listen. When you're done, you can leave the boots in here. I might be napping or something, so just let yourself in." Dylan stood there like he might object, so Connie went inside, leaving him on the porch.

They settled into a routine. Dylan got the boots in the morning, and he brought them back in the afternoon. He didn't seem to need anything more. Sometimes their paths crossed, and he shared something from his day—he caught a frog, he saw a heron, his neck was eaten by a cloud of biting gnats. He was earnest and careful as he described his experiences, and Connie saw that he was really paying attention. He'd be gone four hours, six hours even, but he wasn't sullen. He didn't seem bored. On the fourth day, she caught up with him as he left the boots in the mudroom. He had startled when she asked if he was okay. "Fine," he had said too quickly.

"It's not lonely out there?" she prodded. "Are you bored?"

"I'm used to being alone. I like it." He lined the boots up in their corner.

She waited in the doorway as he tied the laces of his canvas sneakers. "Because I could come with you," she offered, "if you wanted to know the names of the plants or animals . . . "

"Whatever." He stood taller than Connie by a foot, but as thin as a shadow. "I'm seeing how many different plants there are. I'm not quite done."

"But wouldn't that be easier if you knew the names?" Then he looked so confused and threatened, actually, that she didn't wait for a response. "Well, whatever."

And so it was settled. His undemanding but periodic presence marked her days and gave their emptiness some structure. Connie had the sense that her lax oversight offered a similar benefit to Dylan. As long as they looked busy, Ellen might leave them both alone.

8

Connie repacked the basket for Otto. She replaced the zucchini bread with a bag of dried pears and, along with the pamphlet, added a note letting him know he might see Dylan around. One morning, not too early, she took the basket back up to Otto's. To avoid any inadvertent spying, she called out as she entered the clearing but there was no response. Otto's vintage pickup wasn't in the drive, although his sports car was. Connie slid her hand along the amber metal where it swelled like muscle over the tires. It was clean considering the dirt and gravel roads of the neighborhood. If he were a real farmer, the creamy leather interior would be smeared with sticky red clay, but if he were a real farmer, he wouldn't spend his money on a car like that. A real farmer wouldn't have the money to spend.

She climbed up to the deck and set the basket next to the entrance to Otto's tipi. Its poles rose some twenty feet and one trailed a string of feathers that moved in the light breeze. Galloping horses, painted like petroglyphs in faded red and black, covered the tipi walls. It was all very tasteful, rustic and quirky. From the front entrance she could see across the narrowly folded ridges to the Willamette Valley beyond, blue with haze. The first evidence of civilization was the flat buildings of Wilsonville, large pale scabs clustered along I-5 some six miles east. Connie remembered driving to visit her grandparents in California on the old winding roads before the interstate was built, its absence now unthinkable. I-5 was the very artery of culture now, supplier even of tipis, ordered online, delivered by truck.

The tipi didn't have a door, just an egg-shaped hole covered by a flap of hide. Connie ducked in and found herself in an attractive circular room. Heavy Indian-style blankets covered the wooden decking, and in the center of the room on a square of slate tile, a small wood stove vented to the apex. A camp chair near a reading light sat next to an old wooden table which held a small stack of books and one book open, a pad and a pen next to it. It was all immaculate, and the open pages of the book, depicting some diagram, were brightly white in the dim room. Beyond the woodstove, a new Pendleton blanket covered a sturdy looking cot. Connie stayed near the entrance. The place looked like a movie set that shouldn't be disturbed.

She hated every bit of it—the anachronism, the western pretensions, the understated wealth—but she especially hated how attractive it was, how cozy it must be to sit by that fire and listen to rain. Irritation came on like a rash. Next to her, near the entrance, a hotplate, the electric tea kettle, pots, and utensils, were stacked on a storage rack with an engineer's precision. Beneath the rack, an antique pitcher and bowl gleamed in the dull light, the porcelain rimmed with tiny trees in forest green. Connie studied the tableau like she was playing a game of concentration. Then she removed everything and dragged the rack to the other side of the door. She replaced the items so that they were a mirror image of what they had been. But not the handle of the handsome pitcher. That, she angled toward the wall, an unlikely and awkward arrangement. She felt lighter walking home, so light she broke into a jog along the ridge trail and reached the pasture's edge in minutes, her heart pounding and her cheeks flushed. She slowed to a moderate pace, just in case Dylan was watching. She would never say a thing, of course, but she thought it was a funny trick and wouldn't Dylan be surprised to know?

9

April arrived but spring did not. Freezing air slipped off the north-pole like a melting ice-cream cone and pooled over the northwest. Days of cold rain interspersed with freezing days of crystalline clarity. Flocks of migratory songbirds scoured the cold pastures for insects, and the bluebirds that lined the fence posts scattered like brilliant scraps of silk when Connie threw hay to the sheep in the mornings. Dylan must have seen them too, but he didn't speak to her any more than he had the first few days. He had not yet come to her with the list of plants. Would it be a list? Where did he learn the names? She left him alone to see what he would come up with. She thought it was a kindness. He had gone through hardships too, and solitude was the natural condition of the wounded.

But one day, as she heard Dylan return the boots, Connie hurried out to the mudroom and almost told him about the prank she played on Otto. She caught herself, and showed instead where to hose the boots, but the impulse shamed her. Her neediness was a mindless hunger, and she didn't want to burden him. She began tracking Dylan's comings and goings more carefully in order to avoid him. One afternoon when their paths nearly crossed outside, Connie pressed into the cover of a large hawthorn where she waited, frozen by perilous thorns and her fear of discovery. The next evening, she hid in her bedroom until she heard him return the boots. From her window, she watched him climb the hill back to Ellen's. He bobbed as he walked, clutching his satchel close. She waited until he was halfway to the woods before she got a trash bag, her water bottle, and the small bottle of pills she had gathered the night before.

She rattled the pills as she walked, their sound a skeletal companion, friendly and somehow comical. Her home felt like a pressure cooker no matter how much she emptied it, but the changing light of the sky reminded her that the earth still rolled into night and spun through the seasons, and nothing earthly could remain the same. The sheep bawled when she threw hay into the manger. Over the winter, they had churned the yard to deep mud, and they slid and tumbled, their long fleeces heavy with rain and dingy with dirt and dung. From the dark tunnel of her hood, she watched the small flock settle at the feeder. When they were eating peacefully, she went behind them and pulled the brambles from their wool and did her best to rub them clean. The next day, Dolores from the Soil and Water Conservation District was coming out to look at the wetland restoration project, and Connie saw the farm as Dolores might. It looked disreputable, the water trough green with algae and the animals wild and unkempt.

Usually by late March, the sheep would have been shorn sleek and gleaming white. They would be well into lambing, and Connie would be out at all hours, checking for new births. But this spring, her farm would not come to life. No lambs cavorting in the fields, no peas climbing the trellis, no chicks. If the sun finally came out, the blooming fruit trees might get pollinized, but no one would harvest. She dumped the water trough out and scrubbed it clean. Refilled, the galvanized metal sparkled under the gray skies. Connie hoped it would distract attention from the neglected sheep and the way the batten was beginning to peel from the barn.

She continued along the gravel drive to the wetland. Her water bottle bumped her every time she reached down to gather the garbage her farm shed like bodies shed hair and skin. By the time she reached the site, the bag was almost full of old pieces of PVC, scraps of tarp, and wisps of baling twine. She had begun the wetland restoration seven years earlier when Cary left for college and Connie had envisioned new projects to fill her empty nest. Working with her high school students and guided through the permitting process by Soil and Water, they used tractors to fill in the drainage ditch and then drove posts across the newly broad stream bed. Volunteers arrived with shovels and work gloves to pull out the blackberries and weave brush and saplings through the line of posts to begin a sort of dam. Throughout the reclaimed pasture, they planted alder and camas, dogwood and thimbleberry. Every year since then, Connie's students inventoried the species and recorded their observations. And every year the diversity increased. Plants thrived. Insects and birds appeared in greater numbers, and Connie had the satisfaction of prying adolescents away from their electronics to demonstrate that the world can get better. She couldn't teach that anymore. *Better* was a slippery idea.

The bottle of pills in her pocket contained a whole miscellany of family narcotics from Mike's bad back to Cary's illness. Connie's thumb traced the edges of the label as she looked out over the familiar site. The ratcheting song of chorus frogs went silent as Connie reached the pond. She held still until they resumed, then she pulled her hood down to feel the slap of cold rain. The frogs' chorus and the rain conflated and immersed her in a world so completely inhuman that she lost herself for a moment. Water rippled around her ankles while her boots sank in the muck. Someday she would sink all the way into soil and decompose. That was certain, and she could begin now if she chose. Gulp the family's misery pills and wash them down with well water. Decomposition would begin before the moon rose. Dylan would not be the one to find her. Dolores was coming. Ellen would be with her. And Connie would die next to a neat bag of garbage which struck her as appealingly pragmatic. But she didn't take the pills from her pocket.

If there was one single idea Connie had wanted her students to understand, it was that the world was not just a resource for humans. Everything existed for its own sake, she taught them, some mystery beyond usefulness. But if that were true, then she, too, would exist for her own sake and she didn't. When Cary got sick, Connie discovered she existed for Cary. She existed in order to explore the new wetland with the small paw of a grandchild in her own knuckled hand. What good are pollywogs without a child to marvel at their transformation? She squeezed the bottle of pills; it was just the size to fill her fist, its rattling contents so satisfyingly decisive. The problem was, she couldn't forget how hard Cary fought to live even after living was miserable. She searched the wilding site for more garbage. The sun broke through the clouds, and briefly all was a luminous green beneath the bruised sky, but it was nothing she hadn't seen before.

When she got back to the house, she put the pills back in the drawer. She kept them to remind herself every day; she was making a choice.

10

"Hello! This looks great!" Dolores from Soil and Water stood at the edge of the wetland and surveyed the scene. She had a clipboard, and she would take a lot of notes, but first she liked to greet a place.

Connie and Ellen stood behind Dolores, looking over her shoulder to young alders arrayed like soldiers and armored in white plastic against the browsing deer. Dylan loitered behind them.

"We'll be able to take all this plastic off pretty soon," Dolores said as they waded through the gently seeping water. "I bet we see all kinds of new species this spring."

"Who's doing the inventory?" Ellen asked. Both the other women stopped and turned to stare at her. "Will you bring kids out from the high school again, Connie? Or will Dolores get volunteers?"

"I haven't talked to the school," Connie said to her feet as she continued deeper into the water.

"I assumed it would be the same as always." Dolores fingered the new growth on a sapling. "I can ask for volunteers, but the kids did such a good job. It might be fun to find some local friends," she said to Dylan. "Connie's students are a lively bunch. It's my favorite project of the year." She slapped her clipboard against her thigh, winked at Dylan, and looked to Connie with an encouraging smile.

Connie felt a flush of irritation. "They're not my students."

"Jesus, Connie. Call the school." Ellen batted at the reeds with her walking stick and then turned to Dolores. "You remember how it was on inventory day. Loud voices of happy children. Shouts of discovery. It put the entire neighborhood in a good mood. We started to believe in a sunny future."

Dolores nodded. "It's a great thing for kids to get out in nature. You've been spending time out here, Dylan. What have you seen?" Dolores stopped by a small alder that had not survived. The protective wrapping had been pushed up the trunk and the trunk gnawed clean through so that the little tree had fallen, its branches lank and broken.

He shifted awkwardly in the sucking mud. "Same things you see, I guess."

Dolores looked at him sharply. "No one sees the same things," she said. "It doesn't make sense but it's true. So what has come to your attention? Anything unusual?"

"He's a city boy," Ellen said. "It's all unusual for him."

"I wondered about that big pile of sticks," Dylan said, cutting Ellen off. "Where did they come from?"

Dolores brought her hands together in playful glee and raised her eyebrows. "Show me."

They followed Dylan more deeply into the swamp. In the center, a pile of broken branches rose above the surface of the water. Old fence posts and pieces of plastic were jumbled in with saplings and brush.

Dolores smiled hugely. "Beavers!"

"Where?" Ellen searched the surface of the marsh.

"Evidence of beavers," Dolores corrected. "Have you seen any movement?" she asked Dylan.

"Ripples?" He watched the water as he spoke, serious and thoughtful. "Maybe frogs."

"Beavers are mostly nocturnal, but the broken trees, this lodge. It's unmistakable evidence. Probably a young male. Oh," she turned back toward Connie, "I really hope you get the kids back out so Dylan can show them. This would be so exciting for them."

"I've never seen a beaver," Dylan said.

"Not many people have these days, but they used to cover the whole countryside." Dolores extended her arm and swept a wide circle.

"I mean I don't even know what one looks like."

"Look it up," Dolores said with a big smile. "Look it up on the internet when you get home."

Connie scanned the wetlands, noticing the broken trees, and the small pile of branches. The students would be thrilled, for they had discussed the possibility of beavers and the category existed on the checklist. A wildlife camera might get a shot of the nighttime activity, but Connie didn't have a camera. She didn't have students. She didn't have beavers either, she reminded herself, she just lived nearby.

"One thing I wondered about," Dylan said. They all turned and waited while he formed his thought. "Are there lots of places like this?"

"Like this?" Dolores said. "There aren't many beaver dams anymore."

"But are there lots of places where beavers could move in? You know, like this? With fields and creeks and trees?"

Dolores frowned, thinking. "Sure. In the wilderness, the national forests . . . It's harder for beavers in agricultural areas. Dams can cause trouble for farmers. But beavers are so good for water and wildlife, especially in the face of climate change. People are trying to bring them back."

Ellen squinted at Dylan, stabbing her walking stick repeatedly into the mud. "Dylan, had you ever left Seattle before you came here?"

Dylan shrugged and looked sideways.

"Like, have you ever been to the ocean?" Ellen persisted.

"Seattle's on the ocean."

"It's on a Sound. Crashing waves, Dylan. Have you ever seen crashing waves?"

"On TV."

"Have you ever been in the mountains?"

"On TV."

"Jesus fucking Christ!" Ellen whapped the stick down hard and Dolores winced.

"I work with about a half dozen wetland restoration projects in this county," Dolores said to Dylan. "Those are just the ones getting started. There are some places like this on the edges of farms, and like I said, lots more places in the national forests."

Connie turned and waded out of the marsh. What would you believe of the world if all you knew were the suburbs of Seattle? All Starbucks and Safeway, Pottery Barn and Ikea? Every opportunity a retail opportunity and not a dollar in your pocket? Connie walked slowly back to the house. Ten minutes later, Ellen and Dolores joined her.

Dolores sat at the kitchen table in front of a plate of cookies Ellen had brought knowing Connie would not bother with snacks. "I've always loved workbooks." Dolores fingered the white pages smudged with mud. "Filling things in."

Ellen brought tea to the table, but Connie sat without consuming anything. "Where's Dylan?"

"He stayed out there," Dolores said. "I think you have a budding naturalist."

"Ha," Ellen said. "He just wants to keep away from us."

"He showed me every broken tree," Dolores said. "He found a muskrat den. He's a good observer."

The phone rang. Connie rarely picked it up and made no move to do so now. Ellen answered. "Sweet residence."

Connie made a sour face, and Ellen smiled mischievously in response. Then, listening, Ellen began to smile in earnest. She stopped fussing with the tea and looked out the window as she spoke. "We've been out to survey the wetland. We have beavers!"

We don't have *beavers,* Connie thought with something close to anger.

"Connie?" Ellen leaned away from the phone. "You're around tomorrow morning?"

Connie shrugged, but Ellen paid no attention. "Around ten?" she said into the phone. "Good. You can see the beavers."

"Who was that?" Connie demanded.

Ellen smiled. "We can chat later. When Dolores is done."

"Chat? Just tell me who it was."

"I'm leaving now." Dolores closed her workbook and settled it in her backpack.

"You haven't finished your tea." Ellen slid the cup a little closer to Dolores's elbow. "Connie doesn't mean to be rude."

"You're not rude." Dolores smiled and squeezed Connie's shoulder. "I have to drive to the other end of the county." She accepted a baggy of cookies for the road, and Ellen walked her to the door while Connie laid her head on her arms.

Ellen returned frowning. "Were you trying to make that nice woman uncomfortable?"

"Me?" Connie looked up to Ellen standing over her, hands on her hips. "I didn't do anything."

"Exactly. And it's your house, your wetland project, and Dolores made the drive all the way out here."

"It's not really *my* project, and that's her job."

"No one expects you to be the perfect hostess, but you could be civil. You can practice tomorrow morning when Otto comes over to return your basket; his expectations of you are low. That was him on the phone just now." Ellen sat down. She bit a cookie and let the crumbs fall to the table, staring at Connie challengingly. Connie returned her look in a manner she hoped appeared insolent.

"He can leave it on the porch. Better yet, he can keep that basket."

Ellen continued to stare Connie down. She didn't even lick the cookie crumbs from the corners of her mouth. Her presence was painfully vivid, her big head and stern gaze and her bold plaid shirt. She filled the room. It hadn't been enough to clear the counters. Connie imagined stripping the kitchen all the way down to the studs.

"He wants to thank you for your kind welcome."

Connie thought of her trespass and felt her cheeks flush.

"You're blushing. That's surprising." Ellen stood up and wiped the table clean. She put Dolores's cup in the dishwasher and rinsed the tea pot. "But it's a good sign." She stood for a moment frowning, but Connie made no response. "You have tea and cookies. Tomorrow, you can be a proper hostess."

11

The door closed behind Ellen, and Connie remained at the table, listening to the gravel pop as the car drove away. She had been eager for Dolores and Ellen to leave, but not because she had anything to do. She didn't make plans anymore. Once you got them rolling, they had their own trajectory. You never knew where they'd take you. She laid her head down on her arms and fell asleep but woke at the sound of the door. "Dylan?" But she must have heard the door closing. When she got up, she found the boots in their corner. Dylan had already gone.

He had spoken to Dolores more boldly than Connie would have expected. It had cost him—the tremor in his voice, the flush—but he had stepped forward. Ellen might rhapsodize about the youthful shouts of discovery, but Connie's well-heeled students spent a lot of their time complaining. Their cell phones didn't work down in the wetland, and despite their snacks and drinks and specialized outdoor wear, they were bored and cold and anxious to return to a faster pace. Connie exhorted them. She used to speak in almost mystical terms about time spent alone with nature. But what did she know? She had never spent an entire day just listening and watching. Like Dylan had.

The sun set behind the trees on the ridge. Connie switched on the kitchen light and the rest of the house collapsed in darkness. She would like to shrink her life around her tight as a glove. Before he left, Connie's ex-husband Mike had told her *you don't leave room for anyone*, but everything she had done she did for the family. Cary watched her beloved birds from her deathbed, and the many chores crucial for keeping Cary out of the hospital kept Connie busy. But Connie hadn't anticipated how Cary's suffering would frighten Mike, how it would fuel his sense of helplessness until he couldn't bear it any longer. Before he left, he told Connie he could not help Cary because of the way Connie helped Cary, that he could not inhabit the farm because of the way Connie inhabited the farm.

She heated up a can of chicken vegetable soup and picked up a mystery she had started the other day, but she wasn't able to settle, and the television was no more engaging. When Otto came to return the basket, would he confront her about her trespass? Was that the real reason he was coming over? What would she say? *Everything looked so perfect, I couldn't resist?* Her impulses betrayed her. They were petty and self-serving, like her hobby farm and her nature pamphlets. Like her life. She got her jacket and let the door slam hard behind her so that the old porch trembled.

The sky had broken into towering, purple-bellied clouds edged with light so brilliant it hurt Connie's eyes. She kept her gaze averted as she walked down the gravel lane. Out in the barn, her workbench was messy with old projects she couldn't remember beginning. She sifted through the scattered brads and screws until she found a roofing nail. She rolled the large nail head between her fingers and hurried up the hill as it started to hail. She was afraid if she returned to the house for a hat, she would lose momentum and end up beneath the kitchen light, waiting for time to pass. It took very little time to reach the edge of Otto's clearing. A thin coil of smoke rose from the tipi which glowed pleasantly like a lit jack-o-lantern. Otto's silhouette loomed on the tipi wall, apparently reading. Or watching trashy TV on his iPad for all she knew. She slipped around the edge of the clearing to the crouching sports car. Its hood was slightly warm, and she moved slowly, touching the car all the while as she might an animal. She rested her palm on the rear tire for a moment, almost a gesture of reassurance. Then, squatting near the ground, she laid the nail just behind the tire. If Otto was casual about shifting the sports car forward, if he let it roll back at all, it would find its mark. Or not. Providence.

The hail had stopped; the storm cloud slid east. Past Otto's clearing, the lights around I-5 brightened, staining the sky sodium orange. Every year, the glow of the city suffused more and more of the night sky. She had been watching its advance for decades. Making pamphlets, lecturing students, writing to her representatives. And the end of all her efforts was what? She didn't even have a clean conscience. Her life was just a bunch of plans following their own trajectories, and she was like an empty can pulled along behind, some kind of noise-maker. A rock at the side of the drive, just the size of a grapefruit, faced her like an inquisitor. She scooped the nail up quickly and nestled it into the tread. Then, using the rock, she tapped the nail deep into the hard resisting rubber.

12

Although Connie was expecting Otto, her heart jumped when the little sports car came to a stop by her front path around eleven the next morning. Otto jumped out in a manner that might be described as jaunty. The car itself was jaunty. She had always hated that word. Connie did not have much practice in keeping secrets. She understood the verb now. A secret had potential that must be tended. She straightened her clothes and opened the door as he mounted the stairs.

"I'm not disturbing you?" He stopped on the top step, half-turned, ready to leave.

"Ellen told me you were coming." Connie opened the door wider and walked back to the kitchen, letting him follow her.

"I thought she might be here."

He seemed sorry to be alone with her; that was reassuring. "Ellen left some cookies." They had been growing stale on the platter since the day before. She didn't offer to make tea.

"No thank you." He patted his belly and smiled. "I try to avoid sugar."

Connie didn't sit down. "So it's hypocritical to thank me for the jam."

Otto's blue eyes narrowed with amusement as though they shared a joke. He was waiting for her acknowledgement. She looked away, shifting from foot to foot.

"I won't thank you, then," he said at last. "I hate hypocrisy." He set Connie's basket on the kitchen table and sat down. "But I can tell you that I appreciated the gesture."

Connie reached out to pull the basket toward her but stopped. "There's something in it." She slid the basket back to Otto. She felt strangely betrayed by the gift. "You should have just sent the jam home."

"That would be rude. It's also rude to return an empty basket." Otto reached in and took something out of a small paper bag. He extended his arm across the table and held the object in his fist until Connie opened her palm. "It's a pocket sharpening steel."

The object in her hand was heavy for its size, a small metal bar half covered with rubbery plastic. She sat down across from Otto. "I appreciate the gesture."

He laughed. He seemed to think they had a friendly relationship when Connie was quite sure they had no relationship at all. "I thought even if you already have one, they're easy to lose."

"Right." Connie frowned. "I'll try that." If she didn't say anything more, he would probably leave.

"My first plan was to come down here with enough time to sharpen your tools, but things didn't work out that way."

Outside, a breeze rattled rain down from the trees and they both raised their heads to look for a moment. She shifted in her chair. "The tools are sharp enough. I don't do much farm work anymore."

He shook his head in disagreement. "You're a steward." He looked pointedly at her clean and bare kitchen before looking back to her with a friendly expression. "Me too. Caring for tools is a hobby of mine. But I had a flat tire on the way to the hardware store. Took some time to get it all patched up."

"I'm sorry." Connie didn't meet his gaze. He would not be friendly if he knew what she had done. That tiny grain of knowledge changed everything.

"The dangers of a construction zone." He shrugged. "Frustrating, because I thought if I made a good impression by sharpening all your tools, you might show me the knack for listening to worms."

She closed her eyes. She felt queasy. "You don't have to butter me up. There's no knack."

"But I tried," he leaned toward her. "I had my ear to the dirt just like you, but I couldn't hear anything. The backhoe guy was laughing at me. I'm afraid I'll never live it down." He paused. "Did you set me up?"

"No!" She was offended that he would imagine she spent her time planning things for his benefit, then she realized that is exactly what she had done in his tipi and with his car. Her breath grew shallow. "Worms are farmyard creatures." She wished he would go away. "They don't live in forests."

He leaned back and lifted his hands in surprise. It was as though he had tossed something away and was left cleansed. "That shows how much I know. I assumed they preferred a virgin environment."

"A virgin environment? What the hell is that?"

"Unspoiled?"

He was trying to win her over, and she shouldn't engage. She thought of Dylan studying the cold wetland, all alone, every day, expecting nothing. This man expected everything. He would probably get it, too. Why not?

"What's spoiled for one species is perfect for another. For example, you don't want a virgin environment. You want an environment filled with grapes. Worms like an environment filled with manure."

"There you have it." His big hands braced against his knees. He leaned forward slightly. "Biology was not my science."

"Computers."

"Correct."

"Hardware or software?" she asked.

"Software."

"Binary code." Just as she had suspected. "Two dimensional. Open. Shut."

Otto tipped his head to the side. "Like the heart."

Outside Connie's kitchen, the day brightened as the sun burned through the morning clouds.

"Hmph." Binary code was not at all like the paradox of the heart. Not like the swing of breath or the turn from night to day. "Binary code is just another language. Abstraction." She blushed. Otto broke a cookie into pieces and ate a fragment.

Connie didn't want to have this conversation with Otto. Digital. Analog. It was the heart of her problem. There was nothing wrong with her immediate life—a sunny kitchen and a plate of cookies, a forest at her back, for now. But when Connie looked at the whole thing, her life didn't add up. A brown creeper the size of a wood chip hopped up the tree trunk, its feathers so perfectly camouflaged it was almost invisible, but she didn't point it out.

"I should be going." Otto stood politely and began to turn, but he stopped and rapped his knuckle on the table. Connie looked up, startled. He smiled at her. "But I did hope to hear the worms. If you really can hear worms."

She stood abruptly. "You really can. Anyone can."

13

Once Connie showed Otto how to listen to worms, he would certainly leave. She hurried ahead of him so they wouldn't have to talk or, worst of all, to have him ask for a tour. She marched him past the sorry sheep and the previous year's plants sprawled brown and rotten across the vegetable beds. They stopped at a patch of earth covered in old straw stippled with decomposing sheep manure.

"Here."

The garden soil had been supplemented with compost every year for a quarter century, and that life continued to thrive beneath the messy surface. She had to give him credit; Otto promptly dropped to his knees and placed his ear on the mucky ground.

"I hear a soft, steady sound," he said at last. "Maybe water draining?"

At that, Connie leaned down and slapped the ground hard, twice.

"Oh!" He said in surprise. "That's a lot of worms!"

"Thousands, I guess."

Mud smeared Otto's cheek when he sat up, and a piece of straw stuck to the stubble of his beard. His eyes were wide with an enthusiasm that took Connie by surprise. She'd seen the look in children; she'd lived for it.

She wiped her own face slowly from temple to jaw, and Otto, mirroring, rubbed his sleeve against his cheek. Then he put his ear to the surface again. He leaned into the earth as he patted and paused, focused, rhythmic. He sat up. "After a while, they quit responding to the slap."

"I think they can only go so low."

Otto pushed himself off the ground and wiped his hands on his new jeans. "What do you know!" He stood with his feet wide and looked around the garden as though it must be filled with wonders they should discuss. Connie started for home. "Hey Connie?" Otto hung back, still smiling. "Would you show me the beaver? Beavers are mighty exotic to a kid from New Mexico."

She spoke without coming closer. "No more exotic there than anywhere. Beavers used to be all over the country. Any place there was water."

Again, the smile, the wide eyes, the eager student. "I did a report on beavers when I was in fourth grade. Funny how those things stay with you."

Connie turned toward the wetland. "Then you should know they're nocturnal." She hated to picture him as a child, dutifully copying a beaver from the encyclopedia. "We probably won't see any."

The sun was high now and the heat became oppressive in the damp field. Otto plowed through, grass brushing his knees, sweat lining his hairline. Indian plum bloomed along the fence line, and insects swarmed the pendant flowers frantic to make up for the days lost to cold. Otto was seized by a fit of sneezing, and by the time Connie had reached the pond he was still waiting at the edge of the wetland, wiping his nose and looking for a dry passage through. When he spotted her watching, he plunged in. He wasn't dressed appropriately, those fancy leather work boots, but that wasn't her responsibility. By the time they got to the alders, his feet were soaked, and water had darkened his jeans to the knee.

She explained how they'd graded the pasture and planted the trees. She showed him the gnawed saplings as they pushed through the brush. "Over here is the incipient lodge." But when she parted the dogwood, the mound of sticks was almost entirely eclipsed by Dylan. He perched on top of the lodge, his boney knees supporting a sketchbook as his feet dangled in the pond. The water glittered around the dull rubber of Mike's old boots. "Dylan!"

He scrambled down to stand in the shallow water. "That lady yesterday said it was okay."

Connie and Otto waded over to the lodge. As they passed, jellied rafts of eggs bobbed around blades of grass.

"It's the driest place to sit and draw." Dylan stuffed his paper and pencils into his satchel. "I've been careful. That beaver lady said I wouldn't hurt anything if I was careful." He fiddled with the heavy silver chain that presumably secured his keys, as if he had anything to lock.

All around them, the world was turning green, the dull green of the conifers now joined by the tender green of new leaves and the acid green grass. The juicy spring was a striking contrast to Dylan's tar black hair and his grey-black clothes, and yet sitting on the lodge he had looked endemic, a fledgling himself, raw and unfeathered, all bones and cartilage. And he had startled like any animal, facing them defensively because he could not run in those boots.

"You looked like a nesting heron up there," Connie said. Skinny and rough. He would grow into something beyond her ken. "Go ahead and finish your drawing. I was just showing the lodge to Otto."

The man nodded to the boy who ducked his head in reply.

"I have to go back anyway." Dylan turned before he'd finished the sentence and hurried away with hobbled steps. Connie saw the effort he made to keep from walking right out of his shoes.

"That boy is awkward," Otto said as he watched Dylan head back to the farmhouse.

"I lent him those boots," Connie said. "They're too big."

"That's not his only problem."

"He's fine." She felt herself flush, suddenly protective. "I've never trusted slick teenagers, the cute ones, the smooth talkers." She wrinkled her nose. "You weren't one of those, were you?"

"Me? I was terribly awkward."

Connie glanced at him sideways, unsure if he was teasing her, always being so agreeable.

"Really," he said. "I hid out in the chess club."

"Good to know. Slick teenagers grow into petty adults." Otto listened as though she were offering instruction, but his eagerness was beginning to flag. His cheeks flushed and his shoulders rounded in the heat. It must be tiring to be so cheerful. She flicked her hand toward the pile of sticks. "You can see it's a very small lodge. It's unlikely it will attract a mate this year, if at all."

"The poor guy doesn't have a lot to work with. The trees here are very small."

"He got the territory he deserved." Connie turned and began to make her way out of the ponding water.

Otto spoke from behind, but quite clearly. "You know, I envy you."

Connie stopped and looked back in shock. In the last two years, many people had offered sympathy. Some even said they admired her strength. But no one envied her. The notion was horrible, and Otto must have seen this in her face because he shook his head and dug his hands back into his pockets. "The time you've spent here," he said. "I'll read any book you point me to, but that's no substitute for experience."

Connie laughed then, a short, barking *ha* that surprised even her. "Experience is a story we tell to string the days together. But I guess this place is literally in my bones. The food I eat comes mostly from this ground. The water I drink comes from these rocks." These were things she thought about, but when she voiced them, she sounded smug and trite. "Some place made you, too."

"Houston?" He crossed his arms and shook his head. "Houston isn't a *place*. A city isn't. Not in the same way. Where does the water come from? Where does the food come from?" He snorted. "I must be made of freeway fumes."

"You look healthy." She knew she sounded stupid, but she let it stand because she meant it. And it might end the conversation.

He laughed. "Freeway fumes and takeout containers. That's why I left Houston." He rocked back on his heels to look up to his ridge with determination. He might have been a pioneer colonizing the west. "I couldn't explain this to the folks in Texas, but you understand."

Even if he couldn't explain it to his friends in Texas, Connie was pretty sure he'd tried. It was bullshit. Everyone was a part of wherever they existed; there was no alternative. So when Otto said he wanted to be a part of his environment, he meant he wanted to be the part that was in charge.

Connie followed his gaze up the hill where the tangled trees would be replaced by trellises of cloned grapes. "It's my understanding that farming is destructive to natural environments." She turned to leave. "The worms will increase."

"Farming can be good for the land." He called so that his words would reach her as she crossed the marsh. She was acutely aware of how dry her feet were in her cheap rubber boots, boots that would last for years, that required no care other than being hosed down when the mud caked on too thick. She could hardly begin to tell him how little he knew.

"You'll cut down all that oak." Connie stopped and faced him. The world had been wasted by well-meaning people like him. Cancer, asthma, obesity, climate change, mass extinctions—the whole cascading avalanche of suffering was the consequence of the most trivial desires. "Birds will disappear with the oak grove and pests will increase. Hawks and owls won't have anywhere to hang out. You'll get rodents. You'll have to get those canons to scare the Oregon robins off your French grapes."

"I think you're mistaken, Connie Sweet," he said, and she felt a thrill of resentment.

"Not about that."

Connie had discharged her neighborly obligations. She had taken him to the worms and shown him the beaver lodge, and now she walked fast, her vision blurred by tears as though his vineyard plans were a fresh insult. She felt Otto's cloying eagerness close behind. He was foolish and misguided, but that wasn't a surprise, and it wasn't her business. She wiped her eyes angrily.

"Shall we bet?"

"Bet?" Connie didn't stop walking and he spoke to her from behind.

"That my farming will improve the land."

"If growing dollars is an improvement, it will. Is that your criteria?"

"What's your criteria?"

"Diversity." She wasn't sure he could hear her, but she wasn't having a conversation with him anyway.

"Deal," he said promptly.

"What?" Connie stopped suddenly and Otto nearly ran into her. "That's a hopeless bet."

"I'll bet you my tipi." His face was guileless, and Connie began to wonder if maybe he was just a little crazy. He wouldn't be the first crazy person to find his way to a hidden home on the mountain.

"And what do you expect me to risk? What else would you like to take from me?" She hadn't meant to say it like that, but that's how it came out.

He was speechless for a moment. "If you're so confident, you should risk your home, too." He no longer wore the open expression he'd cultivated earlier. His goodwill was not bottomless. "But I'm not asking you to risk anything. Maybe a celebratory dinner." He opened his hands heavenward. He was leaving it up to her.

"We'd have to do plant and wildlife surveys."

"Okay."

"Before you log and then again later."

He nodded, and again Connie wondered what he wanted.

"You understand that you can't win? You can't replace a complex mature forest with acres of cloned grapes and not lose diversity." She waited for him to do the math, but he only smiled, awaiting her agreement. "Okay," she shook her head, "even though I do *not* need a tipi." She pronounced the word distinctly so that each syllable created a brief, sneering smile.

Otto brought two fingers to his forehead in salute.

"If I'm wrong—which I'm not—you can have my house. I won't deserve it," Connie said.

"Dinner will be sufficient. But if you decide to move, I'll pay you for the house and make it the headquarters for an educational non-profit: the Sweet Farm for Sustainable Ag."

Connie rolled her eyes. "It will never happen."

"We'll see." Otto extended his hand. Connie shook it and her own hand felt tough and leathery in his uncalloused palm. "Now I must go and study."

14

After Otto had returned to his illegal dwelling in the tipi in the clearing, Connie returned to her own home, restless and discontent. Outside her kitchen window, a flock of starlings blanketed the pasture, and the ground twitched like the pelt of an animal. Every day now travelers came through—starlings, bluebirds, finches—hungry and on their way to someplace else. The little daisies bloomed in the fields, but the wind barely stirred the oaks and maples, their leaves still secreted in many small wombs along their naked branches. After a quarter century on the farm, Connie knew this was the last chance to prepare—to prune and weed and fix and plan—before she would be flooded by the demands of spring. Still, she didn't begin. She had let the weeds of May triumph each year since Cary's diagnosis when Connie swore off herbicides forever. There was work out there, but it wasn't her work. If we are all cogs in the wheel of the universe, the closest Connie came to spirituality, she was a piece that had broken loose. She was rattling around, jamming things up while Otto was at his tipi studying for their bet, building things, making a five-year plan and a ten-year plan. In Connie's draughty farmhouse, the empty days blew away like last year's leaves.

"I'm thinking of moving," she told Ellen the next day as they walked the mountain.

"Where?" Ellen slowed and turned to read Connie's face.

"Somewhere foreign, I guess. The Midwest? A condominium in Tigard? Some Mexican beach town?"

"Is this penance?" Ellen looked truly pained. "I thought you were past the bargaining stage."

"Fewer responsibilities."

"Oh! Like death." Ellen watched Connie as they walked. "You can't make decisions now; you're depressed. It's not appropriate to abandon your farm."

"Appropriate." A word that adults used to coerce behavior from children. Connie opened her hands at her side, presenting herself as evidence. "Jesus, Ellen. What's appropriate? You've got a Texan in a tipi growing French grapes in the Willamette Valley."

Ellen shrugged. "You're starting to sound like an old cynic like me." She tacked over to Connie's side and threw a big arm across her shoulder. "None of that is appropriate." She shoved Connie gently so that Connie half-stepped to keep her balance. "Anger is a good sign. Better than lethargy."

"This isn't real energy. It's just fermentation." Connie waved her hand over her head. "A burp or a fart."

"Jesus, Connie, what's gotten into you?"

"Last night, Otto bet me his tipi that his farming will make a more diverse habitat. If he wins, he said he'd buy my house. He wasn't serious, and he's bound to lose that bet, but—I don't know—maybe I *should* move."

Ellen stopped right in the middle of the empty lane. Connie walked on until she saw that Ellen wasn't budging. Connie paused, sulking, and used the toe of her sneaker to probe a fungus at the base of a fir tree.

"That's pretty subtle for a man."

Connie kicked the fungus hard, and a piece chipped off. "What are you talking about?"

Ellen caught up and bent into the hill, pulling Connie along. The brisk pace seemed to wind her up. "He wants your house. Then he could live on his vineyard legally, with indoor plumbing."

"He said he'd make it into a non-profit education center."

Ellen dismissed the idea with a toss of her head. "Texans hate paying taxes."

"He's not going to win the bet." Connie didn't want to encourage Ellen's speculation. "And he was only joking."

"There's a fine line between a planner and a schemer." Ellen looked to the clouds; the wheels were turning, and Connie felt a pang imagining a life without their walks. "A good-looking guy used to getting his way probably doesn't understand the difference himself. One silly suggestion and you're already talking about moving." She stopped and clutched Connie's elbow. "Don't fall for it, Connie."

"You're crazy." Connie shook Ellen off. "Always trying to seduce me with drama."

"You'd miss that if you moved to Tigard." Ellen scratched her head, loosening the red cap. It was almost too warm for a hat now, even in the mornings. "Do you remember when we met for the first time?"

"Did I bring you a pamphlet?" Connie had been so proud of them, but her neighborhood had more invasive species than ever and people still built their manure piles in the creek drainages.

"Thank God I avoided that." Ellen grimaced. "I beat you to the introduction because I came down the day after I moved to buy some cheese. You were in the kitchen, and you had cheese draining all over the counter. You were making an enormous pot of chili for the freezer while you helped Cary with her chemistry homework. Whey was dripping onto the floor and your dog was licking it up while you explained covalent bonding. I wanted sage cheese, but you were all out. You just told Cary to go cut some sage, and you mixed it into curds right then and told me it would be ready the next day. You were so incredibly competent."

"I was ambitious. I thought we had a future."

"You have a future. Everyone has a future right up until the moment they don't, so stop with that, Connie."

"You know what I mean."

"I know that I was ready to move in with you. I grew up with six siblings and alcoholic parents. I had never seen anything like you in that farm kitchen. You couldn't be happy in Tigard. It would be like making Matisse paint in black and white. Like Christo and Jeanne-Claude making porcelain figurines."

"For heaven's sake."

"Besides, I need you here. What about Dylan? He needs a mother figure, and it shouldn't be me."

Connie had juggled those chores because she thought they were important, but she had never juggled them well. She could show Ellen the warped and stained floorboards; the dog didn't lick up all the whey. And Cary almost flunked chemistry.

15

Connie left Ellen at her driveway and let herself in through her back door. The front door was broken and could only be unlocked from the inside. Ellen had shown her how to go on YouTube to learn how to replace the mechanism, but Connie only needed one door. The first week after Cary's death, Connie gave away all of Cary's clothes. Then she got rid of the toys she had saved to share with grandchildren. She threw out the ceramic whale Cary made in third grade, the one they used to pin the door open. She sold her wedding china and her mother's silver and the crystal candy dish passed down from her great-grandmother. It wasn't strange to live without those things. It had been strange to keep them and polish them and pretend they stitched generations together.

She took garbage bags to her bedroom and began to bag her own clothes. She saved out one sober winter dress, one skirt, and a summer shift. She pulled the other skirts and dresses off their hangers and wadded them into a bag, then she stuffed the hangers themselves in another bag. She kept ten pairs of underwear and ten pairs of socks. She kept two pairs of jeans and a pair of wool pants. She kept three blouses, two sweaters, and a small handful of tee shirts. By the end, Connie's remaining clothes could fit in a suitcase.

Outside, heavy equipment crawled over Otto's ridge like slow moving beetles. The growl of their engines haunted her even in the basement as she cleaned out the canning supplies. She listened for changes in the engine's pitch and wondered where the bulldozer was among the familiar trees and shrubs and which particular obstacles it strained to overcome. Her attention was excessive, and she tried to get back to her chores, but thoughts of the forest clung to her like a toddler.

Dylan's boots were gone from the mudroom. Connie imagined him seated imperturbably on the nest of sticks. If she went outside, maybe he would let her join him. They could watch the heron stalk frogs in the shallows, and it wouldn't matter if the sun rose and set without them accomplishing a single tangible thing. She took the box of canning supplies to the growing pile of giveaways in the garage, then she gathered a clipboard, checklists, and pens and went to find Dylan.

He would be surprised to see her; she hoped he'd be glad. Or at least that he wouldn't flee. Connie thought she would start by asking Dylan questions, the way Dolores had. She would begin by listening. She hurried down the lane, her eye on the ridge, but Otto's equipment was still hidden by trees. When she got to the marsh, she waded slowly to disturb the currents as little as possible and perhaps to catch a glimpse of Dylan before he knew she was there. But he wasn't perched on the lodge. The stand of red alders blushed with new growth and birds flitted in the dense branches, but his black figure was not among their pale trunks. She scanned the pond surface in case he was squatting to search for pollywogs, but the boy was nowhere.

From the wetland, the clash of rocks and metal was even more audible. They were making inroads: clearing brush, dumping rock and spreading it. Connie suddenly realized Dylan might be up there. She scanned the hill from the fence line, searching the shadows on the margin of the wood. If Dylan was lurking, if Otto didn't know he was there, Dylan could be injured. He would be used to urban construction sites, fenced-off and well-marked, and he might not be aware of the danger. Certainly, Connie had never warned him. And she should have. She hurried up the hill, following the sound of the truck as it spread the crushed rock and packed it down. She didn't see Dylan, but he was so slim, his clothes so dark, he could turn sideways and disappear.

She spotted Otto leaning against a truck pointing to various parts of the forest as a man in work clothes nodded. They gathered supplies and walked together among the trees. Otto pointed and the other man sprayed certain trees with a spritz of blue paint. Beyond the dull green fir needles, a bulldozer the size of a small garage waited beneath a canopy of lacy yellow flowers that were just beginning to unfurl from the maple branches. Connie and Otto had been talking about the vineyard as a simple change of use for the land, but that wasn't right at all, and the bet they made was sick, as though they planned to swap out a family member for a new puppy and catalogue the gains and losses. She and Otto could wager and debate but the end of it all was a forest scraped away from the earth and dismembered. That's what Dylan would see: the logs to the mill, ferns and soft mosses jumbled to rot in the slash piles. The many animals, insects, and birds would dissipate like a final breath.

Connie skirted the perimeter of the ridge. Branches fell as the bulldozer strained against the forest. Clouds of dust billowed into the spring air as rocks thundered from the dump truck. Everything was so much bigger, so much harder and heavier, than a boy. She hurried on to Ellen's, but the house was empty, and Ellen's car was gone. Connie jogged back to the wetland feeling more and more anxious. The site was small, but she might have missed Dylan if he was deep in the grass sketching frogs maybe, or in the bushes with a bird's nest. She squatted for some time at the edge of the pond listening, then she walked the perimeter but saw no sign of Dylan. When she got back to her own house, the boots were already in their corner.

Her hands trembled as she made a cup of tea. Now that she knew he was safe, she was grateful she hadn't found him. She would have had to talk calmly about the logging and its dangers, and yet she felt outrage, resentment, anger—emotions she had no right to. Connie had sold vineyard land because she wanted vineyard dollars, many more dollars than she could have gotten for a forest. If she hadn't sold the forest, she would have had to sell the whole farm. It might have become a dirt bike track or a lavender farm, but sooner or later the forest would have fallen because that was what happened. Everywhere. All the time. When Connie needed to remember that, she communed with the ancient yew tree and she needed to take Dylan up there so he would understand. Life is that which disappears. Every earthly thing—animal, vegetable, or mineral—just changes form. A constant churn of transformation. For the short time they have before they give their bodies back to earth, humans get to watch. Forests fall and children die.

She set the cup down so abruptly the tea splashed and burned her hand. She licked the reddened skin. She should not be guiding young people, teaching them the stoic ways of trees. Dylan was not a tree. He was a person and people scampered. They ran. They fought.

Late that night, she pulled on jeans and a dark sweatshirt. She stopped at the barn for the rest of the things she needed. She took a flashlight, but she didn't turn it on. Her eyes were still stunned from the electric light, and she walked slowly, giving them an opportunity to adjust, but her path was clear and easy down the lane and past the wetland. From there, she struck uphill through the steep open pastureland where she used to graze her sheep before she sold the land to Otto. Her heart pounded from excitement and the climb. At the top of the hill, the forest faced her like the wall of a fortress. She could see the break in the foliage where the path cut through the woods to end on the lane across from Ellen's driveway, but once she had stepped onto the path, she couldn't even see her feet.

Despite the cold, her hands sweat as she held the metal can. She wiped her palms on her jeans as she strained to find the passage through the woods. Slowly, masses began to separate themselves from the wall of darkness, creating space between the trees and shrubs. She proceeded and immediately blundered off the path. It was no good peering into the distance. She looked down, probing the trail with her foot, her arms in front like antenna. Step by step, she went forward in six-inch increments. Halfway along the path, the trail to Otto's would appear on her right. If she missed it, she would arrive at the lane where she could circle back to Otto's by way of his driveway. But she didn't see the path and she didn't reach the lane. She must have made some sort of mistake. Right next to her was a large madrone, its smooth trunk lithe and soothing beneath her hand, but she couldn't remember any large madrone on that trail. She had no idea where she was. Then panic descended. She no longer had any sense of the direction she had come, and the patch of woods was not hers at all but something strange and hostile. She wanted to bolt, to crash through the forest until she reached familiar ground, but it was a dangerous impulse. She gulped air and exhaled slowly. Then she turned the flashlight on and swept it all around. In the light, the forest settled and was hers again. The trail to Otto's was just ahead.

She used the flashlight until she neared Otto's clearing. Then she memorized her surroundings before turning it off. Otto had left a light on over his shed. It probably made him feel safer, but it just made her job easier. With her back to his clearing, the large trees were illuminated by the faint light. She marked most every tree with a spritz of blue paint. The paint made a sound like someone blowing out a candle. Once she had marked the trees, she circled Otto's clearing. She heard him snoring in his tipi, a comical wheezing that made her strangely light-hearted. She timed the spritz of paint to coincide with his exhalation as she marked the shed and then, feeling bold, a long, hissing line down the tipi deck. Her arm dropped to her side, and she began to sidle back to the woods, but before she left, she drifted to the driveway. She left a spritz of blue, like a cold blown kiss, on the driver's door of the vintage pick-up.

Connie walked more quickly back through the woods. She used the flashlight a couple times, just for a moment to keep on track. When she reached the open field, she burst into a run. She still clutched the can of paint, and she let her arm wave freely as her galloping strides carried her downhill. At the bottom, mist rose from the wetland. She dove in and kept running. Her breath pushed against her ribs and her heart pounded, and although the pressure reminded her of her smallness—the fragile mechanisms of the finite body—still she was almost overcome by an exhilarating sense of power.

16

The trucks stayed parked on Otto's ridge all next morning. Marking the trees would hardly set him back at all, but now he knew there were forces against him, and Connie felt almost happy as she went to meet Ellen for their usual walk. The sparkling sounds of springtime filled the morning. No straining engines, no crashing trees. Only the chittering of a flock of chickadees. She felt an almost proprietary pleasure as she listened to the birdsong. All her life, Connie had followed instructions and minded the rules. She had been a team player, but where was her team now? Even the field was dissolving.

Ellen crested the hill and called a hearty hello.

"There was some vandalism up at Otto's last night," she said as Connie fell into step beside her. "Spray painting. Otto came and grilled Dylan about it."

Connie's heart raced ahead, out of sync with her feet, and she felt a swooning vertigo. "But Dylan couldn't have done it."

Ellen looked over with a doubtful expression.

"I mean, he was with you, right?"

"He's a big boy; I don't know where he is all the time. But anyone can tell just looking at Dylan; that boy is not an activist." She curled her lip and Connie wasn't sure if the derision was for Dylan or the fool who'd fingered him. "He internalizes things." Ellen marched on, her arms swinging like paddles. "Always been that way. He doesn't cause trouble. He just tries to fit in."

"Did you ask him?"

"Talking to Dylan doesn't work. He's like a black hole: nothing comes out of him, and things get weird near him." Ellen scooped off her red cap and rubbed her head. "I'm betting Ed did it. That's what I told the Otto."

"The recluse?" Connie had not really considered that her transgressions might stain others. But there would need to be evidence, and she had all the evidence in her barn. She reached deeply into her pockets. Ellen slowed to avoid leaving her behind.

"Who knows what he's up to all by himself?" Ellen skipped a step and bumped Connie to jolly her along. "Personally, I'm relieved he's vandalizing trees. That makes it less likely he's in his cabin building bombs which, admit it, is what we've all feared."

"It wasn't Ed." Connie spoke into the collar of her raincoat. "Everyone always suspects the introverts." No one would guess Connie was responsible. She wasn't sure how she felt about that. She lifted her chin to speak up. "That must have been kind of scary for Dylan. Send him down after our walk and I'll talk to him. I wanted to go over some stuff anyway."

When Dylan sat down at her kitchen table later that morning, Connie was ready. She slid a package of cookies towards him the way she might bait an animal she wanted to tame. Not too close. She wanted him to reach. "You seemed like you belonged in the wetland the other day, perched on that beaver lodge."

"That's the only dry place to sit." He held himself stiffly, as though he didn't want to take up any more space than necessary.

"You looked so content. Like you belonged there."

He exhaled with a small puff of derision. "I can fit in anyplace."

"Right." Connie poured boiling water into the teapot, talking casually. To some teenagers, every approach seems like an attack. "You've spent a lot of time out there. What have you seen?"

"Same stuff you see. Water, grass, trees, and bushes." Dylan pulled a small notebook from his satchel. He opened it and looked at it for some time. "Birds. Frogs. I might have seen the beaver. A splash. Could have been something else."

Connie reached out to take the notebook, but Dylan's long fingers curled around it.

"May I see your notes?"

He looked at her with a rigid expression, his eyes wide, his mouth pursed, like he was imitating an emoji. "They aren't notes." He put the book back in his satchel. "It's not like I'm going to see something you've never seen."

Maybe kids were right to hold themselves aloof from adults, to maintain the pure innocence of their outrage. Connie envied that, her own outrage so thoroughly compromised.

"You might see something new." She spoke reasonably and the effort made her feel claustrophobic. "Otto and I talked about doing a survey of the forest. We thought you could do an inventory, but I'd need you to take notes and share them with me."

"What kind of notes?" Dylan retreated more deeply into himself. "I don't know what all that shit is up there."

"What have you put in your notebook so far?" She hadn't asked Ellen about his education, if he had any learning disabilities. So much to keep track of.

"I just made some drawings." Dylan slumped back in his chair. "I sketched what I saw."

"Good start." She nodded as though sketching was the absolute best way to compile a survey. She gave him a printed hand-out of common native plants, and showed him how it was organized by tree, shrub, and ground plants. "You can get names from this and look them up on your phone. Take some pictures too. Label your drawings. You can make a list from that."

She had to assume Dylan heard and understood, but he gave no indication. Out on the street, a car drove by, and they both lifted their gaze to watch it pass. Dylan looked back to the table and Connie drank her tea.

"Well." She set her empty cup pointedly on the table between them, "have you seen *anything* interesting?"

Dylan scrunched his shoulders and turned sideways in his chair. "They thought I spray-painted the trees."

"So I heard." She ought to end the mystery, but how could she go up to Otto's and stand before that panoramic view, the tasteful furnishings, and well-managed projects and tell her tale? "Was Otto mad?" He must have been indignant to ferret out Dylan, but he would be the sort who would want to get to the bottom of it. "Did he accuse you?"

"Not exactly. He wondered if I'd seen anything. What do I care about those trees? I'm going back to Seattle as soon as I can. Aunt Ellen told them I didn't know anything about anything."

"There's no reason to think you did it. Where would you have gotten the paint?" Connie watched the skinny boy in her peripheral vision. He was closing in on six feet tall, but still insubstantial—all arms and legs. Dylan looked at her quickly, furtively, and even though she knew better, she was suddenly afraid she had paint on her hands.

"Otto marked the trees again," Dylan told her, "and he's going to log around the tipi tomorrow. He put up some wildlife cameras. He said he'll show me any animals he discovers, but I think he's mostly looking for vandals."

Connie nodded. "Will you have a cookie?" She slid the bag closer.

"I'm vegan."

"Oh." She ate another cookie even though she wasn't really hungry. "Do you want an orange?" she asked as an afterthought.

He shrugged and it took Connie a moment to realize he meant yes. She put an orange and some nuts in a yellow bowl and set them in front of the boy. He began eating immediately, stacking the orange peels in a little tower, fragrant and gleaming with oil.

When the food was gone, she took Dylan up to the ridge and had him show her the cameras. She was astonished at how easily he spotted them. She had to make careful mental notes, identifying landmarks, estimating distances, but Dylan just seemed to know. He moved quickly and quietly in the forest, blending into the pockets of shade beneath the canopy. She pointed things out as they walked. She made him stop and look closely at the poison oak that filled the margin of the woods. "Leaves of three, let it be," she told him as she had been told in her own childhood, but the poison oak was only beginning to leaf out, so she made him note the twiggy shrubs and the thick vines climbing the fir trees. "It's terrible in spring," she warned, "even before the leaves are all out."

Dylan brought Connie to the trees Otto planned to save. They were now marked with white paint. Mostly Douglas fir in a rim around the clearing, they were all over a century old, their trunks thick and furrowed. Connie moved among them, looking up into the canopy.

"Forests grow so that they minimize the strength of the wind," she said. Dylan trailed behind her. Maybe he was listening. "Each tree moves differently to break up the force." Without the protection of their neighbors, the saved trees would be dangerous in a windstorm. "These trees don't have any low branches because they grew up in the center of the forest." Connie made Dylan stop and look. "When Otto chops down their neighbors, their branches will catch the wind like a flag." She glanced at Dylan who gazed upward, bored and dutiful. "Look around, Dylan, and tell me the direction of the prevailing winds." She was being petty, but she thought it was worth noting that Otto's plans were as flimsy as anyone's.

Dylan's brow furrowed as he gazed up into the canopy.

"No, look at the forest floor."

"Oh!"

It was obvious to him as it would be to anyone who looked. All the downed timber in the old forest lay with their bases pointing south and their tops to the north. "So that tree there," she pointed back to one of the chosen trees. "If it falls, where do you think it will land?"

"On Otto's shed."

Connie locked eyes with Dylan and nodded. It would serve Otto right.

17

Connie spent the afternoon wiping her counters and mopping the floors. When she was done, the house was scoured as clean as an old seashell. She drank coffee all the way into the evening, and by midnight she was wide awake and buzzing. Once more, she pulled on her dark clothes and walked up the hill, giving time for her eyes to adjust to the dark. The squawking of a juvenile owl pierced the murmur of rain, and the forest around her felt feral and exciting. Connie had to avoid the cameras, but she sprayed most of the trees around the clearing. This time, she painted a simple flower: five scribbly petals and a blotch at the center, obliterating the marks Otto made. She took the trouble because it didn't seem like something Ed the hermit would do. When she was finished, she crept to the edge of the clearing and listened for Otto's snores but found only silence. Even so, she was on the verge of making the rounds, marking the shed, the deck, and the car this time. She had just moved out of the shadow of the forest when she spotted Otto himself, wide awake and seated on the deck near the tipi door. She froze. He was wrapped in a blanket and sheltered from the rain by a brimmed hat. She had to assume his eyes, too, had adjusted. Silently, she dropped into a crouch. He hadn't seen her yet, but if he looked, she would be visible. She wanted to run away, but she would expose herself if she moved. Her foot grew numb as she squatted, and she dropped one knee to the moist soil. Then Otto flicked a lighter to a pipe at his lips and Connie saw his face in the flash of yellow. As the skunk-like odor of cannabis drifted downhill, Otto stared out over the dark forest. He sighed audibly and Connie recognized the voice of loneliness, but she had no time to feel the kinship then. The flash of light would blind him, and it gave her the opportunity to melt back into the woods.

Connie got safely home but couldn't go to sleep. The brush with Otto ought to have made her reconsider her behavior, but it had the opposite effect. She felt triumphant. She cleared the old games and puzzles out of the closet. When she was done with that, she went through the bathroom drawers, discarding old make-up and out-of-date medications, although she saved her bottle of pills as a sort of talisman. She filled an entire bag for the homeless shelter with new bars of soap and bottles of shampoo that her ex-husband Mike had liked to buy in bulk. The excess had always irritated her, but he stopped shopping as Cary's illness worsened. Connie had supposed the presence of death had given him a new perspective. She was wrong, as it turned out. Mike had just shifted his behavior; he became a hoarder of secrets.

At the time, she had been shocked and disgusted at the discovery of his double life. The duplicity had seemed tangled and congested. But now she understood the power in it. A person with a secret has two lives, and two lives at odds with one another cancelled each other out. If she was both a vandal and a diligent householder, then she was, somehow, neither. By the end of the night, all but one drawer was empty, and each empty drawer seemed like a possibility. She went to bed as the sun rose and slept well into the morning.

In the late afternoon, a wrenching crack split the quiet day and the whole earth shuddered. The sheep in the pasture raised their heads and looked toward the ridge as birds lifted from the trees. The sound of something so huge and heavy falling to earth held a dreadful finality. Connie listened to the keening saw, cringing until the snap of separation and the earthshaking landing. She heard three trees come down that afternoon, each felling followed by the high-pitched whine of a smaller chainsaw as the trees were limbed. Just before five, Dylan arrived.

"They're cutting the trees." He looked distraught, his narrow hands balled up in fists that held his thumbs.

"That was the plan," Connie said, leading him in.

"I thought we were supposed to do the survey first."

"As much as we can. The survey, the bet. It's kind of a joke." This was the truth, after all. Dylan's jaw hardened as he swallowed, and Connie regretted her words, noticing too late that he had said *we*. "Otto's just doing some selective clearing to get the roads in. He'll do the bulk of the logging when the ground is drier."

"Look." Dylan pulled his notebook from his satchel and opened it up on the kitchen table. In a large view spanning two pages, he had drawn a whole downed fir, the broken branches and the surrounding shrubbery stripped and mangled by the big tree's fall.

Connie wanted to study the intricate drawing, but she was afraid he would pull it away. She kept some distance as they regarded the elaborately contoured bark, the shattered limbs, the confusion of shadow among the broken branches. The drawing was as detailed as a botanical illustration, but he was bold with shade and line, and managed to express the raw violence that had troubled her all afternoon. Ruin.

"I surveyed the tree," he kept his jaw tight, almost swallowing his words so that Connie had to strain to hear. He turned the page and showed her more drawings of lichen and moss—usnea, lobaria, dendroalsia, and others Connie didn't know.

"How interesting." But she was thinking about the drawing and wondering how she could get a better view. It took her a moment to notice his narrow index finger pointing to something amidst the wreckage of branches.

He flattened the notebook and this time he did slide it over to her. Like the forest itself, the notebook offered rewards to the careful observer—a wren with its beak open in song, usnea sprouting from a lichen scabbed branch. But Dylan was tapping one spot repeatedly, making a soft sound like a dripping faucet.

She saw. There had been a large platform nest in the tree. Dylan had drawn it smashed and scattered on the forest floor. His fingertip rested nearby and there she saw the tiny, fluffy form of an owlet. It had not feathered yet and could not fly. Dylan had drawn it with cartoon X's for eyes. Nearby, another body.

"Great horned owlets," Connie said. "I heard them last night."

"I made a note so you could find them." Tiny print, all capitals: *forty paces from the road between the twisty tree and the big fir.* "I know you're not supposed to move anything before the police come."

"Police?"

"To arrest Otto. For killing the owls."

"Otto's allowed to harvest his timber."

"But not to kill owls."

Connie looked over to the boy as he gazed down at the notebook. His hair was dyed a flat, coal black, but his eyebrows were sable, the left pierced with a small cheap ring of silver. He looked like a child playing dress-up.

"Great horned owls aren't endangered. It would be illegal to shoot them, but he's not responsible if they die from logging."

Dylan didn't lift his head. "But if he'd waited," he mumbled, "they would have been able to fly away. They were *babies.*"

Connie laid her hand on his boney shoulder, barely muscled beneath the black jacket. He startled and she quickly removed it. "There are always babies." She looked at him, not the picture. "Owls hatch their eggs early. In a couple months, the songbirds would have been just as vulnerable. Did you show the pictures to Otto?"

"No." He looked shocked at the suggestion. "He still thinks I painted the trees. I wish I did. Even if it didn't help." He closed the notebook and put it back in his satchel.

"Let's go up and have a look," Connie said. "We can show Otto together."

She got a basket and some pieces of newspaper and followed Dylan. He bent forward at the hips, leaning into the hill, and she had to jog to keep up with his long-legged strides. She was sorry and surprised to see him so upset. She had thought the shell of his apathy was a little thicker, but he was becoming invested in the project. That had to be a good thing.

18

They found the tiny bodies of the owlets flung some distance from the tree. Connie gathered them and laid them on the newspaper in the basket. "Look at the eyes, Dylan." She used a gloved hand to press the fuzz back. The eyeballs were already gone, but the sockets were enormous, the bones startlingly white in the small soft face.

They followed the high whine of power tools to the shed where Otto was installing a counter along one wall. "Knock-knock," Connie said at the open door.

Otto pushed himself upright and set the screwdriver down. "If it isn't my own personal EPA."

"It isn't." Connie stepped across the threshold into sunlight streaming from generous windows cased with fir. The counter Otto was installing was some kind of reclaimed wood, dark with age. "This is the fanciest shed I've ever seen." She placed the basket with the owlets on the counter and slid them toward Otto. "They'd been nesting in one of the trees you felled."

"Ah." He touched the fine fuzz on the owlet's head. The corpse was no bigger than his hand. "I'm really sorry."

Dylan exhaled sharply, but Connie only shrugged. "I explained to Dylan that if you'd waited a couple months, these owlets might have survived, but other nestlings would have died."

Otto lifted the body from the basket and extended the tiny wing. From the soft fuzzy chaos, perfect feathers were beginning to form at the tip.

"But with the trees gone, and the disruption from development," Connie continued, "the parents may not have been able to keep them alive anyway Great horned owls are territorial. They can't just move if their hunting grounds fail."

Dylan pulled the basket away from Otto. He used an index finger to splay a crumpled talon.

"I'm really very sorry." Otto looked just at Connie now. "I don't know what else to say."

Connie crossed her arms and waited, wondering if he would mention the bet. He must see that this was just the beginning of the losses that were to come. But they were interrupted by the crunch of tires on gravel. A truck rolled past the shed door to park nearby.

"It's the logger." Otto hesitated, his hand on the counter near the owls. "I've got to talk to him."

"We won't keep you. I thought you might be interested. It's not often you can see an owlet that close."

"You can see baby owls any time you want on YouTube," Dylan said.

Connie and Otto both looked at the boy, unsure of how to respond.

"The owls on YouTube move." Dylan smoothed the feathers and settled the bodies, side by side. "On YouTube, the owls make noise and eat things." He stroked the down with his index finger.

"I guess we should bury them." Connie couldn't imagine throwing them away and she thought a burial might help Dylan. They returned to the fallen tree and scraped a shallow hole in the soft humus. Dylan laid them in the ground and pushed the soil over them. His hands were pale against the dirt except for black marks on his knuckles, maybe words or letters.

"Life is fragile," Connie said over the grave. Dylan made a grunting sound that might have been disagreement or might have been a stifled sob. His pictures had looked so sad, the violent mess of branches and the X'-d eyes. "They were perfect baby owls, ready to grow quiet wings and fierce talons." A sob rose in her throat like a flooding wave. She swallowed hard and the wave moved up into her head. Tears started in her eyes. "Well," she said, but it came out choked. Dylan looked at her with a shocked expression. It wasn't the owls that made her cry. Owls died all the time and were born all the time. She wasn't crying over owls. She wiped her hands on her jeans and stepped away from the grave. "Other birds will move in. Crows. Ravens. That's what our survey will track." She fixed the boy with a serious look. "That's your job, Dylan. Notice everything. Take pictures. Draw."

"We're like those war photographers who watch without helping." Dylan's lips were thin and bitter.

Connie lifted one shoulder and let it fall. She couldn't deny it. "Pretty much."

"Fucking monsters," he said in a tone of wonder.

19

Dylan's bitter face haunted Connie all the next day. He had opened up, but to what? She thought of the paper fortune tellers she made as a child, counting and rhyming to arrive at a set of choices. Beneath each paper flap, a different future. Choose one. Under other circumstances, Dylan might have opened differently.

She used to teach her students that simply paying attention had its own power. But in the hospital, people paid a lot of attention as Cary died. They had watched and measured every physical system and Cary only weakened. By the time they unhooked Cary from the monitors, her breath was shallow and her body as slight as a child's. The monitors, sleek and well fed, were polished and pushed against the wall to sleep until their next patient. Now Dylan witnessed the last weeks of the forest and Connie witnessed Dylan's growing engagement, and Ellen pretended that everyone benefited, but Connie wasn't so sure.

Connie made scrambled eggs for dinner which left plenty of time for thought, and she thought she had better tell Ellen to find Dylan some more cheerful job. He could work at the humane society saving kittens, and even though the world did not need more kittens, and there was so much it did need, still, that might be best. She washed and dried her plate and silverware and placed them back in the drawer. It would be easier if living were harder, if she had to fetch water from a well and bury her waste; she needed to spend herself but everything she did seemed to cause more trouble. Outside the window, the pastures turned golden as the sun neared the horizon. She laced up her shoes and ran hard down the back steps, her worry replaced by the complaints of her old knees and ankles.

By the time Connie reached the end of her driveway her breath was ragged, and her legs felt leaden. She slowed her pace. Every time her foot touched the earth, she thought—*rest*. By the corner, she had settled into a rhythm: the rebound of her feet on the ground, the carrying power of her breath. Her heart contracted and released as it did every moment of every day. A muscle the size of her fist, with no back up. What a flimsy arrangement! But it hadn't been a failure of heart that took Cary. Blood cancer. A confusion of manufacturing. And as Cary sickened, both from the cancer and then from the treatment, her heart had marched on, carrying her forward into each new moment even as she withdrew into pain, closed-eyed and distracted. Connie, watching, thought her own heart would break, but it didn't. Now as she ran, it asserted its power, and she had come to believe that the heart has its own agenda, separate from a person's ideas, that we are all hostages.

"Connie! Hey Connie!"

She turned to look down the lane that led to Otto's ridge. Annabelle was waving as she approached with Otto. Connie stopped to let her breath slow, waiting for them to reach her. Annabelle's long legs brought her to Connie in almost the same amount of time it would have taken Connie to jog.

"I was just thinking about you, and here you are!" Annabelle put her hands in the back pockets of her jeans and smiled broadly. "Otto! Come meet Connie. I have the best idea!"

"We know each other," Connie said.

"Of course!" Annabelle laughed as Otto caught up. "I knew that! Otto bought his land from you."

"Connie was up at my place just yesterday," Otto added, nodding hello. "Owl-shaming me."

Annabelle giggled as though he'd made a joke. She brushed her long blonde hair away from her face, and leaned onto his shoulder, the two of them facing Connie.

"I was *not* owl-shaming you." Even though Connie had cooled, she felt her cheeks flush.

Otto turned to speak to Annabelle directly, separating himself from her so that the three stood evenly spaced. "Unfortunately, we killed some baby owls with the logging. Connie brought their sad little corpses up for me to see."

"I thought you'd be interested." Connie was speaking too vehemently. She took a breath and started over. "I didn't mean to make you feel bad."

"You didn't?" Otto fixed her with his gaze. Annabelle edged in to lean on his arm, but he didn't look away from Connie.

"Maybe a little. Dylan was so upset." Connie shook herself and jogged in place, eager to get away. "You said you wanted to learn about the place."

"See?" Annabelle said as though she had made some point. "Connie is a very studious person. Otto, if you need to know anything about a plant or animal, call Connie. That's what the rest of us do."

"I was moved by the owls." Otto said, still speaking to Connie. "I'm glad you showed me."

"I wasn't trying to punish you. Death is as common as birth. As necessary. I'll talk to Dylan about that tomorrow."

"Don't talk about death!" Annabelle stamped her foot. "Just now," she told Connie, "I brought a picnic up to Otto because he's always working. I was thinking, what would be fun?" She grasped their shoulders, right hand on Connie, left on Otto, and gave a comradely shake. "I thought we should put in a trail system. Otto can put in trails around his vineyard, and we can hook them up to trails on your property, Connie, down by the creek. I'll add some around my paddocks, and we would have miles of trails. Connie wouldn't have to jog on the road, and I could use them for my horses. I'm going to teach Otto how to ride. I can't believe you lived in Texas and don't ride."

Otto shrugged. "I was in Houston."

The sun slipped beneath the horizon and cold blue shadows crept up the trees. "I gotta go," Connie told them as she hopped from foot to foot.

"We'll talk more about those trails. We can go exploring tomorrow," Annabelle said to Otto. "We can get the workers to clear passages while you've got that big bulldozer up there." Annabelle never wasted any time.

Connie waved and ran as fast as she could up the hill. Her lungs burned. She ran until the muscles of her legs began to quiver. She thought she might vomit. Thanks to her, Annabelle and Otto could ride European horses around a French-style vineyard on a deforested Oregon mountain. But not happily ever after. She had rounded the bend and immediately dropped to a walk. No one got to live happily ever after anymore, and the people smart enough to see that were doubly cursed because they had to watch, fully cognizant, as disaster loomed. It was painfully unfair, just as it wasn't fair that Cary, if she had to die, couldn't have died in a car crash in the middle of a busy afternoon.

Fair had nothing to do with anything important. Connie paused at the top of the hill to look south down the broad open valley. This view was visible every day from Annabelle's summit estate, where her wealthy boyfriend had set her up fifteen years ago with her own horse barn and training facility. The boyfriend made Annabelle his third wife and stayed long enough to expand the house and put in a pool. Annabelle had cheered on every change. The sparkling view of the lights at night! More sophisticated restaurants in the village! And more and more interesting people, wealthy people like Otto, moving to the neighborhood. Connie was glad she'd showed Otto the owls. If she could win Dylan over, she would show Otto and Annabelle every drawing Dylan made.

20

When Connie got home from her evening run, she found Ellen waiting on her porch.

"I'm looking for happy hour," Ellen called, waving a bottle of Pinot Gris.

"You thought you'd find it here?" Connie held her open palms up to the sky.

"I knew it wouldn't be crowded, anyway."

Ellen followed Connie into the house and Connie poured herself a big glass of water as she got Ellen a glass for wine.

"How do you think Dylan's doing?" Ellen asked.

Connie splashed cold water on her face and dried it with the kitchen towel. She drank the water down and then another before pouring herself some wine. She lifted a shoulder in an uncertain shrug. "He's a sweet kid," she said. "I think he really likes being outside."

They went out to sit on the back steps with a view of the pastures and the ridge beyond, now with an unfamiliar gap where the trees had been felled. Connie's eyes studied it compulsively, the way the tongue explores the void left by a lost tooth.

"Those owls," Ellen said. "I didn't think about how sad the project would be."

"I'm sorry about that." Connie took a big swig of wine. Now that Ellen was voicing her own doubts, she felt defensive. "That's the world he lives in. But he's invested in the project, and that's a good thing. His drawings are amazing, but it might be easier on him emotionally if he just took pictures with his phone."

Ellen craned her neck to look right in Connie's face. "His phone?"

"I know," Connie acknowledged. "I'm usually trying to pry kids *away* from their phone, but in this case the detachment might be good."

"Talk about sheltered." Ellen finished her glass of wine and poured some more from the bottle she'd left chilling in the grass. "Dylan doesn't have a smart phone. Where would that kid get a phone?"

Connie felt a sudden cold shame in her belly. "He didn't ever say . . ."

"Of course not. I bet when teachers told him to do his homework, he never told them he didn't have a home," Ellen said.

Connie sat for some time in silence. "I'm going to buy him one."

"I can get him a phone if he needs one."

"No, I want to," Connie said. "You can pay for his service. I just wasn't thinking." This is the world he has to live in, but she could at least give him the common tools. "Listen, I'll talk to him about the owls' death tomorrow. Put it in perspective for him."

"Please don't." Ellen set her glass down so hard some wine slopped out. "Sorry." She mopped the wine up with her sleeve. "You gave me your death lecture once, and I still haven't recovered. I understand the sages used to meditate on the charnel grounds, but you are forbidden to tell Dylan what charnel grounds are. I think I can get him a slot at the ice cream shop."

Connie felt a tightening at the pit of her stomach. "How does Dylan feel about that?"

"He objects."

"He likes doing the survey?"

"I can't say he *likes* anything. He never smiles, Connie. And he stays up all night drawing, and now he's prowling around outside at night. Did you tell him to do that?"

"I haven't given him much instruction." She had given him rubber boots and sent him outside. "He's an artist. I hated to interfere."

"He showed his drawings to you?" Ellen sounded hurt. "That *is* promising."

"Only to show me the owls."

Ellen tossed her wine back and poured herself more before topping off Connie's glass. She leaned back on her elbows and looked up to the rising quarter moon. "I think he should go to the ice cream shop."

"If he wants to." Connie knew that Ellen would recognize the desperation in her voice and the feeling of exposure caused tears to well. She blinked hard to stop them. "But if he doesn't want to quit, give me another week or two. I'll be a better teacher."

Ellen studied Connie as she drank her wine. "Don't get too attached, Connie. He's got problems and you might not be able to help. I'm going to look for options in town."

"Whatever." Connie set her glass aside, the wine sour in her stomach. "Really. Whatever is best for Dylan." She wouldn't get attached. She would get less attached to everything every day.

21

Before her next meeting with Dylan, Connie stocked up on nuts and fruit and hummus and crackers. She cut up carrots and celery and cauliflower. When it was all laid out on the table, she saw she had enough to host a small party. But if she had to talk about death (she would avoid the lecture but couldn't entirely avoid the subject) she thought the subject might be easier if it was surrounded by the comfort of food. When Dylan arrived, he sat stiffly in the kitchen chair. He didn't even pull it up to the table. He kept his distance from the food, his satchel on his lap. Connie dipped a piece of celery into the hummus and ate it noisily. She wasn't hungry and the food made a lump in her throat.

"Eat," she said. "I got this for you."

"All of it?"

She shrugged. It was ridiculous. He kept his distance but reached for a handful of nuts.

"It's what we do in the face of grief, isn't it?" She looked sadly at the blameless vegetables. "I've walked out in those woods pretty much every day for a quarter of a century." She nodded her head toward the window. "Losing the forest is like losing a member of the family."

"Like losing the whole family." Dylan flipped through the pages of his notebook as if to say, *all that and more.*

Connie raised her empty hands. "If we let death shut us down, we would never get up. Think about it; it's as common as birth. Let's go out to the wetland." She stood and waited for Dylan to rise. "I'll show you the survey work we've been doing with the kids over the years so you'll be up to speed when they all come out." She hadn't called the high school yet, but she could set it up that afternoon.

All along the gravel drive, Connie had to keep turning to check that Dylan still trailed behind. His bony wrists poked out from the sleeves of Mike's plaid jacket, but although it was too short it was far too wide for the fine-boned boy; he was a sapling, a whip, a slip of a thing.

"You've seen this place change in the weeks you've been watching—new leaves, insects, birds. Not too many years ago, it was all forest." She waved an arm toward the greening pastureland. "After it was logged, settlers used it for livestock. Even though they trenched the creek, it's too wet to grow much besides grass." The ground became softer as they approached the pond. "Before the Europeans arrived, the native Americans used to burn the fields in the valley to keep the trees out." Connie could hear Dylan squelching through the mud just behind her, so she kept talking. "They did it to encourage the wild camas—the roots were a staple food. These planned burns increased diversity by making more marginal spaces. The edge of the forest and the edge of wetlands will have species from both habitats. It's a liminal space." She turned and Dylan stopped clumsily. "Do you know what liminal means?"

He looked at her out of the top of his eyes, bored, patronizing.

"It comes from a Latin root meaning threshold." Connie turned around and continued walking. "Liminal spaces are margins, ambiguous places." She couldn't be sure he heard her, but she kept talking. "Full of possibility."

They reached the edge of the shallow pond. Connie pulled the clipboard with the survey summary out of her backpack, but Dylan shoved his hands deep into the pockets of the plaid fleece. He had pulled the collar up around his ears, and the jacket gapped an inch above his silver studded belt.

"Most animals change the landscapes where they live—eating, building nests, making trails. Humans have changed this place from forest to field to wetland." Connie showed him the survey. Every year, new arrivals. "Sometimes we change things in ways that benefit other species." She started wading, speaking over her shoulder with more animation, trying to ignite the boy. He looked so cold. "Beavers do too. They kill some trees, but their construction slows the flow of surface water which helps replenish ground water. More sunlight gets through so more plants can establish themselves. Birds and insects follow the plants."

Dylan listened to Connie's explanations and looked where she pointed, but he didn't ask any questions.

"Well," she said loudly. She had wanted to show him the evidence of new life, but she didn't really have anything for them to do out there. When Dylan saw that her lecture was over, he turned around and began to slog back to the house. Connie caught up, hoping to talk about the young wetland, but he shuffled slowly, plowing his feet through the mud. Occasionally, a boot stuck and he'd have to bend down to hold the top to keep from stepping right out of it.

Back at the house, she threw the boots in the giveaway pile and handed him his black sneakers. Their white rubber was stained with red mud and the canvas had begun to stretch and bulge. "You should have told me you couldn't walk in those boots." Connie watched him slowly tie his shoes, irritated by his quiet passivity.

"I told you they were too big when you gave them to me."

"But I forgot! You have to advocate for yourself, Dylan. Speak up and tell people what you need."

"I don't really need anything." He stood and leaned against the wall, blending in.

"Everyone has needs." This was indisputably true, but even as Connie said it, she doubted. She was whittling her own needs down, and it was easier than she ever would have guessed. "Anyway, I wanted you to see that even as we lose the forest, the wetland thrives. Some changes seem good. Some seem bad. But change itself is constant. I just wanted you to see that."

"I see what's *there,* not what used to be there." He spoke to the space next to Connie, as though to her shadow, a smaller and more timid persona who required careful explanations. "That's the thing about drawing. You have to see what's there and nothing else. Right now, you only have half a face." He caught her eye and held her gaze, his own eyes round and dramatic. "That's what's there. Half is lost in shadow. I can't *see* change." He continued to stare, letting some existential question reverberate between them, then his gaze slid away. "I know what you mean, but it's only pretending."

Connie turned her head away from him until she felt the light from the window touch her whole face, as though restoring it to his vision would make some kind of difference. "I don't buy that, Dylan. When you drew the baby owls you drew what was there—the shape, the chick fluff, their little talons. But you did more." She continued to face the window, showing him her face. "You drew those X's for their eyes. But death isn't really there, is it? It's an absence.

"Tomorrow, I'll meet you on the ridge to get you started on a rough map of Otto's forest." It was an ambitious assignment, but Connie thought it might be a welcome challenge. Mostly, she wanted to make him move more, hoping to tire him. If she kept them both busy, Otto's vineyard might fade into the background like the noise from the freeway faded when she focused on the birds. She opened the door and watched him leave.

22

Connie woke the next morning to the sound of rain, her heart pounding from a dream she couldn't remember. As she lay in bed, the darkness faded, leaving Connie with weak daylight and a silly plan to survey the forest with Dylan. She wasn't up to it. The project wasn't any benefit to science, and Dylan wasn't really eager. She couldn't dredge up any compelling reason to get out of bed. Some people managed to die that way; they just quit eating and drinking and moving around, but it wasn't easy. The paradox of dying was that it was fundamentally an act of living, as visceral and effortful as birth and love. And like birth and love, death was a community event. One way or another, every death touches others and changes them. In Cary's case, people fell away from her as she died, as though she were contagious. Once illness became protracted, casual friends disappeared. When illness became terminal, even close friends drifted off, furtive if Connie passed them in the grocery store. And although Connie was hungry for news of life, Cary's old friends spared her the stories of their new jobs, marriages, and babies. Connie had known some of those kids since preschool and loved them still from afar, but she understood their need for distance. When Cary had decided not to travel to Houston for one last debilitating and experimental intervention, even Mike faded away, taking refuge in his office. Cary lived four more months.

Outside, a restless wind shredded the cloud cover, and the trees began to sparkle, scattering rain. Birdsong came through the open windows, a crescendo that broke around the house in chaotic song.

The astonishing beauty of that chorus came like a rebuke, and Connie threw the covers aside, but still she didn't rise. She lay exposed and cold as the wave of praise passed, traveling west with the rising sun.

By the time Connie was in her kitchen drinking coffee, the clouds had thickened and dropped. The forecast called for more rain, and she considered cancelling the work with Dylan, but then what? The days were so long. She rummaged through the mudroom for foul weather gear. Mike's rain pants would be too short for Dylan but better than nothing. She stuffed them in her backpack along with a serviceable hat she was almost sure Dylan would refuse to wear. Everything else of Mike's she threw in the garbage.

When Mike began to separate from the family, Connie let him be. After thirty years of marriage their patterns were well-established and, Connie had thought, well-accepted. She became busy, scheduling nurses and visitors and planning meals. Mike would spend forty-five minutes every morning reading the newspaper with Cary, then he left for work and didn't return until late, usually after Connie had gone to sleep. But one morning Mike paused on his way out the door. He'd waved his hand at the schedule Connie had pinned to the bulletin board. "You think if you plan Cary's life she'll have to stay and live it? Maybe she just wants you to leave her alone." With uncharacteristic drama, he had looked Connie in the eye a moment to let his words sink in. Then he smirked, a horrible little smile of derision that Connie would never forget. He slammed the back door. The porch, already beginning to rot, trembled.

He had spoken from the safe distance of his double life, but Connie didn't know that then. It was a week longer before she happened to see a text filled with emojis. A domestic text with dinner plans, requesting groceries, sending love. From Mike's thirty-four-year-old administrative assistant.

A week after Cary's funeral, when Connie was too spent to argue, Mike packed two suitcases and left. He left the assistant, too. He seemed newly confident, as though Connie had held him against his will all those years and he was suddenly free. For a while, Connie still thought it might be a misunderstanding, but the mud dried on his work gloves and crumbled to dust in the drawer. His farm shoes stiffened and cracked. He didn't want his books or any of the furniture or even the personal gifts he had received over the years. He took his two suitcases and moved to California, where he'd been born and hadn't lived for thirty years, as though his whole adult life had been some kind of detour.

23

Connie skirted the logged area as she went to meet Dylan on the ridge. The few trees that had been felled had been limbed but not yet dragged for removal, and the forest around them was smashed. Life beneath the canopy was usually serene. Big trees filtered wind and rain and protected the tender growth from the searing sun. After a storm, raindrops continued to sieve gently from the upper branches. Now the sudden devastation was strange and alarming.

Connie sat with her back against a fir tree near Ellen's driveway where she would be sure to see Dylan as he came to meet her. English ivy had colonized Ellen's side of the road, and Connie absently peeled the vines away from the trunk as she waited. A fine mist coated her hat and jacket, but her rain pants kept her dry as she pulled the tough ivy roots from the soil. She gathered the ivy and hung the bundle high on a snag to keep it from re-rooting. Across the lane in Otto's woods, tender green sprouts lay trampled and wilting in the rain. When the loggers came in to drag the timber away there would be more destruction. She and Dylan could survey near the lane before then. It might be instructive to notice the unique stages of devastation from the felling, dragging, and bulldozing—to see which species lost out when. She could talk to him about soil compaction. She closed her eyes and listened to the birds and the slow drip of moisture from the branches. When she opened her eyes again, Dylan was leaning against the tree beside her. "You surprised me."

He scuffed his toe in the mat of ivy. "What's this stuff?" After weeks outside, he was not so pale, and the cold morning brought a pretty, boyish flush to his cheeks.

"English ivy." Connie scrambled up to stand beside him. "I pull out as much as I can."

"You weed the woods?"

"Just the ivy. This is interesting, Dylan." She led him more deeply into the forest at the side of Ellen's house. Ivy blanketed the ground and bearded the tree trunks. They stood among the peaceful trees for about five minutes, then she led him across the street where the forest had not yet been disturbed. Immediately, they were surrounded by birdsong. A variegated thrush scratched furiously in the soil at the base of some scrappy berry vines. "What's the difference?"

"It's a mess here," Dylan said. The forest floor was chaotic and uneven. Soil bubbled where a mushroom had broken through last summer's leaves.

"Yes!" She laughed. "That's diversity. Mess! People like ivy because it's so tidy. But nothing eats ivy and it takes over. Fewer plants mean fewer insects which mean fewer birds. Less of everything. I've done my best to keep the ivy from spreading." Soon, three decades of effort would be irrelevant. The ivy would be scraped away with everything else. "But I was losing that war." She unzipped the pack and pulled the extra rain pants out.

"Put these on," she said to Dylan. Above her, manic warbling tumbled down from the canopy. She always meant to learn the birds' songs. Now there were apps for that. It was easier than ever, and she still hadn't done it. Dylan held the pants up doubtfully. "We'll be cutting through the brush," she said turning away from the birds. "You'll be soaked if you don't."

He wriggled into the pants. They were plenty wide but four inches too short. To her surprise he put the hat on without complaint and followed her out to the lane.

"There's one of Otto's wildlife cameras." He pointed to a low branch on one of the young firs. Connie never would have spotted it on her own.

"So near the road," she said.

"He's more interested in vandals than in wildlife."

Connie nodded. She was sure Dylan was correct, but Otto could do what he liked, and she didn't want to fuel Dylan's theories.

They tied a cord around a tree and bushwhacked to run a sixty-foot line along the ridge, fixing the other end to another tree. Connie handed Dylan a role of fluorescent pink surveyor's tape and explained how he should walk the line and leave a flag every twenty feet. Connie left him with that and began to run a parallel line about forty-feet downhill. She got it all fixed and Dylan still hadn't rejoined her. As she waited, she heard the brush of nylon against branches but then periods with no audible movement at all. She retraced her path until she spotted him, stopped at a recently fallen fir prickly with branches.

"Just crawl right over," she said trying not to be impatient. He broke three branches before he made it over then he looked around at the tangled forest with a baffled expression.

Connie pulled a water bottle from her pack and passed it to him. "Keep an eye out for poison oak." She pointed to a bare branch, a furled leaf sprouting from its tip like a candle flame.

"Who lives there?" Dylan pointed high up a nearby fir tree.

Yellow-green maple flowers dripped from ruffled branches. More flowers littered the forest floor like scattered bouquets. Connie searched beyond the lacy foliage to spot the large platform nest. "Could be a squirrel or an owl or a hawk. Those big nests get used over and over by a variety of animals," she said. "You've got a sharp eye."

Dylan handed her the bottle back. "I have sonic eyes," he said.

"*Sonic* eyes?"

Dylan nodded. He was entirely serious. "This force comes out of my eyes and bounces off whatever I'm looking at. I can even see in the dark."

If anyone needed a super-power, this boy did. She was glad he'd found one for himself. "That's convenient,"

He shook his head. "Sometimes one eye gets stronger than the other and it just pushes my head around." He swiveled his head to demonstrate. "Sometimes I have to wear an eye patch."

"I'd like to see in the dark." Connie rummaged in her pack and pulled out some granola bars. She did not have a sharp eye. When she sat still in the woods, her mind wandered. She got to thinking about things and missed opportunities.

"The other problem is my peripheral vision sucks." Dylan put his hands at the sides of his eyes, like blinders. "It's pretty easy to sneak up on me. That's why I'm always kind of nervous."

Connie had never seen him so relaxed. She handed him a granola bar and watched as he peeled the wrapper away. "Have you seen an eye doctor?"

"My eyes are fine; they're just sonic. I was born that way."

"I have good peripheral vision." Connie leaned back and looked without focusing. The whole forest poured in—leaves, needles, light, shadow, movement. Her attention jumped from near distance to far distance, greedy and unfocused.

"Can you see the owl on the third branch up?" Dylan pointed and Connie leaned over to line her sight up, but she didn't see anything beyond the many shades of green. "Over there," he said. "About twenty feet up."

Even with careful instructions it took Connie some time to spot the snoozing owl. It was the same mottled grey as the tree trunk, but visible to Dylan presumably because his sonic eyes distinguished the soft texture of the feathers against the tough tree trunk.

"Maybe she lives in that big nest."

Connie watched the sleeping bird for a minute. After she looked away, she couldn't find it again. "Maybe." She didn't have the heart to explain that another owl would not nest so close to the nest that came down with the logging. More likely, this was one of the orphaned parents. "Birds don't have a home, like we do." She scanned the forest to see what else she had missed, but everything was green and dappled; nothing was distinct. "They only use nests for eggs and nestlings. The rest of the time, the whole forest is their home."

Dylan exhaled sharply through his nose. It might have been a laugh.

"That's funny?" Connie used the tree to pull herself up. She tucked the water bottle back in her pack and tore a ribbon from the roll of surveyor's tape.

"Sounds kind of like my mom."

"The forest is her home?"

"Ha." He scratched his leg before standing. His canvas shoes were wet, and his ankles looked cold where his socks had slouched down. "When we got kicked out of our apartment, she insisted we weren't homeless. She said the whole community was our home."

The fine blade of Dylan's nose made him look skeletal, very much like a nestling, and Connie thought of cowbirds who lay their eggs in other birds' nests where the adoptive parents struggle to feed the strange baby. That's just the way they do it. It's worked for ages.

Connie tied tape to the line where it fluttered, bright and ugly. She sent Dylan on to tie the next piece. He was meticulous as he picked his way through the brush, parting the branches with his hand rather than just pushing through. "Don't touch those branches unless you're sure you know what they are," she warned again. At the rate he was going, marking the lines for the survey would take the whole day. "This is the boundary." Connie tied tape to a wand of hazel above the brass survey marker. She wiggled it to catch his attention.

But Dylan was looking up to the tree canopy, his Adam's apple sharp beneath his chin. Twenty-five feet up, a squirrel froze above them.

Connie cleared her throat and kicked a rotten log. "Dylan."

"Wait. He's posing." Dylan pulled his notebook out, but the squirrel ran as he began to sketch.

"The squirrel held still because of you," Connie said as he drew. "It thought you wanted to eat it."

Dylan kept sketching.

"If you wanted to make your drawing accurate, you'd draw both of you: predator and prey."

Dylan's pencil passed rapidly over the page. "I'm not a predator," he said without looking up.

Connie inched forward to watch him draw. "Basically, humans are predators. Staring is what predators do before they pounce. And with your sonic eyes . . ." Dylan edged away and continued drawing. She followed him. "You say you only draw what you see, but you're leaving out a crucial element—you." She peeked over his shoulder at the sketch of the squirrel, frozen in alarm. "You show the fear, but not the cause of the fear."

"They're not afraid of me. It's because I'm vegan," Dylan said without looking up from the page. "They hold still so I can draw them."

Connie shrugged. "I've known plenty of vegetarians who scared animals." She was thinking of her years of experience with students. The hunters were often the best observers.

"My black clothes too," he said. "I was sitting right by the deck when Otto walked to his shed. He didn't have any idea I was there."

"That's creepy, Dylan."

"Otto is up to something weird."

"You're the one spying. Leave Otto alone."

Dylan made a few more passes with his pencil. "There." He thrust the notebook at Connie.

He had rendered the little animal so carefully that its pelt showed the gradations from its tawny back to its golden belly. Beneath the squirrel, he had drawn himself with his head tipped so far back it looked like it might fall off. Dylan studied the page a moment and then added drops of blood to the neck, as though the head had been severed. Connie rolled her eyes and started walking. "That's funny, Dylan, but it was the squirrel who was at risk." Behind her, Dylan muttered something. She couldn't hear him, as he must have intended, but she was pretty sure he was mocking her, and she felt a flush of gladness. For Connie, the derision of teenagers was a familiar tonic.

24

Connie left Dylan cataloguing plants in six-foot sections centered around the flags they'd left. She had never known a kid so happy to be alone. On her own, she finished laying out and flagging the remaining lines within a couple hours. The lines ran parallel along the hillside so they would have samples from the relatively dry and rocky ridge all the way down to the boggy valley. The project might not have value for science, but Connie was curious, and she wished she had taken the trouble earlier, when what they catalogued still had an uncertain future that she could track. Before she went home, she circled by Otto's place to let him know Dylan would be around the next couple days. She called out to him as she walked down his drive. He came out of the new shed, wiping his hands on a rag.

"More trouble?"

"No, no. Everything's fine." Otto waited by the shed for her to state her business. It wasn't very hospitable of him. "I just wanted to let you know that Dylan and I platted the survey area. I don't know how serious you were about the bet, but the wildlife survey is a good project for him. He'll be wandering around. Let me know if he gets in your way."

"That kid looks pretty out of place in the woods."

Otto looked out of place too. His shirt was too new and the pair of pliers in his back pocket gleamed like the polished bumper of his vintage truck. "He'll learn. Dylan's an amazing artist. He has a knack for observation."

Otto smiled, visibly softened. "You like teaching."

"I don't teach anymore."

He looked at her sidelong, teasing. "Sounds like you're teaching."

"It's something to do."

They gazed out over the valley, suddenly awkward.

Otto took a step forward. "It's good of you to take him on, Connie. I've had some vandalism up here with the logging. Just some tagging, but I can't help wondering if it's Dylan. He makes me nervous."

"It's not Dylan." She spoke confidently, to show him the idea was unthinkable. "He's too passive for one thing. Teenagers can be scary if you're not used to them."

Otto laughed. "I was scared of kids even when I was a kid."

"You're so sociable now."

He tipped his head and smiled. "I make a study of it."

She eyed him sideways, frowning. Was he teasing her?

"Really." He opened his palms at his side. "I pretty much memorized *How to Win Friends and Influence People*. Of course, you set me back when I came down to introduce myself and you were so rude. I thought I must have really screwed up."

"Sorry, Otto. That wasn't your fault."

"I learned an important lesson: call first. See? You're a good teacher even if you are a little strict."

Connie winced. "My skills are limited: taxonomy, transpiration, and time management."

"I'm sure that's only the t's in the long catalogue of your knowledge." Otto studied her a moment. Connie stepped back, self-conscious. "You've taught me a lot," he said. "Those owls you brought? Can you believe those were the first dead bodies I've ever seen?"

"Really?" How many dead animals had she seen over the years? Sheep and chickens, rodents and pets. Slow, wasting deaths from age and the shocking carnage of predation. They were all a different thing entirely from Cary's waxy face, strangely deflated.

"We had a cat when I was a kid, but it was euthanized at the vet's. My dad and mom both had institutional deaths—hospital, nursing home." He nodded, apparently surprised himself. "I could move the owl's wing; it wasn't rigid yet."

"Rigor mortis doesn't affect babies because they don't have much muscle. And it relaxes as the muscles decompose."

"There. I'm learning so much."

How did someone so inexperienced end up with so much power? What kind of a system let wealth be the only qualification? His enthusiastic wonder might be charming if the implications were not so disturbing, and Connie stared back at him flatly, watching his smile fade.

Otto pulled the shiny pliers from his pocket and opened and closed them several times before setting them on the counter. "Annabelle told me about your daughter. I'm very sorry for your loss." He rubbed his hand across his head and looked out the window. "Death is a strange, strange thing, isn't it? It may be as common as birth, but a specific death is unprecedented." He stopped suddenly. "I hope I'm not being insensitive. I spend too much time alone." He caught her eye and smiled in embarrassment, but he didn't look away. "You really did get me thinking."

Connie shifted and turned to watch a hawk circle slowly on an updraft. Otto was right. One death never prepared you for the next one, and Connie's extensive experience gave her no expertise. "You give me too much credit, Otto. You're flattering me."

His face bloomed into an embarrassed smile. "That's part of the program for making friends. Is it working?"

"Oh, me?" She waved her hand in embarrassment as she turned away. "You'd better practice on someone else."

25

Connie returned from Otto's and spent the afternoon and the next morning cleaning out her office space. Old taxes and receipts, files filled with brochures on farming and hiking and local nature areas they had never visited. She bundled up the extra pens and pencils and gathered the notebook paper. She couldn't help but feel that she had prepared for all the wrong things.

"What are you going to do when your house is totally empty?"

Connie looked up to see Ellen, dressed for a walk, standing at the door.

"It will never be empty." Connie put the bag in the give-away pile and pulled on her shoes.

"It will. And other than Dylan, that's the only thing you do."

Connie frowned. "I don't know."

"It's not healthy," Ellen said as she led them out to walk. "Stuff anchors people. Even homeless people have their shopping carts. Taking care of stuff gives us something to do. I guess I could have you clean my house, but I don't really want to." She scratched at her graying curls and then passed her hand over her head, pressing her hair close to her scalp.

"It must be spring," Connie said.

"What?" Ellen scowled as they reached Connie's driveway and started down the road. She looked distracted.

"You're not wearing your red hat," Connie said. "That's one of the neighborhood signs of spring. First the cherry blossoms, then the trilliums, then you lose the hat, and the creeks dry up."

Ellen blew air through her lips and made a sour face. "That little shit ruined it."

"Dylan?"

"He's the only little shit I ever let into my simple, sane life, and he ruined my hat." Her hair had grown greyer over the year, and it looked as though she hadn't brushed it in days. "I'm not so cute without my red cap."

"Maybe it was time for a change. A blue hat next? Yellow?"

"Bite your tongue." Ellen kicked a rock, scowling down at her feet. They crowded to the edge of the road as Fred and Eileen drove past. Ellen waved without even turning her head.

"What happened?"

"Now that he's making some money, he bought himself some fancy drawing pens. He knocked over the bottle of ink he was using to fill them. He panicked and mopped it up with the first thing he could grab." She kept her head down. She looked tired. "My red cap. Jesus Christ, it wasn't even absorbent. There's ink stain all over the cutting board."

"I'm sorry."

"Not as sorry as Dylan," Ellen said and gave Connie a dark look. "I lost my temper."

"That's okay," Connie said. "People get mad."

Ellen shook her head. "Not like that. Not good people."

Connie walked nearer and bumped Ellen's shoulder companionably.

"I shouldn't be raising a kid," Ellen said, and Connie was surprised to hear her voice shake. Ellen coughed and cleared her throat.

"You love him," Connie said. "That will come through in the end."

"Bullshit." Ellen walked faster as they climbed the hill, and Connie hurried to keep up. "My parents loved us. They used to tell us when they were drunk. Tears in their eyes, but no one bothered making dinner."

Connie slipped an arm around Ellen's broad shoulder and Ellen allowed it for a few steps before breaking away.

"And now he tiptoes around me, and I feel like a heel," Ellen went on, "and he's out all night observing wildlife for you, but it just seems wrong, Connie."

"At night? What can he see? He should be sleeping."

"Of course he should! And I thought about slipping Ambien in his soup, but I shouldn't, right?"

"You're not allowed to drug him."

Ellen marched up the steep slope. She held her hands in loose fists as she swung her arms. Connie jogged to catch up.

"It would be better if he got a job in town," Ellen said. "Be around other kids. Get to know some wholesome families maybe. We fought about that, too." Her shoulders rounded into the climb, and she slowed as they crested the hill. She paused to stretch a muscle in her hip. "That kid fucks up every interview," she said shaking her leg out, "He wears these weird pink earrings whenever we go to town. Then he doesn't speak. I've set him up with two potential jobs. These people owe me favors, but they say he won't speak above a whisper. They're not even sure he understands what they've said. You, Connie, are the only one he talks audibly to."

"I'm honored."

"I'm not saying he likes you. He complains about you."

Connie felt wounded, and this surprised her.

"The usual complaints about a boss: you're not clear, you're not fair. Most recently he was carrying on about how you don't listen." Ellen looked across to Connie. "But I knew that."

Low cumulous tumbled across the sky, creating rolling shadows on the ground. Connie and Ellen walked into sudden sun and the wet road steamed. Connie began to sweat. She pulled her jacket off and tied it around her waist. All around, new leaves broke from their branches and the stems of bracken fern lanced the dark ground. Connie suddenly missed the cold suspension of winter. "I'll help him as long as he wants," she said with a vehemence that surprised her. "But if he's going to keep working in the woods, he'll need better clothes. I pulled out Mike's old jacket, but it's too small and Dylan doesn't like to wear plaid. The boots I lent him don't fit him right. You need to get him some."

Ellen hooted and her voice echoed in the narrow valley. "Like chore boots? I know I'm the grown up and I'm supposed to make the rules, but do you think I could get that kid in anything as uncool as rubber chore boots?"

"Then fishing boots. Shit. Bike messenger boots—they must have to keep their feet dry. He's going to get a foot fungus."

"Bike messengers quit being a thing when the internet was invented. Honestly, Connie, you're the one who needs a job in town, but the Ellen Employment Agency wouldn't have any better luck with you. Miscreants and misfits." Ellen raised her arms to the sky, and, as if on cue, a crow swooped and angled away. They looked at one another in surprise.

"I'm not a miscreant," Connie said, and she felt a little skip in her heart. "I'm a curmudgeon."

Ellen scoffed. "You're only fifty-two and you have to be at least sixty-five to be a curmudgeon. There are strict rules for these things. You can look them up online."

They reached the intersection with Ellen's road. At the corner, fat primroses lit the margin of Annabelle's driveway, gold and blue and pink.

"This looks great." Ellen approached a large column of basalt where water bubbled up and sparkled as it splashed down the rock into a small dark pond. Ferns and flowers leaned over the water, and beyond, the red corrugated metal of the barn made an immaculate backdrop. Two glossy horses grazed a green paddock.

"Maybe she's getting ready to sell it." Connie doubted this, but the thought made her happy.

"Oh no," Ellen said. "It's a lure. She's all alone in that beautiful big house right next door to Otto's camp. Otto needs a house."

Connie sped up as Ellen dawdled. She wasn't fond of primroses. Their name described them perfectly. Naïve, aggressively cheerful, like a child's drawing come to life, but in a creepy way.

"I admit," Ellen said, catching up with Connie. "It's hard to watch Annabelle get what she wants because she always gets what she wants. But you have to give her credit; she works for it."

Connie kept her eyes on the road ahead. Annabelle's drive was notably attractive, but other neighbors had spruced up for spring. At the top of the hill, apple trees in full bloom stood out against the purple clouds. As they passed, Connie could hear the hum of bees and saw three new hives stacked on the south facing hill.

"Annabelle's going to have a party for Otto." Ellen picked a blossom and tucked it behind her ear. "Next Saturday. That should have been your job. You should have introduced him to the neighborhood."

Ellen picked more blooms—cherry blossoms, hyacinths, and dandelions. She wove them into her hair as they walked. "Otto's kind of cute. Ambitious. Rich. Maybe I'll go after him myself. If I dressed a little more feminine? Flowers in my hair? Ribbons?"

Connie looked over doubtfully. Ellen was older than Otto, six feet tall and stout as a tree. She had divorced long before Connie met her and had not been with a man again as far as Connie knew.

"You should see your expression!" Ellen shook her head hard and the flowers rained down to the road. One dandelion caught on her fleece jacket and dangled there. "Anyway, you'll enjoy coming to the party and watching me try."

"I don't need to be introduced to Otto." Connie said.

"You're going to get your very own invitation soon. Annabelle's being formal because Otto is a Southern Gentleman. Really. That's what she told me. We're all expected to put on party clothes. I'm telling you now so you can go buy some."

"I'm not coming. Nothing sounds worse to me." Connie didn't care if she sounded pathetic. She felt pathetic.

"You are coming. I promised to be the bartender, and I plan to make everyone drunk. If you didn't come, I would tell you all about it, only you wouldn't know what was true or not and you would be so confused and curious you'd regret your absence for the rest of your days."

"No," Connie said. "I would never need to know the truth."

"You're a scientist, Connie. You care more about the truth than anyone I know."

Connie imagined Ellen's tall tales, spun out day after day on their walks around the mountain. She was pretty sure she would want them to go on forever. She wouldn't care at all if they were true. "I'm not a scientist," was all she said.

Ellen rolled her eyes dismissively. "Some things you have to see for yourself. Annabelle's party will be one of those things. I will pick you up."

Connie started to protest but Ellen surprised her by clapping her big hand right over Connie's mouth with such determination that Connie could taste the salt on her palm. She pushed Ellen's arm away.

Ellen barked a harsh, short laugh. "You don't have any choice here."

26

Two days later, Dylan returned to Connie's kitchen table to show her the map he'd made. He had defined the landscape features in the sections they'd marked—pasture, oak grove, mixed forest, and Otto's clearing—so the map was rather accurately scaled. It wasn't necessary for their purpose, and she hadn't asked him to do anything so difficult, but now that she held it in her hand, she hoped he would allow her to keep it. Down in the bottom corner, near the beaver pond, he'd drawn a large dark band that followed the property line up hill.

"What's this?" She traced her finger over the sweeping band, simple and blank compared to the surrounding land filled with icons he'd made to indicate oak, fir, hazel, maple, and grass.

"That's the new road."

"There's no road there."

Dylan looked at her like she was stupid.

"Near the beaver pond?" Connie tried to think what the boy meant to depict. "There's no reason to bring a road down to the wetland."

"I'm just showing you what I saw."

She felt terrible when he spoke carefully like that. "Maybe a truck drove down there," she said, not wanting to contradict him when they were finally becoming easier with one another. "Left tire marks."

"Left rock," Dylan said. "Just yesterday. And then today they spread a bunch of gravel over that. He'll be able to drive on that all winter."

Connie frowned. There was no point in arguing. "Well." She got up and pulled a fleece jacket over her head before stepping into chore boots. Dylan drifted after her.

She could see the road before she reached the pond. Just as Dylan said, it was built up above ground level with rock and gravel. It followed the contours of the property line so that it ran down hill and turned at the bottom to extend briefly north along the edge of Connie's property. The raised road formed a levee that would effectively block water from draining off the hill into the wetland. Connie wheeled around to face Dylan. "This is insane."

"He's a criminal," Dylan said with an eagerness that made Connie wince.

"A criminal? Stop it, Dylan."

With his skinny legs and his black clothes, Dylan looked like the kind of ominous, solitary crow you might see in a parking lot picking oily morsels out of fast-food wrappers. That's what Connie had made of him—a spy, an opportunist. She sat down on a log at the edge of the wetland. The new road would be a dryer, warmer place to rest but the bland grey-blue of the recently crushed rock was repellant to her. She put her head in her hands with a sense of defeat so profound she thought she might not rise again.

"The road is outside the wetland," Dylan said.

"And the hangman's noose is outside the neck," Connie said and immediately regretted it. "I'm being dramatic. I'm sorry." She knew Dylan stood before her because she could see the toes of the new leather boots Ellen had bought him. The leather was already stained from the wet conditions. He would have been better off in cheap rubber. Ellen hadn't even shown the boy how to waterproof a pair of shoes. She lifted her head to meet his questioning gaze, and when he saw her sad face he extended one hand, as though he might pat her shoulder. She stood suddenly and climbed the new road. On the side opposite the wetland, a small puddle had already formed. "See?" She waved her hand over the water. "This should be draining to the pond. So this road," she said loudly as though Otto himself could hear, "will probably dry up the beaver pond and flood Otto's land. Who benefits from that? It's just stupid." But it was worse than stupid, and while putting a road on soft ground took some work—ground-cloth and rock and gravel—taking one out was an even bigger task.

Dylan stood next to her. "This is not the only bad thing Otto does."

"Are you spying?"

Dylan flinched. She didn't mean to yell, but everything was so corrupted, so off-course, even Dylan. And wasn't it all her fault?

"Okay," Dylan said in his careful voice. "I'm going now, before that lady gets here."

Connie looked up and saw Annabelle approaching on horseback. When she spotted them, she kicked the big bay into a trot. Dylan promptly turned and headed uphill toward Ellen's.

"Did I scare him away?" Annabelle asked when she reached Connie. She pulled the horse to a halt so that Connie's head was level with the top of Annabelle's boot. "He scares *me*. All that black and those weird earrings. Is he gay?"

Connie stepped back. "What's this?" She waved her arm at the road.

"It's brand new." Annabelle gazed up the hill, where the road disappeared into the forest. "Otto just finished and I'm taking a tour. I've got to teach Otto to ride."

"But why?"

"Everyone should know how to ride!"

"No. Why the god-damned road?"

Annabelle's smile faded and she looked at Connie sternly. "Otto has to be able to bring his equipment down."

"But not down here. He's not planting grapes down here."

"Yes, he is."

"That's crazy. This land is too wet for grapes. The soil is all wrong."

"It's those stupid regulations. He needs to have fifteen acres of vineyard to qualify for a tasting room. He decided to leave some trees on the ridge. You know, for the owls and stuff. So now he has to plant down here."

Connie imagined the hillside terraced all the way down to the wetland. It was inevitable, she told herself, and would not be without its own beauty, like the pictures she had seen of the domesticated hills of Europe. The old world. It was all an old world now.

Annabelle's horse stamped with impatience, its big hooves displacing the new gravel. She muscled him back to stillness and held him there, her forearm taut.

"We should have done this years ago." Annabelle tossed her head to indicate the new road. "We could have gotten some use out of this land."

Connie didn't point out that the land was always being used—beavers, owls, and myriad strangers among the small, the furry, the winged, and crawling. The horse began to fidget more insistently, its black tail whipping. Annabelle pulled his nose in toward her knee, and they turned several tight circles before coming once more to a standstill.

"That's about all the standing we can manage right now." Annabelle held firm and rigid, containing the horse as its gleaming skin twitched with impatience. "It's good practice, but we'd better move on." She waved like the Lone Ranger, and the big animal gathered his back legs beneath him and sprang forward, the powerful haunches bunching and extending while Annabelle's blonde ponytail bounced in rhythm from beneath her helmet.

27

Even at ten in the morning, a large congregation bent their heads over the Apple Store's white displays. Connie almost left. For someone who spent so much time in the forest, the lack of shadows beneath the bright and even light was strange and disturbing. But a personable young woman took her in hand, and Connie left with a clean, small box, heavy with phone. She picked up chips, salsa, and guacamole on her way home.

Connie set the containers of food on the table with napkins and spoons. In the clean and empty kitchen, the spread had the incongruity of a picnic which prompted her to add a mason jar full of daisies (she had given away all the vases). But Dylan, when he arrived, lingered on the porch as he had the first day. She let him in before he knocked, and he was unduly startled, like she was psychic and not just peeking through the draperies like any nosy old lady.

"How is the survey going?" Connie led the way to the table with its offerings.

Dylan widened his eyes dramatically as he sat down. At first it seemed like a surprising but gratifying response to the food, but he placed both his hands on the table, as though to anchor it. He didn't pay any attention to the guacamole.

Connie sat across from him and slid the chips closer. "I'm in suspense," she said at last.

"Otto's up to something."

Connie waited but Dylan didn't elaborate. "Like what?"

"Something secret. He doesn't sleep at night."

"That's not secretive."

"He disappears in that shed, all night long."

Connie dipped a chip in salsa and waved her other hand over the bowl to indicate that Dylan should eat too. He touched a chip to the salsa and ate it carefully. Not even a crumb fell to the table. Connie chewed and swallowed. She wanted to demonstrate an utter lack of urgency. This was not a problem. "People get insomnia."

"It's not insomnia," Dylan said. "He went to bed around eleven. An alarm went off at one. He got up and went into his shed. But then he disappeared. When I looked in the windows, I couldn't see him anywhere."

Connie's gut twisted. "Are you spying on him?"

Dylan nodded. "That's my job."

"No. Ellen is not paying you to spy." She sounded petulant to her own ears. She was losing her authority.

Dylan opened his notebook and slid it across the table. She sat back in her chair and folded her arms. From the corner of her eye, she could see he'd drawn a picture of Otto's compound—the tipi, the shed, the driveway, even the parked vehicles—all accurately placed and meticulously outlined in black and several shades of blue.

"Here's the key." He pointed to a note at the bottom of the page and Connie leaned forward again to see. The black outline was labeled *always*. He'd labeled the light blue *10pm* and the dark blue *1am* and midnight blue *4am*. Otto's silhouette was light blue within the outline of the tipi and also as he walked to the shed. Inside the shed, he was outlined with an aura made of all three blues. Other blue creatures filled the page—skunks, deer, raccoons.

"This way, I can draw what happens at different times without redrawing everything."

"That's thoughtful." The drawing showed a place busy with people and animals. If Dylan were to draw her place, it would all be the bland black of *always*. "But Dylan." She leaned across the table, feeling a queasy sense of guilt. "It's not right to spy on people."

"I thought he would be asleep," Dylan said quickly. "I didn't think I'd be observing *him*. I wanted to see if animals stayed away from the new buildings."

She lifted a page and raised her eyes to ask Dylan's permission to turn it. He nodded and scooted his chair away to give her room. He skimmed a chip across the surface of the guacamole as she flipped through the notebook. Some pages were crammed with small sketches, others showed whole panoramas like the drawing of Otto's compound. She stopped to study one page dominated by an old, twisted oak. She knew that tree. A flicker, not to scale, was sketched up near the crown, and a Douglas squirrel the size of the oak trunk stood on its hind legs to the right. All around the margin, Dylan had illustrated lichen and moss in a large scale so that the botanical details were clear. A fly traversed the page, heading toward the upright squirrel. She didn't have it in her to organize his work into something more scientific. It was, in its way, already perfect.

"Who is this?" Connie pressed a thumb against one of the many sketches of an elfin archer. He was drawn in an anime style, his shrewd gaze so focused it was almost malicious.

Dylan scooted closer to Connie. "That's Sylvio." He started to pull the book back, but then paused. "These are his arrows of karma." He pointed to a quiver filled with elegant arrows. "See? He's aiming at Otto."

Sylvio crouched near the large boulder at the top of the ridge. Dylan had gotten the strike of the hill just right, and Connie could easily find the very spot. A tiny shrew peeked from a maple leaf near Sylvio's right foot. All the animals on the page looked toward an unsuspecting Otto just as Sylvio did. The bow was drawn, and the muscles in Sylvio's sinewy arm strained. Even the plants leaned toward Otto. Otto himself had his back turned to the forest. He was in the process of entering the shed. Dylan had drawn him so that the small bald patch on the back of his head shown like a target.

"Looks like Otto's had it," Connie said.

"The arrows of karma never miss."

"Right." Connie bit the word off. Talk of karma always made her mad.

"Arrows of karma might be slow, and they hardly ever go straight, but they never miss." Dylan traced a finger over the back of a skunk, its tail raised in alarm as it faced Otto.

"I don't think Otto deserves the attention. He hasn't done anything wrong."

Dylan spread his palms over the open notebook. "He's killing everything."

Connie shook her head slowly and emphatically. "He doesn't have that much power." She chose her words carefully. "Change happens. If Otto were to die tomorrow, someone else would come along and plant that vineyard."

"You wouldn't. I wouldn't."

"We couldn't afford to. Pretty much anyone who could afford to buy that land would plant a vineyard. Sooner or later, something else will replace the vineyard." Connie tapped her finger over a family of one a.m. raccoons investigating the garbage can. Outlined in the midnight blue of four a.m., a coyote defecated at the head of the driveway. "These are the animals we might expect to see near human dwellings." She was determined to bring the conversation back to wildlife.

"Connie." Dylan had never used her name before, and she looked up from the page. "Otto is up to something."

"But it's not our business."

"He's up to something weird."

"People can be weird. You're weird. I'm weird." She waved her hand around to include them all, the emptying house, the obsessive drawings, the whole neighborhood. "Leave Otto alone. Your job is to observe and survey the forest."

"Otto is in the forest."

"He's really not." Connie spoke the words loudly and clearly. She was surprised to meet so much resistance from Dylan. Maybe it was a good sign, but his insistence was irritating. "Otto sticks pretty close to his little development." She got the checklist and tallied the plants and animals from his drawings. "And if you don't stop spying on him, you can't continue with the project. You'll have to take a job at the ice cream store or join the FFA boys at the farm co-op. You can learn how to raise a steer for slaughter." She set down her pen and looked Dylan in the eye. "I'm serious. You have a future as a wildlife illustrator or biologist if you want it. You could have some influence on the world with those drawings. Maybe that's your destiny." She felt cynical dangling a hero's quest, but maybe that's what he needed.

"Do you believe that? That we have a destiny?"

Dylan looked sharply at Connie. What could she say? What had been Cary's destiny? Suffering and disappointment? If that was her destiny, was she *born* to it?

"I believe that everything is a unique point of view. I mean that literally, scientifically. We don't *have* a viewpoint; we *are* the viewpoint. Our destiny is to explore where we are and share that view. And with your drawing, you are uniquely able to share." She paused so the idea could sink in. "I'm going to give you some assignments. I want you to write them down."

Dylan poised his pencil over the page. He was probably being sarcastic, but Connie ignored that. "First, decide on the section you're going to study. Take photos of plants and animals you don't recognize. I'll show you some apps you can use for identification and some other sites that will be helpful."

"I don't use a phone," he said. "They rot your brain."

"It's just a tool. It depends on how you use it." She reached into her pack and handed the heavy white box to Dylan. He received it with a frozen look. He didn't even open it. "That's yours," she said. "It's not set up yet, but you can use it to take pictures now. Ellen will add you to her plan. Then you'll have access to the internet."

"Mine to keep?"

Connie nodded and he slipped the box into his satchel without a word. He took the notebook back, his mouth drawn so tight his thin lips were almost invisible.

28

Luckily for Connie, her rural neighborhood's idea of party clothes was liberal. If you wore your farm shoes, you should clean the manure from them before coming inside, but if you arrived covered in wisps of hay because you fed the livestock on the way out of the driveway, no one minded. They'd pick the seeds from your sweater when they greeted you. Connie wore wool slacks and a sweater and felt defiantly dowdy as she waited for Ellen to pick her up. To her enormous surprise, Ellen arrived in a full cotton skirt and an embroidered Mexican blouse.

"Look at you!" Connie said. "I've never seen you in a dress."

"I feel like I'm in drag, but I did this for you. You can't wear that." Ellen gestured with disgust at Connie's dark sweater and brown pants. She didn't wait for Connie to respond before going to the bedroom and loudly opening the closet and then the drawers. "Where are your clothes?"

Connie trailed upstairs. Ellen stood in the center of the room with a look of accusation. The closet doors gaped, and every single drawer was open.

"I don't need much." With Ellen in the room, the empty closets seemed like an indictment. Connie cultivated a righteous nonchalance.

Ellen looked at the few remaining garments and narrowed her eyes with determination. She pulled the summer shift off the hanger and threw it at Connie. "Put this on."

Little bunches of flowers covered a dark blue cotton that was so fine and thin it seemed to float as it hung from her finger. "It's too cold for that."

"Wear this over it." Ellen pulled out a plaid flannel shirt. "Those actually look good together."

Connie did as she was told because it was easier than arguing.

"Oh! And these." Ellen threw Connie's cowboy boots at her feet, bruising her ankle.

Connie felt like a rag doll as Ellen helped pull the dress over her head, but time was passing. Every moment took her closer to the end of the party.

"Hell's bells." Ellen shook her head. "You look adorable."

Connie rolled her eyes.

"I'm serious. You've lost all that weight, which you ought to gain back, but in the meantime, you look like a model, and the outfit's great." She dragged Connie to the bathroom mirror and stood her there. Connie hadn't looked at herself in a long time. Her dark eyes were large, and her thin face had taken on a new, austere clarity. The red and blue plaid complimented the discrete floral print, but the whimsical mismatch was belied by Connie's gaze, vacant and fearful.

"You can't see the boots in this mirror," Ellen said, "but they're perfect, and they show off your legs."

"We look like we're in costume," Connie said following Ellen to the car.

"That's the point of a party."

"I thought the point was drinking."

"Right. Drinking in costume."

When they arrived at Annabelle's, Ellen pulled lipstick from the capacious pocket of her skirt and ran it boldly over her lips. "Hold still." She anchored Connie's forehead with one hand while she drew on lipstick with the other. "You're a beautiful woman," she said when she was done. "You might want to forget it, but when anyone else looks at you, they see a beautiful woman."

They had arrived at Annabelle's early so that Ellen could set up the bar. In addition to beer and wine, she was serving mint juleps at Annabelle's request, and she had harvested a big bunch of fresh mint, just the tender tips because the season was so young. When Connie opened the bag, the sharp, clean scent filled the room. She took a deep breath and then another.

"Aromatherapy," Ellen said as she organized the glasses. "That's why I didn't try to talk Annabelle out of the juleps even though any right-thinking person understands mint and bourbon have no business in the same glass."

Annabelle came in with a stack of cocktail napkins printed with wine grapes. She wore tight jeans with heels and a silk blouse in a rich dark pink that contrasted well with her blonde hair and perpetually tanned skin. She stopped in her tracks when she saw them.

"I've never seen you wear a dress," she said to Ellen.

Ellen grinned and spun around. The cotton skirt, brightly printed with bucking broncos, opened like a flower.

"Is that a square-dancing skirt?"

"No." Ellen was defensive. "You have to have the puffy slip for square-dancing."

"Well." Annabelle set the napkins on the counter and fanned them out with a swipe of her hand. "But you, Connie Sweet," she said turning to Connie who was arranging beer in a tub of ice, "you look like you stepped out of the pages of a fashion magazine."

Connie looked up from the beer feeling unaccountably guilty. "It was all I had."

"Lucky you." Annabelle swished out to tend to the pork roasting out back on the big stainless-steel grill.

Ellen mixed up two juleps and thrust one at Connie. "Taste this and see if the sugar is right."

She took a tiny sip. "Tastes okay."

"Then drink up!" Ellen raised her own glass in a toast. "Annabelle is jealous of you. It warms my heart."

Annabelle had a large section of oak burning gloriously on the hearth. A fire seemed almost improper considering that the winter daphne and Indian plum had long faded and the small flowers were all in bloom, but it was cold still, and firelight gleamed on the polished furniture. Annabelle returned from the pork and stood before a home-sweet-home sign printed on a plank of aged barn wood as she surveyed the party-ready room. "I'm ready for a drink."

"Nice of you to do this." Connie said. "Your place looks . . ." she waved her hand to include the whole cozy room, the freshly painted walls and coordinated throw pillows.

"Well." Annabelle smoothed and fluffed her hair. "Home is where the heart is. And neighbors should be friends."

Just then the Stevens arrived with appetizers and behind them, Otto, with a large bouquet of flowers.

"How sweet of you." Annabelle stood on tiptoe to kiss Otto's cheek. She clasped the bouquet to her chest and her cleavage swelled beneath the pressure. "Let's get you a drink." Leading him to the bar, she handed the flowers to Connie. "Would you find a vase for these, Connie? In the mudroom. Snip the stems so they'll last longer."

"Connie, it's nice to see you." He leaned forward, as though to kiss her on the cheek, but Connie held the bouquet between them, nodding to the neighbors who were arriving all at once, right on time. "You look pretty this evening," he said stepping back.

"We were instructed to wear party clothes, and I'm afraid I don't have much to choose from." She looked down to the curled pointy toes of her old cowboy boots. "We do the best we can. Behold the resplendent Ellen."

He bowed, and Ellen did kiss Otto before handing him a julep.

He tasted it and eyed her over the rim of his glass. "You make a stiff drink, ma'am."

"It is my duty and my calling."

He looked at her quizzically, but Ellen stood at martial attention, gazing out at the growing crowd like she was looking over her troops.

"Come on, Otto." Annabelle took his hand. "I need you to consult on the pork."

Connie settled the flowers in a vase. When she returned to the living room, it was filled with neighbors greeting one another. Ellen mixed drinks, teasing and cajoling so that even neighbors who rarely drank alcohol circulated with plastic cups filled with bourbon and mint. Connie left the flowers on the coffee table and stood in the shadows by the fire. She had known most of these people for decades and their faces were dear to her. Fred Olmstead approached in jeans so stiff and new it was a wonder he could bend his knees, but he was perennially spry, tough and leathery beneath a thick mop of startlingly white hair.

"Connie." He embraced her lightly. "I'm so glad to see you here. How are you getting on?"

She squirmed beneath his look of tender sympathy. "All right, Fred. And you? Do you have calves this spring?"

"Oh, hell yes. The day you stop doing the hard stuff is the day you start dying. Eileen," he called back to his wife. "Here's Connie."

"Dear!" Eileen embraced Connie, holding her just a moment too long. Eileen wore an old plaid skirt, turtleneck, and boots, but her thick grey hair was twisted into a fancy bun and held with a rhinestone comb. "You look lovely. I guess we're all pretty cute tonight. I had to pick the staples out of Fred's pants before he crossed the threshold."

Connie laughed and felt pleased despite herself. Maybe Ellen's drink was taking effect. "Pretty fancy." But what she meant was that no one was fancy at all. They were a bunch of eccentrics in glad rags—whatever they could find that were not work clothes. All except Otto, whose crisp white shirt stood out in a sea of plaid. He wore jeans that weren't quite new but were miraculously unstained, and his stylish three-day beard contrasted with the scrubbed faces of his country neighbors. They had all jammed their knotted feet into their cheap city shoes while Otto wore the sort of work boots you'd never find at the feed store. Ellen was right; he was the best-looking man in the neighborhood, but Otto's costume demonstrated his urban background more clearly than even his talk of vineyards and *terroir*.

29

"Have you met the Olmsteads?" Connie asked as Otto appeared at her elbow. Otto greeted Fred and Eileen, leaning in to hear Fred's joke above the buzz of the crowd and then leaning out to laugh. Connie had known Fred long enough that she didn't bother to listen to the joke; still, she shared a smile and rueful headshake with Eileen. She didn't have to hear to know it was the right response.

"Come on, Fred." Eileen took her husband's arm. "I told Annabelle you'd bring up more firewood from the porch."

"Stick around," he said to Otto as they moved away. "The ladies will fill your time with chores. I'm here to drink," he said to Eileen even as he followed.

"This is so nice of you all." Otto tightened the antique bolo tie at his neck and straightened his collar.

"It's Annabelle's doing," Connie said. "And I don't want to take away from the occasion, but you might as well know, nothing pleases this crowd more than a party right here on the mountain. We put on our costumes and drink too much to drive. Everyone will leave their cars up here and stagger home in loud groups. There'll be a second party in the morning when they come back to fetch their vehicles. It's a treat for us."

"For me too, then, though I'm not much of a drinker."

"We'll change that. Just one of Ellen's juleps should do the trick. You'll be a real farmer in no time."

Sheepishly, Otto raised his arm to show Connie his beer. "I've never been able to stomach juleps."

"Don't tell Annabelle. They were in your honor, you being a southern gentleman."

"So she said." Otto smiled. "And I'm enough of a gentleman that I drank one. Then I tried to explain to Annabelle that Texas isn't really The South, but I'm not sure I got through. Anyway, I grew up in New Mexico. Definitely not The South."

"Either way it's without moss, which is exotic for us." Connie took a sip of her drink. She was trying to be pleasant, but she was out of practice with small talk. She looked past Otto to the roomful of neighbors, their cheeks rosy from alcohol. He shifted, reclaiming her attention, but he didn't speak. He stood with a wide stance and in the brightly white shirt, he took up a lot of room.

"I spent a week in Death Valley once." Connie dredged up the only desert memory she had. "It was so austere it felt mythical." Rocks and sand and searing sun seemed to ask existential questions. Connie's own little valley was always talking about what to have for dinner. "Our wet fields and forests are so collaborative," she explained. "Lots of options for food and water and shelter. But I felt like an alien in the desert. I imagine our green hills are equally exotic to you?"

Otto stepped his feet together. He frowned. "No. In fact, I felt an immediate connection here. I never liked the desert much." He picked his beer up but thought better of drinking and set it once more on the table. "You think I don't belong, that I have no business here, trying to grow grapes in the rain."

Connie felt a wash of remorse. She hadn't meant to be rude, but of course he was right. "No, no. I'm sure you'll figure it out."

He turned to look over his shoulder at the crowd. Connie was suddenly afraid he would walk away. She opened her mouth to say anything, but before she found the words, he shook his head.

"Mine was not an outdoorsy family. I'm ashamed to say I don't know the desert much better than you. Then I lived in Houston, and I hear Texas has wildflowers, but I never saw them." He admitted this boldly and stood before Connie awaiting her judgement. "I come to the land late in life, but isn't that better than never?"

Connie blushed and finished her julep in two large swallows, the mint sharp in her nose and the bourbon burning her throat. "Of course." She tried to think of something nice to say. "That's just modern life. All this moving around makes people earthly orphans." She had said too much. Either too little or too much. "I don't mean you're an orphan . . ."

"But it's how I've always felt." He smiled down at her so warmly she felt a shiver of guilt. "Now I've found my place, I'm just sorry I didn't find it when I was younger. I'll never know it as well as you, no matter how much I study."

"I'm no expert," she said, embarrassed. "I know a little bit about a lot of things. Just enough to point high school kids to someone who knows more."

"Like who? Whenever I ask a question about a plant or a bird, people around here tell me *ask Connie*."

Connie shifted uncomfortably. "I've lived here a quarter of a century. All that time should have taught me something."

"I've been glued to a computer all that time. Plenty to learn there, too. I used to think I was on some cutting edge, but I don't know. What I learned twenty years ago is pretty much obsolete now. The field is literally superficial. It comes and goes in a flash." He looked a little feverish, but anyone might, what with the fire and the party and the alcohol. "What you've learned about your land is cumulative. I've read every natural history I could find, viticulture books, gardening books. But I don't have any of that on-the-ground, roll-up-your sleeves experience." He took a long draught then rubbed his head. "Like you all."

"Oh." Connie felt woozy. She set her empty glass on the table and left her hand there to steady herself. "I've lived within thirty miles of this place my whole life. This patina of knowledge," she fluttered her hand to indicate her whole dressed-up self, "it's the moss that grows on an unrolling stone." She had never come close to any of the wonders of the world—not the Nile nor New York nor New Orleans. Every season on her farm fed straight to the next season, the seasons rushed to years, the years strung together so that leaving, even briefly, felt like walking out in the middle of a movie.

"Bullshit, Connie." Otto was a little drunk. He had acquired a new expansive quality. He finished his beer and pushed it to the far side of the table. "To know a place from the aquifer to the trees, through all the seasons, over years. That's the most wonderful life."

"Better than computers," Connie said.

Otto nodded.

"Better than business," she continued. "Better than becoming a merchant seaman or a professional surfer or even a rodeo queen."

Otto looked down and covered his face with his hands. The gesture was boyish and surprising. When he dropped his hands, he was smiling. "You're teasing, but I still think it's better than all that. I'm afraid y'all made me tipsy."

Connie couldn't help smiling back. "I'll tell Ellen. She'll be pleased."

Just then, Annabelle appeared. "Here you are."

Across the room, Fred was telling another joke while Steve Alcott, there with his husband Sam, interrupted at an increasingly urgent volume, "No, Fred. Stop. Don't say it. Don't."

Annabelle frowned. "Otto, let's get dinner going. It's past time we fed this crowd. Maybe the bourbon was a bad idea." She took Otto by the elbow. "Connie," she said over her shoulder, "will you round people up?"

Connie navigated the perimeters of the room and swept the guests toward the table of barbequed pork and the bean salads and beet salads and green salads, pickles and breads. Annabelle never said it was a potluck, but the neighbors brought food anyway. On the sideboard, berry pies and rhubarb compotes waited their turn. Connie returned to the emptying living room to gather glasses and help Ellen.

"You did it," she whispered to Ellen. She felt tipsy. She lined wine glasses up at the bar, then deciding there were too many, took them back down. Ellen brought them back up. "You made everyone drunk. Otto rhapsodized about the land, Fred is telling inappropriate jokes to Sam and Steve, Eileen is on the verge of tears, and Annabelle is afraid she's losing control."

The volume rose as the neighbors coalesced near the dining room table. Blanche and Carl didn't even live close to one another, so everyone was surprised when they formed a team near the table's edge and routed all the people they deemed athletic to the shorter line. This incurred resentment and frank irritation, but no one tried to stop them until Annabelle showed up and told them to get their food and sit down. Blanche was laughing so hard she was in tears and Carl giggled with a strange high-pitched wheezing sound. They went off like naughty children to snicker in a corner.

"It warms my heart," Ellen admitted as she stowed the bourbon and uncorked a few of the bottles of wine people had brought. "Blanche and Carl will start an affair, and maybe we'll get a fight before we all go home. The perfect party."

They hadn't noticed Annabelle, pouring wine for Otto and herself. "That's a perfect *high school* party." She frowned at them both for a moment before turning back to Otto. "This is the wine I was telling you about, the one my friends made." She spoke in a musical voice as she lifted a bottle to show him the label. "We'll have them over for dinner. They could be a lot of help." She set glasses on a little table near the fire, just barely enough room for the two of them.

"She out-maneuvered you," Ellen hissed to Connie over the buffet table. "You had the advantage with your soulful chat in the corner; I saw the way he was looking at you. Then you said something mean, didn't you? Annabelle will keep him all through dessert."

"She can have him," Connie looked down at the plate of meat. It wasn't that she wasn't hungry, but eating was so much trouble. She took a sip of wine.

Amidst all the noise, Annabelle leaned in close to Otto as she spoke, one finger resting on his wrist, its nail lacquered pink to match her blouse. Otto's eyes were downcast as he listened.

"He's looking down her shirt," Ellen said sadly. "Annabelle's breasts are magnificent even if they're not real. You can't compete with that."

Connie looked around, afraid some of her neighbors had been listening, but everyone was busy balancing silverware and sharing recipes. "I'm not competing." It was absurd even as a joke.

Otto placed a hand on Annabelle's shoulder as he spoke into her ear. Annabelle's rosy lips curled into a smile.

Connie and Ellen found a seat on an ottoman in the corner of the den. Ellen was sour after being routed away from the athletic side of the table, and Connie spoke reflexively to distract her. "Dylan thinks Otto is up to something nefarious."

"Like what?"

Connie licked barbecue sauce from her fingers. "He says Otto gets up in the night and disappears in that shed."

"So?" Ellen shrugged. "Dylan gets up at night and disappears in the woods."

"It's a *shed*." Connie set her silverware down to speak more emphatically. "You know, a simple, rustic structure. How does he disappear in a shed?"

"I don't know. How does Dylan cause trouble out here in the *middle of nowhere?* You know, a rural location where nothing ever happens." Ellen bared her teeth and ripped meat from the bone. Barbecue sauce covered her chin, but she made no move to clean it off. "Dylan shouldn't be out peeping in windows. Someone needs to take charge of that boy, and obviously it isn't me." She frowned down at her lap for a moment and wiped her face with the napkin.

"Otto's behavior sounds kind of weird."

"We're all weird, Connie. I mean, look at you. Look at me." Ellen got up suddenly. She returned with a glass of bourbon and handed Connie a full glass of wine. "I've got to get that kid a job in town." She sat back down with an air of defeat. "Something that wears him out so he sleeps at night. Otto's probably doing computer stuff with someone in a different time zone, someplace like India. Vineyards aren't cheap. He's probably making money."

Connie picked at her bean salad.

"Just eat that, raw onions and all." Ellen was suddenly fierce. "Otto's not going to kiss you."

"I never thought Otto was going to kiss me!"

"Well good." As quickly as the fierceness had erupted it collapsed, and Ellen slumped in the chair and sucked the last of her drink. "Otto's going to marry Annabelle. She keeps a nice house, and she makes a mean pork shoulder. They'll host parties like this once a month and you'll all get as fat as me."

People finished their dinners and circled back for dessert. Sam and Steve circulated through the rooms gathering dirty paper plates and Ellen passed hers to Sam with a queenly gesture. She didn't even say thank you.

"Dylan's paranoid. You shouldn't listen to him." Ellen looked around at her pie-eating neighbors. They were animated and flushed, but they behaved pretty much the way they did on any day of the week. "Nothing ever turns out the way you want it to."

30

After dessert, Annabelle put the bourbon away and without exactly lying gave the impression it had run out. Many people gathered their coats and thanked the hostess and left their phone numbers and good wishes with Otto. The remaining party continued drinking beer and wine, assiduously refilling one another's glasses. The conversation around Otto grew loud and teasing. They told tales about cat-eating coyotes, the spontaneous combustion of barns, infamous affairs. They used the opportunity to needle each other while Otto, looking glazed, laughed among them.

Ellen rose and joined them, unsteady on her feet. "Not only are the good old days gone," she said loudly, "they were never here to begin with." She pivoted to face Otto and rocked back on her heels. "Otto, no self-respecting cat would be caught by a coyote. That's what we told the children. Fred runs them over when he sees 'em. And that barn did not spontaneously combust. The kids were getting high in the hay loft."

Annabelle, looking tired, fumed in the corner. Connie pulled herself up, feeling drunk and weary.

"Come on. Let's walk home," she said, grabbing Ellen's elbow.

Ellen turned to Connie. Her momentum made her sway as she looked down and glowered. "And cancer isn't some bolt out of the blue. Remember all the chemicals we used in the good old days? Even made the kids go out and spray the fence lines."

Everyone became quiet looking to Connie with fear and sorrow.

"You were being a good mother!" Ellen said. "None of us knew any better."

Connie waved her hand in dismissal. That was the truth, too; she hadn't known any better. She'd read the labels. She'd thought she was informed.

"Time to go home," Steve said and touched Sam's arm.

"Truth is like a fart!" Ellen laughed. "See how it clears the room?"

Connie nudged Ellen toward the door. Halfway there, Ellen took off on her own steam, slamming the front door behind her. Connie smiled an apology and got her coat. Otto stopped her at the threshold.

"You're a good friend."

Tears welled up. She was drunker than she'd realized. "Well," she began in confusion, but her voice caught, and she ducked out the door. She rubbed her eyes and pushed the hair from her face. When she looked up, she saw the taillights of Ellen's car pull out of the driveway and shimmy down the gravel lane. It was almost nine and the sky was growing dark. Large clouds massed in the southern valley, each one a towering individual presence. Connie felt small and transitory.

"She should not be driving," Otto said from the door.

Ellen had planned to walk home. She was punishing Connie, thumbing her nose at Connie's usual caution. "She hasn't got far to go," Connie said. "And there's nothing to hit but trees. The people are all here."

A few raindrops began to fall, and the smell of coffee floated out from the kitchen.

"Stay awhile." Otto laid a hand on her arm. "I'll walk you home later."

"I should go." Connie pulled her jacket more closely around her and looked down at her bare knees, pale and goose pimpled.

"Nope," Otto said. "Come on back. The after-party is always the best."

"I wouldn't know." But she felt a surge of recklessness. Maybe she would stay to see what happens. She could make up juicy stories to taunt Ellen.

"Let's see." Otto steered her back in the door. "We're scientists. It will be an experiment."

31

Inside, the party had coalesced into two groups. One group gathered near the fire, knotted together in intense conversation. Carl tilted forward on his toes, talking loudly to Fred who leaned against the mantle with his arms crossed, scowling. Six or seven others gathered around, perched on stools from the breakfast bar or standing back, listening. The second group moved through the rooms cleaning and gossiping. When they passed the group at the fire, they shook their heads.

"Come on," Annabelle scolded, her fingers pinching a bloom of plastic cups. "No politics!"

"It's not politics," Carl called after her. "If neighbors can't discuss difficult things, what hope is there for the world?"

Fred uncrossed his arms when he saw Otto. "We were just talking about the vandalism up at your place," he said, interrupting Carl. Otto nodded. "Well hell! You got a gun, don't you? If it was me, I'd sit up all night. It'd be worth it to surprise those tree-huggers with a slug of lead. Oh wait," he said in a mocking, feminine voice, "lead's *toxic*."

"You can't shoot someone for trespass," Blanche said.

"Some asshole's on my land? That's self-defense."

"*Self*-defense is okay," Blanche said. "Not property defense,"

"I don't want to shoot anyone," Otto said. "Some trees were marked." The group parted to let him step forward, but Connie drifted off to clean up the bar area as she listened, her pulse in her ears.

"Your truck, too," Annabelle said as she passed through.

"Your truck? Next it'll be your house. No respect for property rights," Fred said far too loudly.

"Fred," Eileen murmured. "Fred." She raised a hand and lowered it slowly to quiet him, but he just grimaced and looked away from her.

"The truck upset me." Otto jammed his hands in his pockets. "It was so personal."

"That's what I'm saying. A man ought to be able to manage his own land as he sees fit. People don't like logging. They shouldn't log. Isn't that what you liberals want? Choice?"

"Fred!" Blanche started but Otto smiled and waved it off.

"The police weren't convinced it was about the logging. They thought it looked like mischief. Do you all get a lot of vandalism up here?"

"Heavens no," Eileen said. "This has always been the safest place in the world. But everything is changing so much."

Evan stepped forward. He was a quiet man, an electrical engineer who didn't usually talk much in groups. "There was some trouble with equipment at that gravel quarry across the river a couple months back," he said. "The police and the owners would rather call it mischief, because then it doesn't mean anything. But I wonder if activists aren't getting a little more desperate."

"It's not like my logging plans were public knowledge," Otto said.

Everyone looked at him a moment. "You had that party," Blanche said.

"Just for neighbors," Otto frowned.

"Word gets around," Blanche said.

Connie shoved corks into the half-full wine bottles and stacked the recycling in bags on the floor. Blanche was right. As fond as the neighbors were of one another, they didn't generally share their plans. Someone was sure to get upset. A new well might drop the water table. Chemicals drifted on the breeze. Plant trees on your border and shade your neighbor's field. Take down trees and lose windbreaks. They didn't exactly mean to be sneaky, but it was all so complicated. If Otto hadn't moved out to the tipi, if he had hired consultants to prepare the vineyard, managing the project from Houston, would Connie have done what she did? There would have been no bet, no wildlife survey for Dylan. The consultants would have had no qualms, and a little spray paint would not have caused a moment of doubt for them. Poor Otto. It wasn't really fair.

"What people do with their land affects others, sometimes a lot." Evan blushed as he spoke again, and the group was chastened to listen patiently. "I've got a cabin down at Rockaway Beach. They had to get an excavator to clear out the water plant after the hill was logged. Without the trees, the soil washed into the creek that supplies the town's water. The soil was contaminated from the logging so even when they got it cleared away, they had to treat the water. It cost so much they had to raise the water rates. The timber company may own the land, but they don't own the water they ruined. People are getting frustrated that owners aren't held responsible for the damage they cause. Private gain but public risk."

"We got consumer protection laws for stuff like that," Fred said.

"Not really," Carl said. Evan was trembling from his moment in the spotlight, and he stepped back with a look of relief.

"This is a democracy," Fred exclaimed. "Change the law."

"Oh," Emily laughed. "You guys remember how long it took just to get a speed limit on the river road? Ten years? Fifteen? If Patty Blake hadn't passed her files on before she died, ODOT would have made us start all over. We've gone five years now without a fatality because Patty died slowly of breast cancer instead of all at once from a heart attack."

"That's no excuse for hooligans," Jack said. He was clearly angry, and he shifted from foot to foot like a rooster ready to fight. "We all get a tax deferral on our land because it's *supposed* to be harvested. No trees come down, no taxes for the county. No taxes and you don't get schools or roads. All that good public benefit stuff. You got to pay for it. Logging has always been a part of this state's heritage. Trees grow back. Oregon's got as much forest now as it did in the fifties."

"Does it really?" Emily asked.

"Look it up," Jack nodded.

"Well." Connie's heart pounded in a giddy rhythm as she stepped into the group. This sort of talk inflamed emotions but never changed minds. Still, if she was willing to vandalize Otto, but not speak up, she *was* sneaky. "Logged land is counted as forest even when it doesn't have a forest anymore. A clear-cut and an old-growth forest count equally for those statistics. Plus, a lot of forest was lost in the forties. That's why those comparisons always start with the fifties."

"If you care about forest," Jack said, turning to her, "why didn't you protect yours? Why'd you sell Otto the land when you knew he would put in a vineyard?"

Some of the women rose to clean up and get ready to leave. They pitied her and didn't want to put her on the spot. "I needed the money," she said.

"Damn straight," Jack said nodding. "Just like the county needs the taxes. Land has to be productive. I've known you a long time, Connie, and I hate to call out your hypocrisy but . . ." he spread his hands and shrugged.

Connie caught Otto's eye and smiled at him, apologizing because his earnest dreams of sustainability and belonging meant very little to the community he had joined; they all just needed the money. "If we have to log," she said, "these are the forests we should cut. The little patchy forests like Otto's, tucked into rural neighborhoods, are not as significant as the large old forests in the mountains. Old-growth is some of the most productive land in the world, much more productive than these young second and third growth forests."

"You're supposed to be our scientist!" Fred gave her a paternal scowl. "Everyone knows young trees grow faster than old trees."

"We still have some wild animals around here." Eileen came to the group and handed Fred his jacket. "I saw a bobcat out in the hay field last week."

"I saw a cougar a couple weeks ago." The man who spoke had recently moved up from San Jose. No one really believed him. Cougars used to live in the deep rocky ravines at the base of the mountain. Maybe one or two still did, but the new vineyards reached tough fingers right down to the creek beds. Connie hadn't seen claw marks in her forest for years.

"I better be more careful," Otto said with enthusiasm. "Where'd you see that?"

"It was standing right there in the middle of Smith Road. About 6:30 in the morning."

"Harley," someone said softly. Harley was a senescent yellow lab who liked to hang out on Smith Road's warm asphalt.

People stood and carried the last of the dishes to the kitchen where Annabelle looked tired as she put things in order. She wiped her hands on a dishrag. "Listen, Otto, let me give you a ride back to your place."

Connie went to get her coat. She could slip out before Otto noticed.

"I couldn't impose." He laid a hand on Annabelle's arm. "You've done so much already. That was the best barbecued pork I've ever had. And the juleps! What a party."

Annabelle walked him to the door, but her expression soured when she spotted Connie who hadn't quite made it out. "For heaven's sake. It will only take me a moment. I can take you too, Connie. And anyone else," she said loudly looking around at the loose group as they slipped into raincoats and collected their casseroles. "It's dark out."

"I'll enjoy the walk." He opened the door for Connie.

"But I want to send some leftover pork with you."

"You are so kind." He leaned over and embraced Annabelle. "But I don't have a kitchen. I'm not even set up to make a sandwich."

"Then you'll have to come by here for lunch. I can't eat it all myself."

"You've got a deal." He waved to Annabelle and placed a hand on the small of Connie's back. His large hand steadied her as he ushered her out, but she had grown used to the vertigo of solitude, and she twisted away from the support as she stepped into the night.

32

Clouds thickened the sky as Connie and Otto walked in silence, cocooned in their coats. At the end of the driveway, Connie turned to the right to travel down the lane that led to Otto's and Ellen's houses.

Otto hesitated. "I'm walking you home," he said. "I'm enough of a gentleman to do that."

"Okay." Connie continued down the lane. As the dark coalesced around her, her heart slowed and her breath came easier. She was drunk and walking felt bold and loose.

"Don't we go this way?" Otto called from the driveway.

She turned around and lost her balance, staggering to keep her feet under her. She laughed. "It's miles by the road. It'll be faster to cut through the woods."

He jogged to catch up with her. "In the dark?"

"I know the way."

They fell in together, walking shoulder to shoulder, kicking rocks between them along the gravel drive. Because they couldn't really see the rocks, they scuffed along. The noise of their feet was pleasantly like conversation. Every once in a while, they veered into one another's path, bumping companionably. Ellen's car was safely in her driveway. Lights were on in the living room and if Otto hadn't been there, Connie would have stopped in. She was afraid Ellen had gone home and continued to drink, but she didn't want to expose her in front of Otto.

The path to Connie's farm was a dark void in the wall of foliage. Connie passed through and then had to stop. Clouds obscured the moon and stars, but the gravel lane had reflected what light there was. In the forest, she couldn't see a thing.

"Jesus," Otto said behind her. "We'd better turn around and take the road."

"No!" Annabelle's lighted house now seemed like a foreign country. The return would be difficult, the arrival a hardship.

"I could run back and borrow a flashlight."

"As if she'd let you leave again." Connie felt so sheltered by darkness that she spoke freely. "It hasn't been much more than five minutes since we left Annabelle's. Our eyes haven't adjusted yet."

They waited, peering into blackness. Connie put her hand in front of her face. It was visible only as a spot of opaque black in the vague black of the forest. "You know," she said, "Fred was wrong. Young trees don't grow faster than old trees. They grow *taller* faster, but old trees grow a lot more biomass every year."

"You should have said something," Otto said.

Connie frowned. Whose side was he on? They stood in the void, waiting for the dark to resolve into a landscape. Otto was invisible, but Connie could hear him breathing and feel the gravity of his presence as he waited with her. She took a step forward and stumbled on a bush.

"It would only take a moment to run back for a flashlight."

"No, no, no, no." Connie sang the words, a whining entreaty. "You don't have to come. I'll be fine. It's only a little ways before your new road. Then it will be easy again." A flashlight seemed like a violent solution. It would crack the night open. "I can almost see now." The bushes and trees began to separate themselves from the dark, pulling away from the trail to show the path through. Connie walked slowly, feeling her way with her feet.

"Ow!"

"Otto?" Behind her, sticks snapped and branches brushed against fabric.

"Where the hell are you?"

"Right here." She saw him now, a hulking shape moving haphazardly and far too quickly. She heard the scrape of another impact. "Slow down, Otto. Can you see a little now? Use your feet to find the path." She talked to keep him oriented. He reached her, panting slightly. "We're almost to your new road." She took his hand and led him, using her other arm to feel the space in front of them. The path was well-trodden and if Connie had been barefoot, she could have followed it easily, but her stiff cowboy boots muffled the feel of the ground. She saw the pasture now, beyond the last line of trees, plain as an empty bowl. Connie pushed through. A blackberry vine caught her leg and ripped a shallow gash across her knee as she pulled Otto out of the forest. They stopped on the clean gravel of the new road. Moonlight leaked from a break in the clouds and stained them with pearly light. Connie dropped his hand.

"That was scary, Connie."

"What could happen to us here?" She looked down into her dear little valley. What could happen to her here was what could happen to her anywhere—illness, loss, death.

"What about the cougar that guy saw?"

"The one that was standing in the middle of the road in daylight? I'm not worried. Big cats are secretive. Harley's a little small to be a mountain lion, plus he's a dog, but he's the right color, he goes around on four legs, and he hangs out in the middle of the road. New neighbors tend to spot a lot of mountain lions and bears. The rest of us aren't so sure. We used to have cougars up here. I never saw one, but I've seen the trees all clawed up. I can show you the scars. If we do it before you log," she said, remembering.

They both realized there probably wasn't time. The quarter moon slipped free from a scrap of cloud and the pale road lit up. They walked easily along the even surface.

"We should have brought a flask of julep, Otto. I'm not quite drunk enough to ask you why the hell you had to put a road into the wetland."

Otto stopped. "Are you upset again?"

Connie kept walking.

"I did it for the owls, Connie." He hurried to catch up. "I decided to keep a bunch of trees on the ridge for raptors. But I have to have at least fifteen contiguous acres of grapes in order to have a tasting room on the property, so I have to plant down in that lowland. The laws here are very complicated."

The owls were already dead. Now the wetland was threatened. What could she say? That's what happens when you learn from experience—your solutions are always for the last problem. The moon disappeared and the road dimmed again to a blue grey line, bifurcating the soft darkness of plants.

"I was glad you spoke to me about the owls," Otto said from the darkness. "I should have thought of that myself. You're a good teacher."

"Hah." He was playing her.

"And I have a lot to learn."

She lengthened her stride, almost desperate to be home alone. A sudden wind came up and bent the grasses as the trees soughed. Connie's knees felt raw, and her toes hurt from the boots. She pulled her jacket close. They reached the wetland and had just crossed over onto Connie's property when the clouds opened. Huge raindrops slapped their faces, and a furious new wind stirred the trees. A large branch crashed to the road behind them as rain began to rake the field in wind-driven waves.

Connie ran for the sheep barn. "In here," she called to Otto. They ducked inside and Connie used her jacket to towel her hair and wipe the rain from her face. "What a squall!"

She climbed onto a hay bale and pulled her dress down around her clammy knees. Hay scratched her through the thin cotton and the bale was too firm to be cozy, yet she thought there was nothing as comforting as rain on a metal roof. "It won't last long," Connie assured Otto, but the rain kept beating down on the little barn and wind circled the structure and shook it. Inside, the sheep chewed and snorted, and the sweet smell of hay mixed with the scent of manure. Connie nestled into a corner where loose hay gathered.

33

"You should tell me a story," Otto said from the dark. She couldn't see him in the gloom of the barn, but his voice was near.

"I'm the wrong person, Otto. I have information, but I've never had adventures."

"I don't believe it."

Connie searched her memory, but she only had domestic stories. They meant a lot to her, but they weren't the sort of thing to entertain others.

"What about hopes and dreams?" Otto's voice became playful. "Maybe you wanted to be an astronaut? You still study rocket science online at night?"

Connie was quiet for a long time. "God, Otto. I thought everyone knew I was hopeless."

"Grief doesn't preclude hope. Hope isn't a betrayal," he said softly.

Tears started in her eyes; the alcohol had made her sloppy. But hope *was* a betrayal, looking forward at all was a betrayal. And as for dreams, did the devilment of Otto count? Not his downfall, just devilment. Among all that, she couldn't think of a thing to say out loud.

"If you were truly hopeless," he said, speaking boldly now above the clattering rain, "you wouldn't be so bossy."

"Bossy? You're the one always looking for advice."

"I'm new here."

"We're all new here. Every day. I could share information about the forest, but it's on its way out, and you're a forward-looking kind of guy." Rain pounded on the metal roof. She had to speak up and raising her voice made her quarrelsome. "I don't think you want a teacher. You ask for help to flatter us, to win friends and influence people. I don't mean to criticize," she added. "It's a practical goal and an effective technique."

He laughed. "Busted."

They listened for signs that the storm was easing; it was time to go, but new gusts worried the barn siding and kept pulling rain from the sky. Otto shifted on the hay. Connie had the impression he'd laid down, but she couldn't see a thing. "That," he said from his new position, "is what I like about you."

"My succinct summaries?"

"*Succinct* is a nice way to put it. *Rude* is the word that came to my mind, but you're honest. You weren't an only child like me, I bet. You're too bold. You must have had siblings to sharpen your wits on."

"Two sisters," Connie confirmed. "But we didn't live together long. My sister Felicity was twelve when I was born, and Grace was fourteen. I was a surprise. Constance was the cross my family bore."

"Ah," Otto said as though something had been made clear. "Complications. It's good for people. If I had a big family, I'd be better with people, not so awkward."

"You're pretty smooth. I don't know what you think you're missing."

A stir on the hay indicated Otto was sitting up again. "I'm missing the ties that bind. It's not healthy."

"And you think a family would solve that? Oh, Otto." Connie lay down and stared up into the dark. Her eyes had fully adjusted, and she could discern some shapes, the outlines of the windows, the hulk of the hay loft. "Ties that bind indeed," she repeated. "For as long as I can remember, Felicity explained how our parents had planned to retire to the beach when she got done with high school, but they couldn't because of me. I felt so sorry for them. And guilty."

"I know families aren't perfect," Otto said. "Interesting families aren't. But you have something to belong to."

"Or something to be excluded from." Connie's heart began to hammer against her ribs, a small insistent harangue, and she exhaled and inhaled. "You know," she tried to find a joking tone, "you can't be alienated all by yourself. You need the help of others."

"Connie."

He spoke her name with sympathy, but she heard the warning there too. She must sound self-pitying. "Everyone has their wound, right?" she said defensively. "It's a birthright. We all get a big sorrow to keep us company all our life.

"Grace was killed in a car accident when I was ten and she was just twenty-four. Weird, huh? That's just about Cary's age when she died." Connie understood that conjunction was not causation. But still. "I worshipped Grace. We all did. Felicity got bitter and my parents got old." Everyone knew the wrong daughter died. "My mom got breast cancer when I was fifteen. After she died, poor Dad was stuck with me."

"Oh, Connie."

The sorrow in Otto's voice made her cringe. She had this effect on people; there was nothing she could do but wait it out.

"So much loss. I can't even imagine. I'm so sorry."

Connie shrugged. Otto couldn't see her, but the gesture was like a familiar cloak she wrapped herself in. "Wars, poverty, disease. Plenty of people face a lot worse."

"Not relevant." Otto spoke softly but with great assurance. "Those are hard knocks. I admire your bravery."

"Courage isn't a choice. I did what I had to."

"You're wrong." He had shifted, and his voice was clear. "People told me how you took care of your daughter. I see how you care for Dylan now, and Ellen. The wetland. The owls. To continue to love in the face of loss takes courage."

"Not relevant." Courage, fear—what difference did it make? "Life changes fast when you're young. After Mom died, Felicity got married and moved to Santa Barbara, and Dad retired and followed her there. I finished high school from a one-bedroom apartment within walking distance of school."

"That's harsh."

"It was my choice. I guess he would have taken me to Santa Barbara."

"You did your own shopping? You made your own meals?"

"Dad sent me money. I was resourceful."

"So you weren't the cross they bore. And you grew up to be a resource for the people around you."

Connie stretched her legs out and leaned into a bale. The darkness was so complete it was almost like being alone. "It seemed like the least I could do."

34

Otto's raincoat rasped against the coarse hay as he found a new position. "Maybe we all do get a sorrow. Like a fairy godmother's gift," Otto said. "My sorrow is sort of banal."

"Unless they're horrendous, all childhood wounds are banal." It was a comfort, really. "I showed you mine."

Otto laughed, and from his voice Connie could tell he was lying down again, looking up into the dark. "Kids didn't like me," he said. "There you have it. And in sixth grade I overheard Robbie Perez say I was like a zero *before* the number. Just irrelevant. Even the nerds didn't like me."

"What did Robbie Perez know?" In the close shelter beneath the rattling tin roof, Connie was glad to join his team.

"Robbie was a great guy. I was devastated."

"Well, I'm sorry. Whatever you are, I don't think you're irrelevant."

"Not anymore." Otto must have turned onto his side, because now his voice was softer, directed toward her. "After Robbie said that, I made a vow."

Rain sluiced down the roof to splash in the puddles that surrounded the barn. Connie had only installed a gutter on the uphill side, where the door was.

"I quit trying to make friends. I studied and played with computers. I designed a game that got popular, and by the time I was out of college, I was making more money than my parents."

His voice grew stronger as he spoke, and he delivered the last sentence like a punch line. Interesting to consider that being a zero wasn't the problem. The problem was being a zero in the wrong place. Everyone wants to matter. It's the root of all evil. Connie found herself losing interest. The rain was not so furious. She was cold. She should be home in bed. "I guess you showed Robbie Perez," she said as she sat up and scooted to the edge of the bale, ready to stand.

"Oh, no." Otto was still prostrate on the hay. The pocket of shadow where he lay might have meant anything—a carcass, a tarp. "No, Robbie Perez is a prince among men, and I'm still at risk of being a zero before the number."

Connie scuffed her boots against the rough floorboards. Her toes felt numb. "Otto, you're getting maudlin." He groaned, and she flicked her hand into the shadow to slap him lightly. "But I started it."

"You did," he said, sitting up.

They listened to the rain. Connie could run home and towel off and be in a warm bed within ten minutes. But how would Otto get home? He'd get lost in the dark. She should give him a ride. Complicated.

"Robbie Perez married his high school sweetheart and coached Little League. They raised a couple foster kids, bless their hearts. At our twenty-fifth reunion he was even nice to me."

"Popularity isn't everything." How many times had she said this to students? It made her tired.

"People like Robbie Perez are the glue that holds society together."

"Hm." Connie stared into the dark thinking of how to exit. She could just leave Otto. He'd make it home sooner or later. "*Is* society holding together?"

"If not, it's because of people like me," Otto said promptly. "That's what brought me to Oregon."

Otto huddled back against the hay, not making any move to leave. He had quit talking, but he had more to say, and the imminence had a sort of gravity. Connie could feel his stubborn inertia. She sighed and pulled her feet out of the punishing boots. She scooted back into the soft loose hay and tucked her legs underneath her to warm them. "Sounds like you have a story."

"People like you," he said, "you probably can't even imagine someone like me. How unattached. When I turned fifty I realized I could have dropped off the face of the earth without anyone really noticing. Maybe my *work* was important, but *I* was still a zero before the number. I had a midlife crisis." He was silent a long time and then groaned and Connie could imagine him dropping his head in his hands. "See?" he laughed. "I told you it was banal."

"Tell me the story anyway." Connie swept wisps of hay into drifts around her, insulation as the night deepened. She tugged handfuls from the bale to block the drafts.

"It starts at the beach." He paused for drama; Connie appreciated the effort and stretched out on the hay, wriggling into the loose and scratchy blanket she had created. "I did not go to play in the waves; I went for research, to observe the well-adjusted people who share leisure time together—picnics, playing Frisbee, football— that kind of thing. But it didn't look fun." Rain still beat down on the metal roof, but not so furiously. "At the end of the day, when they dragged their kids off to dinner, I was just happy I wasn't in there with them eating spaghetti."

"Some of those people wished they were someplace else."

"How about all of them?"

"Some of those people were having a great time."

Otto sighed and began again, in a portentous voice. "And then," he reached out to poke Connie, but because he couldn't see her, his hand hit her shoulder awkwardly. "A flock of sandpipers landed on the beach." Otto shifted on the hay. Connie imagined him lying on his side facing her. She couldn't know; it was too dark. She felt like a kid at a slumber party. She rolled onto her back and stared into the blackness.

"I'd never seen sandpipers before, the way they chase the tide. A bunch of clowns. Then all at once they lifted into the air, and it was a transformation. They became a perfect fabric of birds, a ribbon on the breeze."

Flocks of birds, schools of fish, herds of antelope. An individual was nothing, a dot in the grid, and yet the whole miraculous display was nothing but individuals. It was a mystery.

"It's mathematical," Otto explained. "Each little body would just get blown around, but when they knit themselves together, they become something else. Individually, they are ridiculous. Together, their elegance and coordination stunned me."

All an individual had to do was hold their spot. They would be borne aloft. Connie's eyes filled with tears, the soft kind that rise silently like a spring. She let them spill down her cheeks, and she knew it was just because she was drunk, but there, in the darkness where no one would see, crying for the heavenly image was a luxury. But heavenly was the problem. She wiped her eyes with the back of her hand. "That's only the first part of the story," she said, "because it doesn't explain how you ended up here."

35

"I've set the scene?" Otto's voice was closer to her now. "You understand that I was moved to seek connection?"

"I understand."

"Good. That's the revelation. The rest of the story is boring. I became a farmer to be connected to the land and the seasons. A vineyard because I love wine and I didn't want to replant every spring. I came to Oregon for the growing conditions and land prices."

Connie stared into the darkness. Fabric tore. It rotted. When fibers began to fail, the whole matrix unraveled. A mess.

"I wanted a place to hold me. To be rooted like you."

"Me?" Connie grunted. "My position is precarious; I'm just trying to get along."

Otto burst out laughing and Connie recoiled, confused. "You better do some soul-searching," he said. "You don't make any effort to get along."

The hay beneath them had grown warm from their body heat, and Connie was comfortable among the quiet animals, listening to the wind as it pulled at the siding, more gently now, and rattled the aluminum gate outside. She could feel the warmth from Otto's body in the air between them. He was very near, and then suddenly Connie felt his hand, laid on the hay near hers so that their fingers touched, perhaps by accident. She listened for the sound of his breathing, but she heard nothing. He must be holding his breath just as she was. She slid her hand closer, just a little, to see what would happen. He clasped her fingers and his nylon jacket rasped against the hay. His other hand touched her thigh briefly as he found her in the dark. Then he brushed her hair back, teasing the stems of hay away from her forehead and smoothing the skin of her cheek. All at once his lips were against her own. Connie leaned into Otto and gripped his shoulder as he encircled her waist. He turned her and laid her down, drawing her close in the circle of his arms. She felt him harden against her thigh and she softened, opening to his touch, to the feel of lips and hands. The sheep stomped and chewed. Connie was no more an individual than the sandpipers. Even her vandalism, which had felt like shocking acts of disruption, were only incidents in a wave of protest spreading across the forests of the west. Otto pressed against her, and she felt such relief she trembled.

Desire became more insistent, and he shifted her again to find his way past her coat and her clothes. He cupped her breast and slid his hand down her waist, fumbling with fabric to reach her skin. She let him arrange her, glad to be an offering, someone else's fate. He pressed his thigh between her legs, hiking her dress up, and ran his hand along her naked flank from knee to the swell of her hip. She tangled her legs with his legs, feeling the pressure of him along the full length of her body.

"Connie." Otto leaned on his hand, then shifted to sit. "Connie, we're drunk. I can't do this. It isn't right."

"Otto."

"No." He sighed as she sat up and straightened her clothes. "I'm going to be a gentleman and walk you home unmolested." He drew her in to lean against his shoulder. "But in a little while," he whispered into her ear. "When the rain stops."

It was April; the rain might never stop. She should just go home. But his arm on her shoulder was heavy and sheltering and there was no reason to hurry. The next thing Connie knew, she could see the outline of the barn rafters. Through the dusty windows, the sky lightened to indigo. Otto squeezed her gently, then slipped his arm off her shoulder. "Guess we fell asleep." His voice was gruff, embarrassed.

"The sun will be up soon," she said.

He moved away from her. "I guess I told you all my secrets last night."

"Nothing too surprising," she said. "The mountain is full of strange ambitions. It's a dreamy place."

"I'm not a dreamy person." He zipped his jacket. "You wait and see. My vineyard will be famous. I'll get this place on the map."

Her head hurt and her throat was scratchy with barn dust. She patted his knee and stood quickly. "I'll be fine from here. Thanks for walking me home." She left before he said another thing.

Otto phoned the next day as a gentleman would. The message was friendly and noncommittal. It asked for nothing specific, and Connie didn't see any reason to return the call. The following week, she stayed close to home. She didn't walk the trails near Otto's property, the spot, he had claimed, that would finally put their mossy neighborhood on the map. As if that was something she should celebrate.

After that, when Connie needed to fill the long spring evenings, she ran north, away from Otto's lane and Annabelle's cheerfully blooming driveway. The memory of his kiss, his body pressing against her, returned at idle moments. She would push it away, but when her mind wandered, it fell to remembering his dry, slightly chapped lips and how the stubble of his beard grazed her cheek. It had been a long time since she had been kissed. Even when she and Mike still had a physical relationship, kissing had fallen out of their repertoire. Their communion took on a sideways, glancing character that she had accepted with the other disappointments of a long-term marriage. She had thought she didn't care, but she found herself closing her eyes to conjure the smell of beer and hay and Otto's freshly laundered shirt. She was ashamed of the turn her thoughts kept taking, but worse still was the humiliation of imagining that he understood the effect of his intimacy, that he had it all mapped out, and he was patronizing her, a woman of such limited experience.

36

"You look terrible," Connie said glancing at Ellen as she tied her shoes.

Ellen rubbed her face hard and swiped a hand over her hair, but she was still puffy, her cheeks mottled with small scaly red patches.

"But here I am, exercising with you anyway. What a friend!"

They walked up the drive at a brisk pace. Connie's recent thoughts were too embarrassing to share. The restless heat at the core of her flared and dwindled, and Connie would not reveal to Ellen what she didn't really understand herself. They were all the way to the corner before Connie finally asked, "Are you alright?"

Ellen shook her head like an old bear, her shoulders swaying with regret. "It's a good thing I never had children. A couple months of Dylan and I'm all in."

"What's up?" Connie walked sideways to keep an eye on Ellen whose arms swung stiffly as if she were pushing things out of her way. Her scowl never wavered. Not a hint of a joke.

"He's depressed. And acting weird. He's on the computer or his phone all the time now."

"Maybe he has an online friend." Connie hoped so. "Maybe he's looking at porn."

"He's reading boring, horrible stuff about the environment." Ellen walked on without elaborating, and Connie fell back to continue at her side.

"You've been losing sleep worrying about him?"

"No. That's part of the problem." Ellen still avoided looking at Connie. "I sleep like a log. That's why I look so bad this morning. I woke up late. Ran over to your place while I was still half asleep. I was up late drinking margaritas with Stephanie Whitcomb."

"From the ice cream shop?"

"Trying to get Dylan a cheerful job. I'm a good drinker, but Stephanie, she has a problem."

Connie felt her heart sink, and it brought a physical chill. "Did you get him the job?"

"Sure. Stephanie'll hire him. Plus," Ellen said, opening her eyes wide in mock enthusiasm, "she's invited me to join her bocce team. That's because of my drinking expertise. It doesn't matter that I suck at any game involving a ball."

"When is Dylan starting?" If Connie could keep Dylan part-time, she'd try hard to be more cheerful.

"Dylan won't. Oh, Connie, we had such a horrible fight last night."

Ellen stopped for a moment in the middle of the street, her face wrinkled with pain. Connie thought she might cry, something that had never happened before. Over the long course of their friendship, Connie had seen Ellen meet trouble strongly, loudly, not always effectively, but always energetically. Now she looked tired and old.

"Teenagers can be dreadful," Connie said softly. "Cruel, even. They don't know any better."

"It was me." Ellen leaned into the hill and walked faster, her stiff arms swung angrily. "I was the one that was dreadful. All those fucking margaritas. I got home around two and Dylan was still up. His face was all bluish over that computer screen; he looked like a ghoul. I told him he got the ice cream job and he said he wouldn't go. I lost my temper."

"It probably wasn't as bad as you remember it."

"It was worse. But I'd made all that effort—I don't even like margaritas. I'm feeding him, housing him, buying him boots, and it's not like he ever says thank you."

"Living with you might not have been his first choice either."

Ellen scowled at Connie. "That's just what he told me. He said he never wanted to live out in the sticks with me, an old drunk who can't even cook. I have no business with a kid. I explained that no one else wanted him. Not his mom or his dad or his grandparents. I didn't see any friends stepping forward to take him in."

Connie felt a withering in the pit of her stomach. "Did you tell him how much you love him?"

"No, I didn't tell him because I didn't love him right then. Right then, he was an enormous, thankless imposition. That's pretty much what I told him." Ellen kicked a rock down the road, scuffing her sneaker hard into the asphalt. When the rock skittered across the street, she followed after. "He could hurt himself." She kicked the rock again and lost it in the ravine. She looked over to Connie, her face sagging. "I'm not exaggerating. He's the sort, right?"

Connie sidled over to Ellen and slipped an arm around her waist. She leaned her head on her shoulder, but Ellen kept marching along. "Have you talked to him since the fight?"

"He was sleeping. He'll still be sleeping when I get home. He stays up all night, but how can I stop him?"

"You could stay up until you know he's asleep." Connie spoke gently because she knew the suggestion would be taken as a rebuke. Ellen often drank in the evenings and when she drank enough, sleep came over her like a sort of death.

They walked on in silence. Thin clouds evaporated beneath the rising sun, and the day was bright and fine, but Ellen only watched her feet. "I'll apologize," she said after some time. "I won't make him work at the ice cream shop. Then I won't have to drink margaritas with Stephanie, and I won't have to join her bocce league. They probably wear funny clothes, right? Like croquet players. Now I won't have to do that. And that will be a relief, and I'll have all kinds of energy and emotional reserves." Ellen looked up from her feet and offered a false smile. "I'll be a tactful parent-figure." They reached Ellen's drive and stopped near the mailbox. "But while I'm working on that, you're our best hope," Ellen said. "Will you do whatever you can for him? I know you are already, but what I'm saying is, feel free to interfere."

37

That afternoon, Dylan did not show up to check in. Previously, Connie wouldn't have cared, presuming he could manage himself well enough. But now she sat restlessly over a table covered with snacks, including vegan bars she had made herself out of chia seeds and peanut butter. Their fussiness rebuked her. She'd even gotten a couple bottles of kombucha because she thought it might be the sort of thing he'd like, but the kombucha grew warm and the hummus got crusty as she waited. She called but got no answer. Finally, she packed up the food to carry to Ellen's. If she didn't find Dylan there, at least she could leave the food.

Up on the ridge, the trees still stood. Otto hadn't continued logging after they showed him the owls, but the reprieve was certainly temporary. He wasn't going to change his carefully drawn plans. He could have asked her to help him think through the tradeoff between wetland and trees if he truly valued her knowledge. The question would have given him an excuse to call. If he had wanted an excuse to call.

She found Dylan up at Ellen's still in pajamas, lying on the couch, staring out the window through his right eye. He wore a patch on the left eye, a cheap plastic thing that looked like it came from a pirate's costume.

"Hello." Connie set the food on the table and waited for him to turn, but he only grunted in response. She walked around to the foot of the couch. "Some trouble with the sonic eyes? Are you okay?"

He moved a little, as though he might sit up, but then resettled. He made a sound in his throat. It might have been a greeting.

"I brought some food for you." The room was stuffy, and she opened a window. "Some kombucha, too. Have you ever tried it?"

"I'm not really hungry."

Connie got two glasses. "I'd like to try it anyway." She handed him a glass, but he set it down without drinking.

"Berry flavored." Connie took a sip. "Not too sweet, a little fizzy."

"I've tried kombucha," Dylan said in a weary voice.

"Come on. Sit up." She swung his legs off the couch and sat down near him. He had not yet begun to grow a beard and his skin was thin and translucent. She laid the back of her hand against his cheek, feeling for fever, but Dylan curled up like a spider into the far corner of the couch.

Connie dipped a piece of celery into hummus. "I thought you'd have more notes for me to look over."

"I didn't go out."

She waved a broccoli spear toward Dylan, but he looked frightened and tearful, so she ate it herself. "Why not?"

"I've been doing research." He tossed his phone onto the coffee table and slumped more deeply into the couch.

"Our time is limited."

Dylan frowned as though he was in pain. He looked like an invalid, and the couch with its nest of blankets and food within reach seemed like a sickroom. Connie turned to the forest beyond the window, but that was no consolation because she couldn't see it without thinking about how the whole ecosystem would be wiped away in a morning's work. Once it was gone, the bare hillside would be a new place entirely—rocky and sunny with no relation to the layered community that had preceded it. As though the forest had never been.

"So what have you learned?" Connie tapped the discarded phone with her fingernail. She had always wondered where animals went when their forest was logged. They didn't wander around the devastation the way humans did after a house burned down. If the TV news showed cougars dazedly pawing through slash piles, would people be more sympathetic?

"Otto's logging next Monday."

This was hardly surprising, but Connie felt a sinking dread. *Monday* was plain and real and inescapable.

"So I've been doing what you wanted," he said. "I've been learning about the condemned." Dylan used his toe to slide the phone to the far edge of the table. "Lichens live for thousands of years." He buried his face in the couch cushions, and Connie had to strain to understand him. "People used to use them for medicine, but they soak up pollution so they're not safe anymore. Overall, one million species are at risk of extinction." He paused to look at her, both accusing and supplicating. "We only know eight million species total. One million out of eight million. We're not doing a wildlife survey. We're doing a wilddeath survey."

Connie bit a piece of celery and made herself chew it slowly. "What we don't notice might never have existed." She spoke as gently and firmly as she could manage, but even as she spoke the words, she knew they weren't true. "We honor what we notice," she added more correctly.

Dylan wrinkled his nose and closed his eye. He held the expression a long time before he looked at her again. "You said humans are basically predators. We *eat* what we notice. More than forty percent of all amphibians are gone now. I've never seen a salamander, and I probably never will."

Connie nodded as he spoke. Salamanders migrate. She used to see them for a few days every year, crawling slowly across the roads. A mystery. She'd always meant to learn where they were going, but Dylan was right; it wasn't relevant anymore.

He shifted on the couch to face her fully. "Scientists think we've lost ten percent of insect species. Nobody really knows, because we don't know much about insects, but there are a lot less bugs, and the birds are starving. Sometimes birds fall dead right out of the sky." His voice rose, keening.

"I'm sorry." She could think of dozens more examples of loss, but she couldn't find the words to make it okay. This was not some current event she could use to hone her student's skills. She bowed her head and squeezed Dylan's knee through the blanket.

"I want to die like those owls—all at once."

Connie leaned over to hug him. He did not move toward her, so she encircled his whole corner, draping her arms around the couch along with his boney shoulder.

Dylan winced. Then he did start to cry. Like a little boy, his face crumpled and his nose began to run and he turned his head to the back of the couch. She slipped the eye patch off and gently rubbed the mark left by the elastic until he turned away. Tears were better than anger. They were better than his ghostly lethargy. Connie drank kombucha and gave him time. After some minutes he began to settle, but he didn't lift his head.

"I'm never having kids," he said into the couch. He pulled the eyepatch back on and pressed his face into the cushion. "Having kids is a crime. It's bad for the world, but it's really mean to the kids."

Connie looked down at the energy bars she'd made, so many more than they could eat. The hardest thing about young people was their pure and blameless expectation.

"I don't mean it like that," he said.

Connie startled and looked up.

"Saying that about kids. I know your kid died. I didn't mean to hurt your feelings."

Connie shook her head. "My daughter, Cary." She had never even mentioned her name to Dylan. "I wish she had died all at once."

Dylan regarded her from the corner of his right eye. "How old was she?"

"Twenty-five. She had leukemia."

He met her gaze and nodded solemnly, his lips pressed together. The masculine gesture was queered by the plastic eye patch, but Connie felt exposed as he acknowledged her loss. She had no right to his consideration. Embarrassed, she began to reach for the food but stopped herself. Who was she to reject his kindness? She faced him squarely and let her grief sit between them as she met the gaze of his one eye. Maybe it was sonic because she had to steel herself to stay there. She nodded, acknowledging the gift of his sympathy.

Dylan relaxed back into the couch and wiped his nose on the cushion. He spoke without lifting his head. "You talk about witnessing, but witnesses only get traumatized."

It might be so. Connie got up and closed the window. She rewrapped the hummus and the vegetables and put them in the refrigerator.

Dylan leaned forward to talk to her in the kitchen. "If Otto gets arrested, he couldn't build the vineyard."

"Dylan."

"He's up to something. And if he gets arrested, he can't log."

Connie sighed. Conspiracies. Secrets. Unwholesome fuel. She paused at the door. "Tomorrow, I'll come up here after Ellen and I walk. You and I can go out together. You can tell me everything you've learned. Not about Otto, but about the crime." She paused for emphasis. "You have to have evidence of a crime."

He balanced his chin on the back of the couch as she put on her jacket. "I have evidence."

He was uncharacteristically confident. She nodded seriously, to honor that confidence, and he seemed to grow a little in the shelter of her regard. Then she waved her hand in the air, circling it comically over her shoulder in a gesture meant to dispel the sickroom aura. "Now get dressed. Eat some lunch. We'll go over everything tomorrow."

38

The next morning, Ellen and Connie walked through a heavy, blowing mist that beaded Ellen's coarse hair and made it sparkle. The planet had passed the equinox and although it was only a little after nine, the sun was already high and bright beyond the thinning clouds. The mist that clung to the treetops peeled off in puffs like smoke from an extinguished match. All along the lane, white trilliums gleamed in the shade of trees.

"I'm meeting Dylan at your house after our walk." Connie spoke breathlessly. Ellen kept up a brisk and angry pace, her long legs covered a stride and a half for every step Connie took.

"He's better," Ellen said. "He stayed in all night. He was having an off day yesterday. Maybe he was sick."

"Maybe." Connie made an effort to lengthen her stride. "I don't think he's eating enough."

"He just picks at the food I serve."

"Do you have snack foods he can eat?"

"I buy tons of that stuff. The other day I threw out a whole packet of lunch meat he never even tried."

"Ellen, he's a vegan."

Ellen looked over in surprise. "No, he's not."

"He said he was."

"He just doesn't eat. Maybe it's the depression. I bought a big package of string cheese. Kids usually like that, but he never opened the package."

"Vegans don't eat cheese."

"What?"

"No animal products. No dairy products, no eggs."

"Not even milk?"

"Almond milk. Soy milk. Not cow's milk."

Ellen's pace slowed. Her brow furrowed. "No," she said at last, coming to some conclusion. "He would have told me."

"Maybe I misunderstood."

They walked on for some time in silence. Strips of blue sky began to shine through the clouds.

"If he's a vegan," Ellen said at last, "he must be starving. It's ridiculous. He would have said something."

They parted at Connie's driveway, and Connie went home to change into forest clothes and gather the surveys. When she arrived at Ellen's, she found Dylan at the kitchen table eating an orange while Ellen paid bills at the desk nearby.

"You ready?" Connie asked him.

"Almost," he said, sucking juice from his fingers.

"Did you get enough to eat?"

Dylan shrugged.

"You're vegan, right?"

"Yeah."

Ellen wheeled around. "No, you're not."

Dylan rolled his eyes.

"Why didn't you tell me?"

"You knew that," he said. "How could you forget last Thanksgiving? Mom threw that drumstick at me?"

Ellen faced Dylan, fierce with accusation. "You must be hungry. Why didn't you say something?"

"I told you, Aunt Ellen."

"No, you didn't."

"You just don't remember."

"Bullshit. What's a vegan anyway?"

"No animal products," Connie said, to give Dylan cover. She took an old envelope and a pen from the desk and sat next to him at the table. "Let's make a shopping list."

Ellen stared at them.

"What would you like?" Connie asked.

Dylan shrugged.

"That's no help," Connie said. "What do you eat at home?"

"Crackers."

"What else?"

"Peanut butter."

"And?" Connie looked over to see that Dylan's cheeks had flushed slightly. He stood and threw the orange peel in the compost.

"Whatever I can find. I'll finish getting ready." He turned and slipped upstairs.

"I saw you eating cheese," Ellen yelled after him. "I can't believe he didn't say anything," she said to Connie.

"He says he did."

"He should have said it twice, for Christ's sake!"

Connie continued. *Nuts*, she wrote. *Tofu, beans, hummus.*

Ellen snatched the list. "I can do that." She pulled her shoes on and left, leaving Connie alone at the table.

After a few minutes, Dylan returned from his room, descending the staircase like a shadow. There wasn't much to that boy. Not much color, not much heft. Just a sliver.

39

Connie felt large and clumsy as they walked together toward the woods. It was a bad sign. She needed to be nimble to carry out her plans. She needed to learn Otto's schedule; Dylan could probably tell her that. She also needed to find out if Otto had added or moved any cameras, and this was information Dylan might not know.

"Who's that?" Dylan pointed to a small brown bird in the laurel at the border of Ellen's yard.

"It's a song sparrow." The bird hopped to a higher branch and cocked its head, looking down as Dylan drifted behind. They crossed the lane to the forest path. Connie walked sideways, turned toward Dylan to encourage his approach. As they moved, the bird did too, flying to another branch just over their shoulders.

"It's peoplewatching," he said, but when they entered the dense woods, it came no farther.

"Let's sit here a little while and see what we see." Connie settled on a mossy rock. If Otto were monitoring the forest for vandals, he would almost certainly post a camera near the trail to Ellen's. "Have you surveyed this part yet?"

"No." Dylan leaned against a log nearby.

They sat in a thicket of snowberry. Around them the forest floor looked undisturbed, roped with blackberry vines and honeysuckle. Connie couldn't see any cameras.

"She'll never admit it," Connie said at last, "but Ellen feels terrible about not feeding you."

Dylan had opened his book to sketch the bulbous form of a conk growing from the side of a senescent fir tree. "I'm fine." He didn't look up from his drawing.

"She wants to take care of you, but she's not sure how. You could help her Dylan. Tell her what you need."

"I don't need anything," he said without looking up.

Connie exhaled and focused on the sound of his pencil, almost silent as he outlined, then the breathy rush of shading. She had been a patient teacher, but it hadn't been a virtue. She had enjoyed the uneven and variable ways knowledge seeped into a student's understanding. She had faith it *would* seep in. But that kind of learning took time. Now, it was all she could do not to yell at the boy. "Food," she said at last, modulating her voice. "Like everyone else, you need that. Water." She shifted on the rock, extending her legs. "Shelter, clothing, education, love."

Dylan reached into his bag and a screeching jay appeared above them, but Dylan only pulled an eraser out. He had completed the conk and was now drawing the tree and the tangle of ferns at its base. He used the eraser to carve smeary patches of light from the darkly shaded trunk, and suddenly a coarse grey nap of lichen lit by sun appeared on the page. To Connie, it looked like magic. He moved up the page and began drawing the branches and the blurry texture of the distant needles. An endless project, drawing the world.

"You know, no one really took care of your mom and your aunts when they were growing up," Connie said. "They never learned how."

Dylan quit drawing. When he spoke, he spoke to his page. "I know. The Finnegan sisters couldn't take care of a cat. I don't take it personally."

But taking things personally is exactly what people do and young people do it most of all. That had been the most grotesque burden of Cary's illness: *Why?* At the end, a certain peace descended, but it came from capitulation, and it was not beautiful. Death was nothing if not personal, and she wanted to yell at Dylan: *You are the entire universe!* She stood and broke the conk from the tree. Dylan looked shocked.

"For your health," she said, handing it to him.

"What is it?"

"A conk. Ganoderma. You might know it by its Japanese name reishi. The mushroom of immortality, herb of spiritual potency."

Dylan accepted the conk but did not put it in his bag. "Not so immortal for the mushroom."

"Accept it without guilt." Connie took the fungus from his hand and tucked it into his bag. "This is just the fruit. The fungus still lives in the tree. For now. Come on," she said. "You can finish here later."

As they walked toward the survey line, Connie pointed out trillium, some beginning to redden. In the grasses near the pasture, they found wild iris in shades of purple and blue. She made Dylan look closely at the veined patterns on the translucent petals. While he sketched, she tried to memorize their beauty, the smell of grass and blossoms, all of which she would never see again, not here, not like this. Whether from invasive species or logging or development, forests like hers disappeared as fast as puddles on a hot afternoon, but they weren't rare yet, and this wasn't some last-chance opportunity. It was only *her* last chance. If they counted the patches of yerba buena and catalogued madrone, if they mourned the owls and harvested the conks, was that love? Was it care?

"I saw a squirrel back there, but no other animals." Connie glanced through the survey list. Most of the mammals on it she had seen only rarely if at all, and never when she was looking for them.

"We didn't stay long enough," Dylan said. "And you were talking the whole time."

"I was not." She could still hear the sound of his pencil, feel the burden of her patience.

"Most of the time."

She supposed it was true. "Is Otto still filming?" She asked as casually as she could manage, and as she spoke she felt the kindling power of the secret.

"He said he was taking the cameras down this weekend," Dylan said. "Then Monday and Tuesday they'll cut the trees." Dylan recited the schedule as though it had nothing to do with him. "Wednesday they'll haul them away. Then the bulldozers come in." He broke a twig from a tree and snapped it into three even pieces that he rolled between his fingers. "But that's not all he's up to."

"I don't want to hear about the spying."

Dylan dropped the pieces of twig to the trail and rolled them with the toe of his new black boot. "You're a liar." He didn't sound mad. He was stating a fact.

"What?"

"You tell me to talk, to say what's on my mind, then it turns out I have the wrong thing on my mind. Aunt Ellen won't listen to anything about Mom. Mom doesn't want to hear anything bad at all—no downers. And you won't listen to anything about Otto even though Otto is a criminal." Dylan held his elbows close to his sides. Shivers ran through him like wind over water.

"I'm sorry." Was he actually feverish? It had been easy to dismiss his unwholesome appearance as his own choice—the black clothes and late nights and troublesome diet, but he was right; they all had some idea of what they were going to do for him, but no one asked him what he needed.

"I have a dilemma," she said. "Let's sit and watch here for a moment." She indicated a log next to the path.

"I'd like to finish that line I started yesterday," he said without moving.

"Please, sit with me." She settled on a low log and after a moment, Dylan sat on the far end. His bony knees jutted up to his armpits. He shifted, obviously uncomfortable, and Connie felt worse. "Are you okay there?"

He grunted and stretched his legs out. They extended across the path. "I'm fine."

"I can see you're concerned." She spoke slowly and deliberately. Dylan kept his mouth tightly closed, his face like a wall. "But you're *spying* on Otto. I would not want to be spied on like that. Neither would you."

"He's a criminal . . ."

"I feel responsible," Connie interrupted, "because I asked you to observe. I feel like I led you astray. If I get information from your spying, I'm spying too, plus I'd be using *you*. It's wrong in so many ways." But she was using him already. He had told her about the cameras and the logging schedule. These were not things Otto had shared with her. She felt her cheeks flush.

"But this is important," he said. "If Otto gets arrested, he can't build the vineyard."

"Then you'd better go to the police." Connie didn't mean to be dismissive; she just wanted him to step back from the drama, but his eyes sharpened, and she could see him thinking.

"How do I do that? Do I just call them?" He was utterly serious.

"You'd have to have some evidence."

"I have plenty of evidence." He was frowning. "All they have to do is search his shed. They'll find his secret room."

"You'd have to have evidence that didn't come from trespassing."

"That's not fair." Dylan kicked at a stick in the path. "Just because he's rich enough to have a secret room. He can hide anything."

Dylan was pale, his nose pinched, his mouth hard. Connie wasn't sure how to respond. She didn't want to be another adult who didn't listen. "Okay." She already was an accomplice. "What's he up to?"

Dylan's foot began to tap against the forest floor. "He's working for the oil companies." He spoke quickly, staring into the forest as though he were looking for something. "They're hiding oil spills and blaming methane on cows."

"Cows burp methane," Connie said reflexively teaching, "but I don't think you can blame them; they can't help it."

Dylan looked askance at her and shook his head with impatience. "Oil and gas drilling release methane. Maybe a whole lot of methane. Otto knows that and he's trying to confuse people, blaming it on cows and undersea volcanoes."

"I don't think confusing people is a crime."

"It's not just that," Dylan said with a vehemence that startled Connie. "I read the memos. They know they're causing climate change, and they're lying about it. Just straight-up lying about everything." Dylan's eyes darted to Connie and then to the woods and back. She could feel his tension rise like a humming engine. She reached out to touch his shoulder, but he shook her off. "He's doing his work at two in the morning," Dylan said exasperated. "From a secret room."

"And that's odd." Connie lifted her hands, palms forward. She waited for Dylan to take a breath. "Why write memos in the middle of the night?"

"I guess he doesn't want us to know. I'll show you the emails."

"You have his emails?" Connie felt sick. "*There's* a crime." Ellen wasn't a big fan of doctors, but maybe Connie could convince her to take Dylan to see someone. "You're getting carried away," she said gently.

"I thought you cared, but you don't. Is it because you're old? The world is dying," he said. "We can't do nothing."

We can't do nothing. Connie didn't know much about psychology, but after Cary's death, she knew a lot about the mental strain of helplessness.

"Just look at what I've found," Dylan said. "You'll see."

"What you've found is illegal. I wouldn't know how to evaluate it anyway."

"So we're not going to do anything?"

Connie had no idea. "If we went to the police, they might arrest *you*. You have no business with his private emails." He waited while she thought. "Maybe you're too focused on Otto. If he's hiding stuff, can you expose what he's hiding?"

"How?" Dylan frowned. "I mean, I just did. To you. And what difference did it make?"

Connie held her empty hands up to the green canopy. "I think we're out of our territory."

Dylan nodded once, as though closing a lid, his animation replaced by a mask of brittle derision.

"I'll do some research." She wanted him back. "Maybe we can find some allies out there. But absolutely no more snooping."

His face softened then, just a little. It broke her heart.

40

Dylan went back to Ellen's for lunch. Connie hoped new groceries had arrived in their absence. After lunch, he would return to the woods to survey. Not drawing; just listing. Time *was* running out and Connie wanted to be sure they had documented the basics before the bulldozer came.

She skirted Otto's compound, staying among the brush where she would not be visible from the shed or his tipi. The remaining forest was remarkably free from traces of Otto. No new paths perforated the understory, only the single walking trail Connie had built long ago, and there was no evidence Otto used it. That very day, Douglas fir towered like church spires and yellow sporophytes glowed over beds of velvet green moss, and where was Otto? He said he envied her familiarity with the long story of their mountain home, but the forest was telling that story day by day by day to anyone who took the time to listen.

She searched for the cameras Dylan had showed her earlier. She'd been confident she'd be able to find them again, but the first was not where she expected. She returned to the path and struck out in a new direction with no success. She ended by wandering, peering into the branches of each tree she passed. Otto might be moving them frequently, trying to catch the vandals, and she felt a jolt as she realized that she might be recorded, perhaps watched from the moment she set foot in the woods. The image of Otto in some secret bunker, scanning banks of webcams like a B-movie mastermind, came like a scene from Dylan's fever dream. Just in case, she peeled lichen from a branch as though that was what she'd been after. She was a liar, like Dylan said, and probably Otto was a liar too. Maybe it was a condition that came with age and they couldn't help it, like cows burping methane.

Past a clump of hazel, she saw Otto himself as he wedged one foot and then the other into the edges of the ladder riser. He rocked gently to test his stability and only when he was sure it was solid did he take another step. Connie considered slipping away before he noticed her, but she steeled herself and stepped forward as Otto reached out to a camera strapped high on a branch. He moved deliberately, like an old man. Dylan's suspicions must be crazy. Otto was too careful to be a criminal.

"Hello," she said. He startled, and she reached out to secure the ladder. "We forgot to tell you if you live alone, you're not supposed to climb a ladder without calling a neighbor. Farmer rule."

"Hi, Connie." He turned and extended an arm awkwardly as though to touch her shoulder or shake her hand, equally impossible under the circumstances. He wiped his palm on his back pocket and turned back to the tree. "Time to take these down. The logging starts Monday." He unstrapped the camera and handed it to Connie.

"Can Dylan check the recording for animals?"

"Sure." Otto folded the ladder and leaned it against the tree. He paused for a moment and then turned back to her. "I got to tell you, that kid gives me the creeps. He's always lurking."

"He's an excellent observer and an incredible artist. He could go on to a career in field biology or illustration. He really is gifted."

Otto put the camera in his pack and knelt to tie his shoe. "I'm glad to hear you say so. Otherwise, I'd think he was up to mischief." He looped the lace into a bow and tugged twice before he stood. "He was out here at eleven-thirty the other night."

"A lot of forest life is nocturnal."

"What can he see in the dark? When I asked him, he said he has sonic eyes."

Connie shrugged and smiled. "Sonic eyes are his superpower."

"Huh." Otto pulled the ladder away from the trunk and tipped it on its side.

Connie looked down the hill, through the layers of trees. She couldn't imagine them gone. The whole mountain might as well become a plain, the creeks turn into boulders. "It's hard to believe it's all coming down." Not inevitably like rain or snow, more like Christmas decorations after New Year.

"I'm leaving the oak trees on the ridge." He rubbed his palm over his stubbled chin and looked directly at her for a moment, his blue eyes sharp. "For raptors."

"I think you'll be glad." There wasn't anything more to say. She took a step back.

He touched her arm, staying her. "I don't want to keep you." A smile came and went. "But I do want to thank you. For all your good advice."

"You're welcome." His palm was warm, and she suddenly imagined Otto embracing her. She shoved her hands in her pockets and looked toward the horizon.

"I'll have to put grapes in the lowland, but I can experiment with some German whites just for fun."

"By the beaver pond."

"I know. I screwed up."

"It's your hill. You get to do whatever you want."

"I wanted to make you happy."

She blushed. "Forget about that." Her words came out harshly. She cleared her throat.

"That's what Annabelle said. The thing is, Connie, between you and the land-use laws, I have to walk a very narrow path. The beaver might be okay." he said. "The vineyard will be biodynamic."

"Fancy compost." As soon as she spoke, she regretted having let him draw her in. The sun on her back started a thin trickle of sweat between her shoulder blades. It was getting too hot for jackets, but she didn't want to take hers off while she stood there with Otto.

"I'll punch a culvert through to fix the drainage," he said at last. "The equipment is coming tomorrow. I'll talk to them about doing that. You know, I do appreciate your candidness."

She did not say he was welcome because she couldn't believe he was really glad, and, of course, she wasn't really candid.

He picked up the ladder, balancing it on his shoulder. "Can I make you some tea? I've got a pot in the shed."

"Oh . . ."

"Or coffee? Water? That's about all I have. Unless you want scotch?"

"I could have a quick cup of tea." She was still not being candid. She was imagining the secret room. She could see for herself.

41

Connie and Otto found their way past the logging rig and bulldozer into Otto's well-organized compound. The shed took the central spot opposite a covered work area. It was humbly sided with corrugated metal but well-trimmed with wood. An exotic antique door on heavy iron hinges dominated the front wall. Connie didn't recognize the wood. From the dense, dark color, she guessed it was a tropical hardwood. Otto fitted a key in the deadbolt and pushed. Inside, a new maple floor gleamed, and the long counter Otto had been installing when Connie came with Dylan reflected squares of sunlight all along its length to a gleaming stainless-steel sink.

"You plumbed your shed?" She didn't mean to sound accusatory, but it was all so fancy.

"I confess to the sink and a small bathroom," he said. "I'll have a lab in here."

"It's very nice." The fresh drywall was painted a sophisticated shade of ochre. The room was nicer than any part of her house. "I don't think you can call it a shed."

Otto filled an electric teakettle at the sink and brought two cups down from a shelf of dishes. "If I call it a lab, it makes me sound like some kind of mad scientist."

While the water boiled, Connie used the bathroom: just a toilet, sink, and a small shower. The whole building was a simple rectangle about twelve by twenty feet including the bathroom and closet.

There wasn't anywhere to disappear, and Connie felt a sinking at the pit of her stomach wondering if Dylan was actually delusional.

Otto handed her a cup of green tea and seated her at a small desk with a view out over the valley while he perched on a stool nearby. She inhaled the fragrant steam and sipped carefully. If she gave him the opportunity, Otto might bring up their night together, and she could apologize as necessary. But Otto only smiled, waiting on her it seemed.

She set the mug on the desk. "Now you've been to a neighborhood party," she began.

"We should sit outside." Otto hopped off the stool. "While the sun's out."

Connie followed him to two camp chairs looking down over the valley. Each chair had an oak round for a coffee table.

"I don't spend much time in the shed; I'm either out here or in the tipi."

He was avoiding the topic of their intimacy just as he had avoided her since that night. His discomfort made it all worse, and Connie felt a growing embarrassment. "Do you still do other work? Besides the vineyard?"

"Nope." He blew the steam from his tea. "I worked for oil companies. It was interesting technically, but, well, the oil industry . . ." He looked sideways at her.

"I drive a car, Otto. Like most everyone else, I'm dependent on the oil companies. So," she raised her cup toward him. "Thank you for your service."

He shook his head in a dismissive acknowledgement. "Congratulate me on turning over a new leaf. And I'm counting on you for more advice."

Connie wrinkled her nose, wincing at the flattery. "You know, I'm not a great naturalist. Dylan can tell you I'm too restless to be a good observer. If they were giving out awards, I might get one for participation. I'm a steady presence, but that's about it."

"I don't think that's right, but anyway, I'm reassured." He watched her sharply. "I heard rumors you might move."

"Where did you hear that?"

"Several people. At the party. They were all tipsy, and it sounds like they were wrong. I hope so."

"This neighborhood." Connie wrapped her hands around the warm mug. "I bet they go through my garbage." She took a gulp of tea and held the cup high, near her heart. "I've been cleaning my house out. Farmers are such packrats, they think if you're getting rid of stuff you must be moving."

"Everyone would miss you. People around here speak highly of you."

"You're flattering me again. I thought everyone agreed I was rude."

Otto laughed. "Like when you told me the only thing wrong was my being there. It's true. That was the rudest neighbor interaction I've ever had."

Connie suddenly saw herself as she must have appeared to him—dirty and cranky and strange. She blushed, her discomfort on display, and the blush deepened.

"Don't take it to heart!" He leaned forward and patted the table for emphasis. "I don't have much to compare you with. I hardly knew my neighbors in the city. Anyway, everyone tells me that even if you aren't a great person to meet, you are a very good person to know. Now that we're past the meeting stage, I'd hate to miss out on the knowing."

Connie acknowledged the compliment with a smile. The motley collection of people on the mountain got along because they found at least one thing they could appreciate about each of their neighbors. When Connie's name came up, they wouldn't say she was bossy or judgmental. They would say: *she knows a lot about the woods.*

Out over the valley, clouds made a patchwork of shadow over the farms and suburbs. Connie had spent time on that knoll over the years, but that was before Otto's clearing had revealed the view. Now she could see all the little buildings in the valley, full of people she didn't know, doing things she didn't understand. The world was bigger than she had remembered, and maybe more accessible. "Have you lived a lot of different places?"

"Just Houston and Albuquerque. Here." He shrugged. "I've travelled a lot. What about you? Do you ever get away?"

"I spent some time in Mexico when I was in college." She laughed, thinking how long ago, but she remembered almost every day of that visit. Strange customs, strange language and money and people. Even buying a cup of coffee had been an adventure. "I was determined to grow up and travel the world, but then there was always so much to do here."

When Otto held her in his arms and stroked her hair, he had kindled a thrumming restlessness. It stirred her now and she pressed her mug of tea hard against her breastbone. She couldn't remember the last time someone seemed hungry for her, as Otto had seemed. She was a fool; hunger was predatory. She set the empty mug on the oak round and shifted to stand.

"More tea?"

"I've got to get home." Her house would be cold after being empty all day, and down in Connie's smaller world, the late afternoon light that warmed their shoulders would be blocked by the hill. She carried her cup toward the shed door, but Otto took it from her hand.

"I'll take care of that."

The brush of his warm skin startled her. "Such a host. I'm afraid you put me to shame."

"If that's true, I'm glad." He rinsed the cups in the sink as Connie stood at the door, half in, half out. "So far in our acquaintance, I worry that the shame has been all mine."

"Otto." More flattery. But he must be apologizing for the kiss finally, his way of putting it behind them. She smiled in acknowledgment. "Then that, too, is my shame." She shoved her hands in her jacket pockets and edged further out the door. "Thanks again. I have to get back and get things organized so Dylan can wrap up the survey."

"It's good of you to take him on." Otto walked to the threshold and laid his hand on her arm. "That boy worries me."

She stepped quickly away from his touch. "He'll be fine." Her voice sounded strange to her own ears, cheerful and false. She hurried away, waving once as she turned up the lane, just in case he was still watching.

42

Connie went home by way of the high road rather than cutting down through the field. From the edge of the road, the hillside fell away sharply, and the broad valley spread south all the way to the horizon. Connie's home had been built in a fold of the mountain and her personal patch of sky was narrow, but now her thoughts expanded beyond the bottled obsession with Otto's kiss. She thought about Dylan. He wasn't fine. Otto was obviously not a criminal, and Dylan might be having a serious mental breakdown. She'd have to talk to Ellen, but would Ellen take it personally? Or blame Connie? Walking quickly, Connie turned from Otto's lane onto the paved road and was startled out of her reverie by a shriek.

"Connie! You scared me!"

She hadn't seen Annabelle weeding among the primroses. "Sorry! I didn't notice you."

Connie would have kept walking, but Annabelle removed her gloves and thwacked them on her thigh to knock the bark dust off. "What do you think?" Annabelle eyed the flowers and glanced back at Connie. "How's the curb appeal?"

"It's always cheerful up here."

"Have you been working on your survey with that little zombie of Ellen's?"

"Annabelle."

Annabelle pursed her lips. "You know what I mean. That boy is strange and scary."

"I've been having tea with Otto." Connie enjoyed watching Annabelle's face cloud. Connie lifted her hands to the sky in an uncharacteristically blithe gesture. "He has such a beautiful view up there."

"I'm glad that man took a little time off. He works too hard. But he probably wanted to talk to you about your house."

"My house?"

"Obviously he'd love to buy it. Then he wouldn't have to use up his vineyard land. Don't look shocked. It's too big for you!" Annabelle looked up her own driveway, past the bright flowers and fresh red bark dust. "I sometimes wonder what I'm doing here all by myself and my house is smaller than yours. But I've got the horses. You know," she said shrewdly, "Otto would be willing to pay a premium for a house next door to his vineyard. He's holding off on building the winery just in case your house works out. If you wait too long, you'll miss the opportunity."

"He didn't say anything about that." But he did ask her about plans to move. While she was distracted by thoughts of kissing, he was thinking of other things entirely.

"He's afraid you're already facing too much loss. He's a very sensitive man. But you're not sentimental, and anyone is better off knowing their options. You should think about it because you could probably name your price. You can tell Otto a little bird told you of his interest."

A little bird? Did Otto trot that sandpiper story out for all his conquests? Unlocking the door of her cold and draughty farmhouse, she felt even worse. The house itself wanted an owner who would replace the roof and redo the septic system. Someone else who would finally deal with the dry rot under the deck. Otto would get a couple more acres of vineyard if he didn't have to build, and the new road by the beaver pond would connect the properties very conveniently. That might have occurred to her earlier if she hadn't been so blinded by her own obsessions. She wasn't a guardian anymore; she was an obstruction. Out of sync, her disharmony disrupted everyone around her, even the blameless. Even Dylan. She crawled into bed early rather than turn the heat on, but she didn't sleep well. In the morning, the sun rose obscurely behind a curtain of rain. If it weren't for Dylan, she might not have gotten up at all, but she thought of him and his eye patch. She had a responsibility.

When Connie got to Ellen's house that morning, Ellen and Dylan were both still in bed. Connie let herself in the kitchen door and brewed a pot of coffee.

"I didn't think it could be burglars," Ellen said from the foot of the stairs. "I don't have anything worth burgling."

"Come on," Connie said. "Get dressed for a walk."

"I'm going back to bed."

"Bed won't help you. Coffee, fluids, a nice walk in the rain."

Ellen's face was puffy and mottled, and she winced slightly as Connie disposed of the empty scotch bottle and poured a finger of amber liquid down the drain before putting the glass in the dishwasher. Connie washed the dishes in the sink, wiped the counters, and poured the coffee while Ellen dressed. Ellen looked even more disreputable dressed than she had in her pajamas. They drank coffee silently and watched rain slide down the windowpanes.

"Do you want some breakfast before we go?" Connie pushed aside the unopened plastic packets of strange vegan food. Mostly the refrigerator was bare. No eggs, no milk, no fruit. The vegetable crisper held one potato sprouting a thicket of stalks.

"I couldn't eat."

"That's good. You don't have anything." How long had it been since Ellen had come to her house with groceries? Ham and cheese and fruit and nuts.

"Not true," Ellen said. "Look at all that shit for Dylan."

Seitan, baked tofu, noodles coiled like worms in shrink wrap, all in varying shades of brown. "Does he like that stuff?"

"No," Ellen said too loudly. "Nobody in the whole fucking world likes that stuff. That stuff is a penance for the eaters and a punishment for the shoppers. Penance and punishment is why Dylan's a vegan."

"So get real food," Connie said.

"Dylan only eats crackers." Ellen put her coffee cup in the sink and went to the mud room to pull on her shoes. She grunted as she bent to tie them.

Outside, rain slapped the brim of Connie's hat and dripped to her raincoat. She wondered if Dylan had stayed in last night, but she didn't ask Ellen because she was afraid Ellen wouldn't know.

"I'm worried about you," Connie said at last.

Ellen just grunted.

"I'm worried about Dylan, too."

"I sleep in the same house he does every night." Ellen stomped in the puddles so the brown mud speckled her black nylon rain pants. "That's more than my sister did."

"Dylan's losing it."

"He's fifteen. He might be anorexic."

"He's paranoid. Seriously, Ellen. He's delusional. He needs therapy."

"Whoa," Ellen said.

"The counselor at school could recommend someone good."

"Whoa," Ellen said more loudly.

"It's serious." Connie leaned over so that Ellen could see her face beneath the broad hat brim and the dripping screen of water. She was sure she looked concerned, but Ellen only looked away.

"He's a kid, trying on different ideas." Ellen looked straight ahead, her mouth was firm and bitter. "Send him to therapy and suddenly he gets diagnosed with a condition. My sister was fine until she went to therapy. She was wild, but we all were. Then she goes to therapy and suddenly she has all kinds of diseases. She's bipolar with ADD and anxiety and each new condition gets a new drug. She hasn't been herself since."

They walked on in silence. The rain let up and Connie took her hat off, letting it hang down her back from the chin strap. A breeze lifted the hairs away from her forehead which was a relief because everything seemed so heavy—the grasses just beginning to seed were beat down, and daisies dragged their white petals in the mud.

"He thinks Otto is a criminal. Some kind of environmental fraud, all very complicated. What if he does something violent?"

"Criminals are often violent."

"Not Otto. Dylan."

"Dylan's not going to do anything violent. Dylan can hardly get out of bed."

"He was ready to go to the police. I only got him to back down because I promised to help him. It's beyond me, Ellen. I don't know what to do." Connie was almost crying. The desperate frustration she felt was a surprise even to herself and it got Ellen's attention.

Ellen stopped, blocking Connie's path. "There's nothing you can do. Most of the time—as you know—" she spoke those words with a cruel emphasis, "there is nothing you can do but watch. Just like you're teaching Dylan. We get to watch things fall apart. It's a fucking depressing lesson, but at least it's the truth."

They stood in the center of the lane, looking at one another's familiar faces until the strangeness broke through. When had Ellen's hair turned so gray? Connie usually thought of Ellen laughing, but Ellen's cheeks dragged the corners of her mouth down, and her forehead fell into a deep furrow between her brows. Ellen began to walk when the rain started again. Connie left her hat off and felt the large drops wet her hair and drip down her forehead.

"That was my last bottle of scotch," Ellen said. "I promise I won't buy another. Will that make you happy? It will probably kill me."

"It won't kill you." Connie felt sullen and hopeless. "Will you buy real groceries?"

"Maybe."

"I don't think it's enough, Ellen. I really don't."

"It's a start."

When they got back to Ellen's, Dylan was at the kitchen table with a cup of coffee and an open package of crackers.

"I'm going to make you a real breakfast," Connie said, "because we have to finish up the survey today, and we need to be at our best. What do you like?"

"I've eaten."

"Crackers don't count." She opened the refrigerator. "Seitan? Tofu?"

"That's for dinner. Aunt Ellen says it has to last the whole summer because she won't go back to the food co-op. She says the people who work there nest in the onions at night and the whole place grosses her out."

"I never said that," Ellen said.

"Yes, you did. You just forgot."

Connie closed the refrigerator door. "Brunch at my house," she said. "I'll go down and get it started. Dylan, you get ready to work. Bring your notebook."

Dylan closed the cracker box and left the table. He shuffled like an old man as he climbed the stairs.

"He should live with you," Ellen said, sitting down and putting her head in her hands. "I'm not cut out for this."

Connie wasn't sure what she could say. She stepped behind Ellen's chair, wrapped her arms around her shoulders and laid her cheek on the top of Ellen's head. "Everything will get better."

"Don't," Ellen said, shaking her off.

43

Back at her own home, Connie cooked oatmeal with bananas and prunes. When Dylan got there, she served it in a bowl smeared with peanut butter. On top, she added hazelnuts and blueberries she'd frozen for Cary. He ate the whole thing as though it were part of his job. Engines had been whining up on the hill all morning, but no trees had fallen. Connie felt like both she and Dylan were holding their breath.

"I'm afraid you won't get to draw today," she said. "There isn't much time. I want you to go through your notebook and draft a summary of everything you've noticed. It doesn't have to look pretty." As she said it, Connie realized she'd never seen anything from his hand that wasn't graced with detail and imagination. Perhaps it was tiring. "Just scribbles, really, because we'll go over it together to make sure it's complete. You're welcome to work here."

"I'll go back to Ellen's," he said.

"You sure?" Connie wanted him to stay. That day, as they waited to hear the trees fall and feel the earth shudder, she wanted company. His company. Dylan would understand.

"All my pens are up at Ellen's."

"But nothing elaborate," Connie said, feeling suddenly lonely.

He stood, leaving his empty bowl on the table.

"Don't go over to Otto's," she said. "Stay away from the work area."

Dylan looked at her, his dark eyes blank.

"I mean it."

He nodded and left, and even though he was in his leather boots now, he shuffled just the same.

Connie's old farmhouse shook as Dylan shut the door. Maybe the dry rot had spread from the deck supports into the house frame itself. If that were the case, it was worsening every moment. She watched Dylan slouch up the hill toward Ellen's. Rain fell steadily, but he didn't flinch. Water must be dripping off his nose and down his collar. His stoicism made Connie's heart twist. She would like to shelter that bravado, to celebrate it even, but it was beyond her. Since Cary's death, as her farm dwindled and her study of nature lost relevance, Connie had held on. But the effort compromised her, and compromise may be a mature and reasonable response to the intractable problems of living, but it was insidious. She'd gotten good at it. Now she could accommodate any outrage. It wouldn't blow her apart, not the way youth gets blown apart. Connie was sorry for Dylan, but she envied him too.

She looked around her husk of a house. The extra pots and pans—gone to Goodwill; the souvenirs of a life's journey—given away. She had sold the old rugs and donated the stained couch, shed the heavy curtains, and she had swept. Every day, she swept the dry floors and moldings. Her house was scoured. Her whole life had been scoured since Cary's death, but it didn't give her clarity. It didn't give her peace. She had relied on the dignity of an honorable life to hold her ground beneath her narrow sky, but what was honorable? And what had she accomplished? While Otto, and all the enterprising people like Otto, hired bulldozers; they brought in big equipment.

She kept some bleach in the laundry room and more bleach in the garden shed to sterilize her tools. She sharpened the pruning shears and adjusted the beam on her headlamp. All day long, she'd waited to hear the trees fall, but she'd been spared. She'd heard trucks moving and the brief whining saws tuning up but then silenced. They were waiting for better weather tomorrow. After all, the logging itself would not take more than a day, two at most, a small number of trees in the end. A few more days to clean up, build the slash piles.

When the sun went down and everything was ready, Connie took a nap. She didn't set an alarm; she was sure she would wake up at the appropriate time, and if she didn't, that would be providence. But she awoke at one am, her head clear and her body ready. Even though the rain continued, Connie did not put on rain pants or a jacket. She needed the silence of soft clothes—jeans and a dark fleece and a black wool cap that held the headlamp without slipping. Connie went out the back door, a bottle of bleach in each hand. The clouded sky seemed to lift above her as though making room, but in the woods, water still fell from the fir trees in sloppy drops that were loud against the maple leaves. She could hardly hear her own movements; only her pulse beat in her ears, that task-master. She skirted Otto's clearing, but everything was dark and peaceful.

The logging rig was parked out near the lane, the gas tank conveniently located away from the clearing, on the forest side of the road. Connie turned the headlamp on briefly to unscrew the gas cap, but she didn't need to see in order to open the bleach and pour it down. The tank, prepared for the workday, was almost full of gas so it began to overflow almost immediately. She panicked at the smell of gasoline and the way it disappeared into the hungry earth, but she spotted a bucket waiting by a spigot near Otto's deck and, hoping the gas would float, poured more bleach, letting the surface gasoline overflow into the bucket. The smell was foreign and ugly in the mossy night, but it was too late for second thoughts. She screwed the cap back on the quarter-full gallon of bleach. She left the bleach by the rigs and went back to the spigot to cut a two-foot section from the hose there.

The bulldozer's tank faced the clearing and would be visible from the tipi door, but Connie moved like a shadow in the conspiratorial rain. She wrenched the rusted cap open and inserted the hose to siphon the gas. The bulldozer's treads were so high she could lean her forehead against the coarse rubber as she sucked up gas and fumes. When she tasted petroleum, she pulled her face away and spat, then let the gasoline fill the bucket. Then she pulled the siphon out and tossed the hose back by the spigot. That was habit; putting things back where you found them. Funny, under the circumstances. She emptied the rest of the bleach into the dozer's tank.

As she was tightening the gas cap, the sound of chimes startled her, and then a light went on in the tipi. She froze. Otto's silhouette rose and moved toward the opening. She hid behind the bulldozer. The smell of gasoline was fainter now but dangerous. Otto crawled out the low opening and unfolded to his full height on the edge of the deck. Connie looked over her shoulder to locate the entrance to the faint path into the woods. As Otto came down the stairs, Connie edged toward the trees, ready to run. He opened the shed door and flipped the switch. Light spilled onto the grass outside, and Connie, hidden in the shadows, moved closer as Otto shut the door.

Through the window, she watched him make tea, just as he had for her that day. He flipped open his laptop while the water boiled. She couldn't read the webpage from where she sat, but it looked like a page of tractor implements. She would explain to Dylan that new farmers had to do a lot of shopping and older men often couldn't sleep. But Otto didn't take his tea back to the laptop. He carried it to the back of the room, opened the closet door, and turned out the shed light. The laptop glowed abandoned on the counter briefly before turning itself off. Connie pressed her face near the glass, but Otto wasn't anywhere in the small open room. She walked around to the back of the shed where the steady low hum of a fan blew into the syncopated raindrops. Over by the heat pump, concealed among its pipes and plumbing, Connie found a small vent near the ground blowing warm air out into the damp cool night.

Why would Otto have a secret room? It was neither cheap nor easy to put a basement into a basalt mountain. She sheltered under a fir tree to wait. If he was in there less than an hour, maybe it was some kind of temperature-controlled storage room. More than an hour, and maybe he had some shameful habit—pornography, gambling—she didn't want to think about it. If he stayed for several hours, he must be working on something, just like Dylan said. She settled the bleach jugs near the trunk and pulled her cloth jacket close around her chest. It was damp now, and Connie shifted her weight from leg to leg, bending deeply at the knees to generate some body heat.

Within an hour, Connie's teeth were chattering and her fingers and toes grew numb. Otto was up to something, something secret and hidden. And Dylan wasn't crazy. Stoic Dylan. Stubborn Dylan. Clear-sighted Dylan. Connie left the shelter of the tree and made her way to the forest edge where bushes crowded the clearing. She kept her gloves on, examining the shrubs until she thought she'd found the right one. She turned the headlamp on briefly to see the glistening oil on the new triad leaves, then she cut it carefully at the base and took two strongly budding branches up the deck stairs to the mouth of the tipi. She had time. Otto would almost certainly turn the shed light on as he left. Even if he didn't, she would hear the door open. Peering in the tipi opening, she turned her headlamp on once more, just long enough to locate Otto's bed and estimate its distance. With one more glance toward the shed, she slipped into the circular room. The bedcovers draped from the end of the cot, as Otto had thrown them when he rose. She laid the branches on the bottom sheet and lifted the blankets back over them. Then she lay down on top and rolled back and forth to rub the oily leaves into the fabric. Raindrops tapped the canvas, and Connie felt a surprising sense of arrival there on Otto's narrow cot in the windowless room. Maybe it was a defining moment—rubbing poison oak into sheets was as mean a thing as she could conceive—or maybe it was simply the magic of a dry tent in the rain; she wanted to stay. But if Otto caught her, she'd have to explain what could not be explained, and she'd be more entangled than ever. She rose and pulled the covers down as they had been. She took the branches back to where the white jugs shone like twin moons and discarded them before gathering the empty jugs, one in each hand. The shed was still dark. The fan still hummed discreetly on the back wall.

She couldn't sleep once she got home. She soaked in a hot bath until she felt warmth seep back to the core of her, but she soaked in the dark, as though she were hiding, like Otto in his secret basement room.

44

Connie never slept that night. She lay in bed until the sun rose, and when it was light, she got up and removed the pictures from her walls. She took the botanical paintings from the dining room and gathered the pictures students had made of the wetland. From her bedroom, she took the family photos and the portrait of Cary. Cary's image never left her anyway. She stacked the pictures neatly against the wall behind the living room couch. Nothing remained but the most necessary furnishings. It was impossible to tell what sort of person lived in that house now. She could be anyone.

"Are you leaving?" Dylan looked around at the bare walls and empty rooms.

The question took Connie by surprise, although it shouldn't have. "Not right away," she said in a jovial voice, as though they were both joking.

Dylan stepped sideways into the room, two notebooks clutched in his hands.

"I did the summary."

Connie took the book and opened it as Dylan looked over her shoulder. She could feel his anxiety. "Are you hungry?"

"No."

"You sure?"

"Yes."

Dylan's meticulous lists stretched on for pages. He had organized everything quite logically—large mammals, small mammals, birds, trees, shrubs, herbs. "This is good." She explained the phylogenetic taxonomy, and how she wanted the final list organized. She almost went to fetch an old textbook for him to use, but then she remembered the books were all gone. It didn't matter. He would be more comfortable getting his information from the internet. They both stared at the list, realizing what it represented.

"I thought they would have started logging by now," Dylan said.

It was almost eleven and Otto's ridge had been silent all morning.

"Big projects," Connie said as off-handedly as she could manage. "There's always some last-minute snafu. But it will happen."

She hadn't done anything that would change the course of events. She wasn't even sure if one gallon of bleach in a tank that must hold hundreds of gallons would have an effect. She hadn't balanced any scale of justice. She had only changed her own course. Even if she was never caught, she had done something terrible, something she could never tell anyone, not even Ellen. She could no longer call it vandalism. She had crossed a line.

"I know you'll do a beautiful job with this, Dylan. I'd like you to follow the order I've shown, but I hope you'll illustrate the list however you think is best." She wanted him to understand his value. "I would treasure it." He chewed on his cuticle, watching her doubtfully, and indeed, her bare walls were an indictment. She drew the sketchbook towards her and asked permission with her eyes. Dylan shrugged.

"Isn't it weird," he said, "to replace a whole place with a list?"

"It's not a replacement." Connie didn't look up. She opened the notebook. "It's like keeping photographs of someone who has died."

Dylan made a wry face and scanned her bare walls. Connie ignored him. The animation of his sketches surprised her anew. She flipped to the back to see what he had done since she last checked. A mole with paws like catchers' mitts looked nonplussed. Then pages of wildflowers—trillium and fawn lily and iris and one perfect calypso orchid. "Where did you find this?" Connie asked.

"By the yew tree." Dylan pointed to his location notes. He used a GPS, and the coordinates had no meaning for Connie.

"Ah." It was too late to run up and see it herself. "I'm surprised. They need a particular bacterium to germinate so they only grow in old-growth forests." Her woods had been logged at least twice since Europeans had moved to the area two hundred years ago. But no one ever logged the yew. She had thought of forests as old growth or new growth, as wilderness or suburban, but of course it was not so simple.

On the second to the last page, Sylvio was just lowering his bow to his side. He looked across the page to the tail of his arrow. When Connie turned the page, she found Otto's tipi. Its contents were visible through the canvas, and Sylvio's outsized arrow had punched through the tipi wall, its head buried in Otto's bed. Connie looked with a feeling of horror.

"At least Otto got away," she said at last, trying to joke.

"No, he didn't."

"I meant from the arrow."

"No one gets away from the arrow."

"Dylan, why don't you tell me what you found at Otto's?" Her throat was dry as she asked the question. If Dylan shared information, they became complicit; she in his spying and he in her vandalism. But she supposed they already were.

The look Dylan gave her was not grateful or relieved, it was challenging. "He has a computer room hidden in the basement."

Dylan's narrow palms rested on the notebook, and it seemed to Connie that he had laid his hands aside as one might set aside the pen. "One day he forgot to lock up and I snuck in. I hacked his computers." Dylan paused; he was proud of himself. Connie winced. "I have copies of his files."

The drama was bad. Her curiosity was bad. "What did you find?"

"Emails. Memos. From oil executives. They're hiding spills and research. To deny climate change. They *know*, and they're hiding the evidence. Those are crimes, right?"

Connie rubbed her forehead. She didn't know what she expected, but she felt let down. "Why would he need a secret room to write memos in the middle of the night?" It didn't add up.

"He's hiding crimes." Dylan said stubbornly. "He doesn't want anyone to know."

"But he wouldn't be hiding from spying neighbors. He doesn't expect that," she said with obvious frustration. "If Otto's afraid of getting caught, it would be because of the memos themselves, and they're already floating around in cyberspace. Besides," she spoke sharply, "it's illegal to break into someone's home even if it helps you prove they stole something."

Two spots of color bloomed on Dylan's cheeks, and he held his arms tight against his torso. "He's not stealing *something*. What is wrong with you? They're stealing the whole future."

Dylan's face was pale and pinched. From his perspective her complacency was insane, not his outrage.

"If Otto is really doing what you say, I don't think the police would care. People don't go to jail for memos. But hacking into someone's computer? That could get you into real trouble."

Dylan's lips whitened as his mouth hardened.

"It isn't fair, but . . ." She watched him withdraw, his dark eyes glazed with a sort of dull contempt. "I don't see what we can do."

Connie ducked her head to look him in the eye. She wanted him to see her sympathy and her certainty. They sat in silence for a moment, and then he wilted. The stubborn rigidity drained away. He slumped and dropped his gaze.

Connie turned the last page and there on the back was a drawing of Dylan himself. He was walking away, and the drawing captured his long-legged shuffle, looking down, his jacket up near his ears. An arrow had pierced his chest from behind, and blood fell in single droplets to the ground where a path of strange flowers bloomed beneath a cloud of insects.

Connie felt cold at the pit of her stomach, something indigestible. "Dylan . . ." She wanted him to erase the arrow. "Does it hurt?" she asked.

"Of course."

"Why don't you do something nice for yourself? Why not?" She tapped her finger against the page. He could draw himself a treasure, a lover, a message from God.

"Whatever." He took the notebook back and closed it.

"Anyway, finish your work up here." She didn't want him to go off alone. She didn't want to be left alone. "I'll set you up at the desk and make lunch later." Her house was cleared of clutter, ready for use.

"I'm sorry, Connie, I'll work better at Ellen's."

The patronizing dignity irritated her, but she had earned it. She was old and tired, and if she had ever been effective, those days were gone.

"Go home by the road. Don't go through the woods today." Connie wanted to embrace him or slap him, to make some sort of contact, but she didn't have that right. "Stay away from Otto. Stay

away from his shed." She gripped Dylan's shoulder for a moment.
He looked startled, as though she had hit him.

45

When Connie was alone, she lay down to take a nap, but sleep would not come. She watched the sheep out the window as she wondered how she usually filled her time. She heated a can of soup and ate without enjoyment. After lunch, she heard the snarl of a chainsaw, and the first tree fell. The earth shook, and the flock of sheep exploded, stampeding to the far end of the pasture where they stayed in a thick clot. Connie's rickety house winced then trembled. Chainsaws keened almost constantly after that, the staccato rhythm of limbing and the deeper, straining whine of the saw that felled the trees. She could keep from looking, but she couldn't ignore it. The sound of crashing trees and howling saws came closer and closer as the loggers moved down the slope. She curled up on the corner of the couch and buried her face in her arms. This was how Ellen and Dylan found her, forty-five minutes later.

"Come on," Ellen said, flinging the door open. "We're going out."

"Where?" Connie lifted her head. Anywhere else seemed like a good idea, but she couldn't imagine getting there. Her nerves hummed with the chainsaw, and when the trees fell, she felt the shuddering in her bones.

"Clumpy's. I'm going to buy you a burger and a couple drinks."

"I'm not dressed." Connie looked down at her sweatpants and tee shirt, but she didn't have the agency to change, to choose a blouse, to brush her hair.

"For Clumpy's? Yes, you are."

Ellen picked up Connie's purse and looked inside. "Is your wallet here? Do you need your phone?"

Dylan got the phone from the counter and dropped it in the purse while Ellen shooed Connie up from the couch. Connie followed them to the car without looking at the ridge. The light seemed different, but she kept her eyes down and once inside, she closed them altogether.

It was barely five when they slid into a booth, but the room was dark, the blinds drawn against the glare from the parking lot that surrounded Clumpy's like an inland sea. Over the bar, a television glowed bluely. A few men sat beneath it drinking beer. Only one other table was taken. Cheryl came over right away and would have chatted, but Ellen shook her head and ordered two Manhattans and an iced tea for Dylan.

Connie didn't think about the trees falling on her hillside. She didn't think about the shattered branches and panicked wildlife. Separated from the violent immediacy of the logging, she thought about how she had rubbed poison oak in Otto's sheets. The rash wouldn't have shown up yet, but she had been thorough in her method and if Otto was sensitive, he might actually require medical attention. Vandalizing the equipment was one thing, and you could call it ecoterrorism. But rubbing poison oak in Otto's sheets was something else.

"Otto talks about sustainability." Ellen paused to sip from her drink, her elbow out to balance the liquid in the shallow glass. "The sustainable part starts after the forest comes down. What bullshit."

One night on those sheets would probably cause suffering that would last two weeks regardless of treatment.

"Just like all those so-called environmentalists jetting around to see Costa Rica and Croatia and China before it's all ruined. Ha. It's all ruined." Ellen took a righteous swallow.

Another night on poison oak sheets would be worse, intensifying the rash and covering a greater percentage of the body.

"That's why I don't drive," Dylan said.

"You?" Ellen sat back, apprising him. "You failed your learner's permit test."

Dylan's cheeks flushed and he took a quick drink. "I decided not to try again. The world doesn't need more drivers." He looked over his shoulder to see if the fries were on the way.

Even once Otto got the rash, he wouldn't suspect he was exposed from his sheets. He might sleep in them for days. That kind of exposure could be dangerous.

"Anyway." Ellen set her glass down. She leaned across the table and brought her big face close to Connie's. "I'm really sorry about the forest. It's lousy for all of us, for Dylan and for all the critters that lived there, but it's particularly hard for you, and I'm really, really sorry."

"Thank you. I appreciate it." The Manhattan had not untied the knots in the pit of her stomach, but it had loosened them. Connie slumped down and laid her chin on her stacked fists. "As you get old," she said with a nod to Dylan. "You lose everything bit by bit right up until the moment you die, when you lose it all at once. If you live long enough, you'll even lose things you thought couldn't be lost—salamanders, snow on the mountain, whole forests."

Cheryl brought the burgers. Dylan had fries and a salad. No one was very hungry.

"Mountains." Ellen took a bite of her burger then set it back on her plate and pushed the plate away. "Remember when Mount St. Helens was a whole mountain? Now look at it. Who'd have thought?"

"My forest wouldn't have survived much longer." Connie sat up and took another bite of her burger. "Doug fir and cedar are dying all over the mountain."

"I heard that two thirds of all birds in the US are facing extinction. Think of that." Ellen shook her head.

"That beaver moved into the wetland," Dylan said.

Both women shrugged.

"Well, it's *possible* for things to get better." Dylan stirred a French fry in the little paper cup of ketchup, but he didn't eat it.

"Chances are he won't find a mate."

"If he found a mate," Ellen said, "and they had a big family, where would the babies go when they grew up?"

"There's not much option for dispersal," Connie agreed.

"The culvert by Smiths?" Ellen asked. Connie had to laugh. Ed Smith sprayed the banks religiously so they were always free of plants. The dirt was covered by a scum of brown moss.

"Annabelle's new pond!" Connie imagined the flowery garden in a wreck of saplings and spreading water.

Dylan ate the fry he'd been playing with. Connie wondered if they were cooked in lard. Did he think about things like that?

Ellen pushed the empty glasses to the edge of the table for Cheryl to gather, making room for more drinks. "That makes me want to get a beaver and take it up there."

"No!" Connie took a hurried sip of the fresh Manhattan. "I was kidding. Annabelle treats her water for algae. That would be cruel to a beaver. Cruel to any creatures that followed, frogs, muskrats."

"Muskrats?" Ellen asked.

Connie nodded.

"I've never seen a muskrat."

"Don't look now." Connie laid her head back down on her arms.

"This isn't funny," Dylan said.

Both women turned to him. He sat upright, his hands on the table, the fries unfinished. Skeletal wrists poked out of his black jacket. His fingernails were bitten to the quick.

"A beaver in Annabelle's pond is funny," Ellen said.

"No," Connie shushed her. "It's not funny." An enormous well of sorrow opened deep inside her. She sat up straighter, like the teacher she had been, rigid and careful. "Humans are driving other species to extinction at an accelerating rate. We're pushing the whole climate system to catastrophe. Science understands that now, but the people in charge are still mostly worried about stock returns. It's crazy. We know how bad it is." Then why did she feel so inauthentic, like a drunk trying to act sober?

Only later did Connie consider that Dylan, sheltered by the innate optimism of youth, hadn't understood how bad it was. She had meant to console him, but it was a condemnation.

46

It was dark by the time Ellen dropped Connie home. Connie's house made a black silhouette against a starry sky where stars never used to be. She walked up the path slowly, feeling like the sky was falling, but that might be due to the drinks at Clumpy's. She slept heavily and when she woke, she waited until she held a mug of steaming coffee to her chest before she stepped out to the back porch to look at Otto's hillside.

The forest was gone. A stubble of stumps poked through an understory trashed and trampled. Huge logs were strewn casually like a giant's toys. Connie sat down on the steps and leaned her elbows on her knees. Sunlight poured onto the wasteland, flattening the scene. She could see all the way to Otto's tipi which really wasn't very far. The forest had once seemed infinite to her, ever mysterious and never fully explored. But nothing on earth is infinite, and this was a very small parcel of land. The size of a pasture, the size of a vineyard.

"How are you doing?" Ellen came around the corner of the house and stopped to share the view.

Connie looked up and shrugged.

"I can see your roof from my house. With the right wind, I think I could send you messages by paper airplane." Ellen sat down on the step and Connie scooted over to make room. "I used to like to make paper airplanes. I'm going to try it."

A backhoe sorted through the debris on the ridge like an ant moving larva.

"Do you have more coffee?" Ellen asked. "I've had a busy day already. I hate for days to be busy before noon."

Connie filled the only other cup and brought it out to where Ellen waited on the step, elbows on her knees, her big head in her hands. Connie sat next to her, and Ellen rubbed her head hard. "The police came by this morning. They wanted to talk to Dylan." She looked worse than tired. "I'm a failure," she said in a tone of complaint, "but you didn't help much either. They wanted to talk to Dylan about more vandalism up at Otto's."

Connie watched the log truck position itself to receive its cargo.

"Bad this time. He put bleach in the gas tanks."

"He's not a vandal," Connie said. "He didn't do it."

Ellen reached over and patted Connie's shoulder. "Yes, he did. And I don't blame him. But that's one of the things that makes me a failure. I should blame him."

Connie stood, agitated and unsure. "Did they arrest him?"

"They threatened to." Ellen waved her hand in a gesture of fatigue. "Sit down. Otto won't press charges. As long as Dylan makes some reparations. That's what we need to figure out. We could have him pay back the damages, but that would take a long time and Otto doesn't care about the money. He thinks maybe some kind of community service. He thought you might have an idea of the best way to handle it. Otto doubts my parenting ability, but he thinks highly of you."

"Dylan didn't do it." Connie set the coffee on the porch and began to pace toward the hill, but she didn't see how she could climb it, not through the rubble. She stopped.

"Connie, he confessed."

"No."

Ellen stood and laid her heavy arm across Connie's shoulder. "I'm sorry. This is too much all at once. I'm a fucking failure all around."

Connie looked into Ellen's tired, kind eyes, and burst into tears. Ellen wrapped her arms around Connie, but Connie did not deserve comfort. She pushed free while tears began to stream from her eyes and her nose ran. Even though she had a number of important things to say, she couldn't line the words up. Once the tears started, Connie felt like they might never end. She sat back down on the steps and put her head in her hands. Ellen patted her back and waited, and then waited some more.

Outside, the bulldozer growled as it pushed the wreckage into piles. Connie tried to speak to Ellen, but she hiccoughed with sobs and her inability made her cry more. Ellen got a quilt from the bedroom and wrapped it around Connie's shoulders and helped her to the couch.

"You're a little scary," Ellen said, frowning. She made Connie lie down. Connie wasn't tired or weak and that was part of her sorrow—the burden of energy, strong arms and a thundering heart in a world where they served no good purpose.

"You rest," Ellen said from the door. "Cry yourself out. Everything will be fine." But Ellen didn't look fine as she stood with her hand on the knob. She glanced at the shaved hillside and grimaced.

"But Ellen." Connie tried to swallow her sobs and her chest lurched.

"We can talk later. Nothing has to be decided now." Ellen opened the door and paused. "We'll take care of everything later." She stepped out and shut the door carefully.

Eventually Connie had to go to the bathroom. She drank the cold coffee. Eventually, she got up and washed her face in cold water and rinsed and dried her cup. There was some atonement in ignoring her hunger, but other responsibilities could not be ignored. She pulled on jeans and laced up heavy boots. She did not go by the road but cut straight up the hillside to find Otto. The trails were gone of course, buried beneath debris, and Connie had to clamber over logs and push through branches and the wreckage of the understory. The loggers paused, unsure of the meaning of her presence. One raised an arm and shouted at her, but she ignored them and continued to struggle over the difficult terrain. She wasn't really in their way, and when she tripped, the men went back to work, mollified by her trouble, seeing that she would be her own punishment.

Connie found Otto in his shed. He straddled a stool as he worked on his laptop. The familiar smell of coffee was strong in the small room. Connie stood at the open door and waited until he looked up.

"Connie!" He paused as he noted her appearance, her swollen face and the twigs that had caught in her hair when she passed through the waste of the forest. "Come in."

"No," she said from the door, and then, thinking better of it, she did enter.

Otto offered a seat, but Connie shook her head.

"I did it, Otto. I was the vandal."

"This is about Dylan." He sounded disappointed. "You don't do that boy any favors by protecting him. Jesus, Connie, you're a teacher. You know that."

"I'm not a teacher anymore, and I'm not protecting him." She had exposed him. It took all her reserves to keep from dropping to the ground. "I did all of it. I marked the trees and poured the bleach in the gas tanks. I did the truck first. I was more successful with the bulldozer because I drained some gas out. To make space for the bleach."

Otto set down his coffee cup and turned to face her. "Really? You did all of it?"

Connie nodded.

He considered her for a long moment, then he turned away and scratched the back of his head. He turned around quickly, as though to ask her something, but he didn't speak. Connie stood before his gaze, exposed and humiliated. "I'll pay for the damage."

Otto walked out the door. After a while Connie followed and found him looking over the logged hillside. Her house was now fully visible from the site. Beyond, blue-gray clouds crowded the tops of the mountains.

"Tell me how much I owe you," she said as she passed behind him to take the road home.

Otto caught her hand and pulled her back roughly. "Are you working with someone?"

She held her breath, frightened. Who would she be working with?

"You could have spoken to me." He looked like he was sick of her, really physically ill, but he didn't let go. "I'm not the enemy. You could have spoken to me."

She did not demand her hand back; she didn't think she had the right to demand anything. "Losing the forest . . ."

"You didn't lose it. You sold it." He dropped her hand as though throwing it away. "You sold it and pocketed the money then came back with all this righteous bullshit. What else?"

She looked at him blankly.

"You stole the camera too? A souvenir?" He walked a few steps away then turned and faced her from a distance, his lips curled in disgust. "You don't need to pay me. I won't send you to jail. You need mental help. This isn't grief. It's insanity."

Heat rose from Connie's gut to her chest, and she was surprised by the visceral objection. She was mean, hypocritical, ineffective—she could make a long list of her flaws. But she wasn't crazy.

"Forests all over the world are being razed faster than they grow. The coral reefs are dying, and the ocean has a garbage gyre the size of Texas. For no good reason. Otto, think of it," Connie pleaded. "*That's* insanity."

"Bullshit." Otto waved his hand violently toward the denuded hillside. "This isn't the problem. It's just easier to blame others—me, even Dylan takes the blame." His voice rose, and the birds quit singing. "But this isn't some fucking wilderness I've spoiled."

The neighbor's houses crowded near, and already the forest was hard to remember. Not only was Connie's house fully visible, light glinted from Ellen's front windows and Annabelle's red barn crowned the hill. With good construction and the right breeze, a paper airplane might reach any one of them. This piece of land could never have contained a whole forest; it was too small.

Connie turned. She had to go to Dylan. To apologize.

"I'm serious about getting help, Connie." Otto had gotten himself under control and his voice was clear and even.

Connie nodded without turning around, lifting and dropping her heavy head so that he would see from behind.

"If you don't, I will prosecute," he called from behind, then his hands were on her shoulders. He spun her around.

She felt like a rag doll in his grip, which was only right. Her opinions could be as irrelevant as the lichens that once colonized the trees. She saw a flash of movement in the fringe of bushes at the edge of the clearing. "Dylan?" She twisted and Otto dropped his hands. They looked briefly toward the remaining ridge of trees, but there was no evidence of anyone. Otto stepped away from her and wiped his hands on his jeans. His disgust was palpable. If there was help to be had, she wouldn't refuse it, but for what exactly? She searched his face a moment, abject, but he looked away. She wasn't his responsibility.

47

Connie went straight to Ellen's house from Otto's. Ellen's car was gone, but Connie wanted to talk to Dylan alone anyway. She peered through the window into an empty room. Dirty dishes sat on the table amidst piles of paper. More dishes lined the kitchen counter. The backdoor was unlocked, and she let herself in.

"Dylan? Hello?" His bedroom door was open, but his desk chair stood empty by the beat-up old table where he liked to draw. In the room down the hall, Ellen's bed was unmade and the shades were still drawn. Connie picked a damp towel off the floor and hung it in the bathroom. Downstairs, a small puddle of brownish soy milk congealed in a cereal bowl. The whole room smelled like old food. She rinsed the dishes and loaded them in the dishwasher. Looking for soap, she found a dead mouse in a trap. It was stiff as cardboard and had to be scraped off the board. She added the trap to the dishwasher and turned it on.

In the old days when living was harder, people might have said Cary was spared by death. These days, living was often easy, one pleasure after another, but the future was getting hard. The skies grew heavier with smoke every year. Cement and steel heaved up from the earth and stiffened the exuberant soil. The birds that Cary loved were dying. Cary's life had been sweet in childhood, and maybe that was enough.

Connie opened a window and the breeze lifted papers from the counter to the floor. A zoning variation letter for a meeting that had happened the week before, an expired coupon, the phone number for the ice cream store. She gathered them into a stack and put a ceramic cat on top to keep them down. Connie tried Dylan's new phone number, leaving a voicemail and text, but she wasn't surprised that he didn't answer; he usually kept his phone silent. She wiped the counters and swept the floor, filling the dustpan with crumbs as hard as gravel, but still Dylan hadn't come in. She wrote a note: *Dylan, call me as soon as you get home. Connie. 11:25.*

She went home to wait, but no one called, and Ellen wasn't picking up. Later, she left a second message for Ellen, begging her to call, and still Ellen ignored her. Otto must have spoken to her. By evening, Connie realized none of them might ever speak to her again, and though she felt bereft, she saw the wisdom in it. She saw the justice in it. She should be bereft.

She didn't get a call until after three the next day and it was Otto. "I'm coming down to talk to you," was all he said before hanging up. Maybe he had changed his mind about pressing charges. She looked around her own kitchen. Not a dish in sight and the room was as clean as a wind-scoured beach. If they took her off to jail, she wouldn't have to worry about what she left behind.

She waited for Otto out on the porch. Across the pasture, the oak trees, always last to leaf out, glowed yellow-green against trunks furred with moss, but in another month they would be tough and dusty. Otto's old truck came rattling down her driveway and pulled to a quick stop at her door. He held the door frame as he eased himself out. Connie could see he was in some kind of pain, and all at once she realized that when she had confessed to the vandalism, she forgot to tell him about the dangers of his bed.

"Otto!" She stood as he made his way down the path. Prison seemed a reasonable, surprisingly workable option.

Otto slowed as he approached her. "You know?" He walked toward her quickly, frowning as she waited. "It sounded like . . ."

His voice trailed off and he sat down heavily on the step. "Connie." He patted the place next to him, his voice stern, his face sad. "Dylan's in the hospital."

Connie gripped the railing and sank, her legs gone all watery. "He's hurt?"

"He's going to live," Otto said in a rush. "He's going to live," he said again. "Ellen's with him now."

"An accident?"

"Overdose." Otto laid a hand on her shoulder as he looked her in the eye. Connie stiffened beneath his touch. She felt suddenly afraid. "But I found him in time, Connie. I'm so glad I found him."

Connie's gut twisted and a sort of vertigo took her. She felt hollow, as if she might fracture and the pieces of her just blow away. She leaned into Otto's hand.

"After you left, I couldn't work. I went for a walk in the woods. What's left of the woods." Otto squeezed her shoulder hard. "I found Dylan laid out in the dirt like some kind of vampire. He was so cold. I gave him CPR until the paramedics got there."

"He saw us." Connie remembered the glimpse of movement in the bushes as Otto held her.

"He hadn't been unconscious long."

"He saw us together," Connie said with anguish. He must have seen Otto gripping her shoulders. It might have looked like an embrace.

"He wasn't on a path, and he was sort of hidden by branches, but he was dressed in white or I wouldn't have noticed. Sweet Jesus," Otto dropped his head in his hands. "He would have been bulldozed with the slash. It's providential that I found him. I never go out there, but you got to me."

Providence? Then what was the opposite? What do you call the force that led Connie to visit Otto before Dylan? She closed her eyes and her lungs shrank in her chest. Her bowels shriveled, but still her heart beat on.

"He'll be okay?" she asked softly.

Otto laid a hand on her leg. Connie moved away and it fell to the step. "Maybe. He was mighty close to death, Connie. But I got there so soon."

Connie laid her head on her arms and pulled her knees in tight to her chest.

"Young people are resilient."

Connie did not think they were, but there was no point in talking about it.

Otto scratched his calf through his jeans. "I wish I'd never come to Oregon."

"It's my fault." Connie wanted to crawl out of her skin and let the husk blow away. "Every bit of it. The forest. The owls. I knew what would happen when I sold you a vineyard." Her hypocrisy was sickening, and her callousness towards Dylan could not have been more complete if she had tried. She sat up straight and looked Otto in the eye. "I promised Dylan I would help him get you arrested and instead he saw us together. When you grabbed me, it might have looked like an embrace."

"You were going to have me arrested?" Otto scratched his calf again and looked out toward the trees.

"Dylan was paranoid," Connie said. "He'd been spying on you, and that's my fault too. He thought you were doing something criminal, so he stole your emails. He wanted to go to the police, but I convinced him to wait. I told him I would help him." The cold lump in the pit of her stomach was growing. Her legs felt far away and useless.

Otto stood and looked toward the road. "He's right; I am doing something criminal."

"It's none of our business." Connie didn't want to know anything about anyone anymore.

"I hack into oil company emails." Otto spoke as though he owed the information. As though she'd asked. She looked away, but Otto wasn't paying attention to her. "Nothing very organized," he said, still watching the road. "Just to see if I can find anything interesting to leak."

Connie stared at the patch of dirt between her feet. "You could get in trouble for that."

"It's pretty low-stakes."

Connie felt a flare of objection, a sudden intolerance for secrets. "Then why do you sneak down in the middle of the night? Why the super-secret room?"

He looked at her now, and she saw his disdain. "Super-secret? Jesus, Connie. It's just a basement. That's where I'll put the barrels if I ever get the winery done. In the meantime, it's cool down there and not likely to get broken into. I work at night when the oil company offices are closed. If I get lucky, I expose some of the industry's secrets. But you're right, I could get in trouble." He turned away and closed his eyes as he rubbed his neck. "Don't tell anyone."

It had started with her, and now everything was unraveling. "I've got to see Dylan."

"Let me drive you."

She should go on her own, but her heart beat with a destabilizing cadence, and she wasn't sure she could drive. She couldn't quite catch her breath despite shuddering inhalations that filled her with vertigo. "But not go in together," she said.

"No," Otto agreed. "But I want to see him too if he's well enough to talk. I blamed him out of sheer prejudice. That poor kid got grilled by the police." Otto's mouth twisted into a look of disgust. "Of course it was you."

48

Connie sat stiffly against the door of Otto's vintage truck. Neither she nor Otto spoke during the half-hour drive. They went into the hospital together, but Otto waited by the nurse's station as Connie entered the room. Ellen sat in a chair by the side of Dylan's bed with her hands clasped over her spreading belly. She looked angry and worried. Dylan just looked tired.

"So don't tell her," Dylan said.

"I can't keep something like this from your mother, for Chrissakes."

"Yes, you can." He shifted in his bed, and when he reached for his plastic cup of water, he spotted Connie. He frowned and turned back to Ellen.

"Hello," Connie said from the doorway.

"Connie!" Ellen glared. It wasn't exactly a greeting. Dylan didn't say a word. "He's going to be fine." She tapped Dylan's shoulder, something between reassurance and rebuke. "He came to right after they gave him the naloxone and spent the rest of the day puking. They just have to keep him here for observation. And they'll have to give him a psychiatric assessment." At that, Ellen looked over to Dylan. "They require it," she said to him, grimacing.

"Dylan, I have to talk to you." Connie approached his bed, but Dylan looked past her toward the television mounted high on the wall, his sonic eyes dull and sullen. Cartoon characters raced around an alien landscape. "Otto's outside," Connie said to Ellen. "You could get a cup of coffee with him. I want to talk to Dylan alone if I can."

Ellen frowned briefly. "Don't upset him." But she shrugged and picked up her purse. "It's late enough for a beer. Text if you need me," she said to Dylan, giving Connie an acid look of warning.

Connie scooted the chair close to the bed. She snapped the TV off and laid her hand on Dylan's forehead. He winced at her touch, but she didn't withdraw. She stroked his hairline, and he closed his eyes. She didn't trust herself to speak a single true word. Instead, she smoothed the line of his cheekbone, running her finger along the bluish shadow beneath his eyes. One clenched vein fractured his milky skin from his left eye to his scalp, like broken porcelain poorly mended, but it was the only part of his face that looked fully alive.

"We almost lost you," Connie said at last, filled with shame. They had thrown the boy into the fraying world without any kind of safety net. One tear seeped from beneath Dylan's lid and rolled down to the crisp hospital pillow.

"You don't need me," he said.

"You don't know what I need." Connie leaned over him until he opened his eyes. "Why did you confess to the vandalism? You didn't do it."

"I would have, if I'd known what to do."

"I did it," Connie said.

"I know. You didn't even keep yourself from getting recorded. Even though I showed you where the cameras were. I took it before Otto saw." When he mentioned Otto's name, he frowned.

"Why did you lie?"

Dylan turned his head away. Outside the window, the neighboring building belched steam over a sea of cars.

"Everyone already thought it was me." He turned back and faced her. "The plan would have worked perfectly if I had died. Now everything is worse than ever."

"Dylan, you're supposed to be alive. We need you. The forest needs you." She sounded trite and stupid to her own ears, but it was what she meant.

"The forest is gone."

"There are other forests."

"Not for me." He closed his eyes again, looking pained. "It doesn't make any difference. I'm going back to Seattle."

"That doesn't make any difference," Connie cupped his cheek with her cold hand. "Wherever you are, I will look forward to seeing you and your drawings. As I did when I didn't look forward to anything else."

"Knock, knock." An orderly peered around the curtain, a big smile on her rosy lips. "I brought your dinner," she said in a lilting Caribbean accent. She set a covered tray on Dylan's table and arranged the food and silverware where he could reach them. "You eat all of this, you hear?" She had to stand sideways to fit in the narrow aisle between the bed and the bathroom door, but she was deft and efficient as she adjusted his bed and arranged his pillows. "We got to fatten you up, boy. If you don't eat enough anyone might start to feel low." She paused at the door. "Anything else you need?" Dylan shook his head, and she bustled out.

Connie lifted the cover from the tray. A glistening steak nestled next to mashed potatoes and green beans in butter. A salad filled one side bowl and chocolate pudding filled a second.

Connie gazed forlornly at the dinner. "Did you tell them you are a vegan?"

"I can eat the salad."

"You have to speak up." Connie put the cover over the food and chased after the orderly, returning after a few minutes. "I think I got you a peanut butter and jelly sandwich. Not a lot of vegan choices. You could have had salmon, an omelet, or chicken broth." Connie shook her head. "They don't feed you any better than we do."

"Whatever."

"No." Connie felt a flush in her chest that flooded up to her face. Anger, she realized. "No," she said again. She reached over and pressed his call button. "When that nurse comes in, you tell her you're a vegan and you explain what that means."

"I'm leaving soon. It doesn't matter."

"I won't let you leave until you tell that nurse how to take care of you."

The nurse entered as Connie was talking. Sensing the disagreement, she raised her eyebrows and waited. Finally, Connie broke the silence. "Dylan has something he needs to tell you."

"I'm a vegan," he muttered.

"What?"

"A vegetarian. I don't eat meat."

"Do you want an omelet?"

"I don't eat eggs."

"Tell her what a vegan is."

"I don't eat any animal products."

"Like what, Dylan?" Connie prodded.

His eyes were half-closed, and his lips barely moved as he spoke. "I don't eat eggs or dairy products. No fish."

The nurse frowned. "You ordered steak."

"It came with a salad. I thought I could eat the salad."

"You're underweight," the nurse said. "You should eat meat."

"Or at least eat more," Connie said, feeling irritated. "I think a peanut butter sandwich is on its way," she said to the nurse, "but could you mark his chart or something?"

"He's scheduled to meet with a nutritionist about his weight before we release him tomorrow."

"Well," Connie said, "that will be fine."

After the nurse left, Connie leaned in and patted Dylan's arm. He flinched. "See?" she said, sitting back. "Tell people what you need. Don't take everything on yourself." Dylan closed his eyes and after some time, Connie thought he'd fallen asleep. She didn't know what medication he was on, or if the opioids were still in his system. Then another tear slipped out from beneath his long lashes. "Tell *me* what you need," she said, leaning in. She brushed the tear from his pale cheek, but he brought his hand up and wiped hers away.

"It's the drugs," he said. "I'm fine."

"You are not fine." Connie waved her arm around to take in the hospital room. Dylan was not hooked up to any monitors, but they lined the wall like functionaries eager to step forward. "Don't lie to me."

"Then don't lie to me." Dylan's eyes were rimmed with red, slow now and heavy with anger. "You said you'd help me get Otto arrested. Now he'll probably arrest you. I should have died. I only cause trouble."

"He won't arrest me. Anyway, I would have confessed even if you'd died." The surge of anger Connie felt was alien and ugly in the hushed hospital, and she struggled to contain it. "You would have caused a lot of trouble then. Dying doesn't stop your effect on the world. You don't get to opt-out."

"It would be better." He turned his head away. "You wanted to be left alone. Aunt Ellen wanted to be left alone." He was trembling.

"It doesn't matter what people want." She spoke so sharply Dylan flinched. She softened her voice. "Think about it. Everyone wants clean air and water, right? Everyone wants healthy forests and a stable climate. So what? Everyone also wants their own car and trips on airplanes. Wanting is a field of weeds." She had wanted Cary from before the moment of conception, and that singular desire had seeded a jungle: she wanted a healthy child, an educated child, a strong and well-adjusted child. Then she wanted a grandchild. Connie felt grief rise like a wave from her gut and she turned away from Dylan to look out the window. "I never wanted anything more than I wanted my daughter, but I'm probably the reason she got cancer. All I could do was watch."

Dylan rolled over and reached out to touch her shoulder, his fingers rigid and tentative. "That kind of watching." He patted Connie, an awkward, light tapping. "I think she was glad. She must have been scared, but you stayed with her." Dylan pulled his hand back, and with a slight, mewing sound of despair he rolled to his side, drawing his knees up to his chest. "I got those new boots, and Aunt Ellen said I'm not a real vegan because they're leather. What else is there? Plastic? Is that better? All that special food she got me came in plastic packages. Is that better? Everything I do is wrong."

"You're just one person." Connie reached for him, and Dylan's narrow back shuddered beneath her palm.

He twisted away from her hand and faced her. "I was going to do one good thing and get out of the way."

"Dylan, you can choose a lot of things, but you can't choose to get out of the way. You *are* the way."

Outside, the sea of cars drained from the broad black lot to the roads and highways. Connie stroked Dylan's forehead and he allowed it. Soon, his breathing smoothed and deepened. As he slept, his face became innocent, and it was enough to sit in the darkening room in the presence of his youth.

She heard a mild commotion out in the hall. The sound of a gurney slapping the wall and Ellen, "Fuck!" Then, "Sorry!"

Ellen entered the room with Otto just behind. He caught Connie's eye and winced apologetically.

"Dylan." Ellen leaned over his bed and placed her large hand on his forehead. He startled, a look of confusion and fear as his eyes flew open. "You are fucked stuck here with me, but your Mom's worse. I'm so sorry; you're just fucked."

"I'm going to take Ellen home now," Otto said. "Connie, could you drive her car back?"

"I'm perfectly fine, Otto." Ellen put her hands on her hips. "You and Connie should go out to dinner." She looked around the room and leered for a moment, then she remembered Dylan and patted his shoulder. "I need to tell Dylan. His mom and me, we were fucked too, with our fucked-up parents. Getting fucked is something you share with your ancestors. It gets passed down for generations."

"Come on, Ellen," Otto stepped towards her. "You said you'd make me a drink."

"You should drink with Connie," Ellen turned away from him. "Connie didn't get fucked by her ancestors like we did, Dylan. Connie got fucked by her future and it's been working its way backwards into her past." Ellen wiggled her fingers past her face, showing how a contaminating future might reach back.

Connie grabbed Ellen's hand and pulled her toward the door. "C'mon, I'll take you home. You can make me a drink. Otto needs to talk to Dylan."

"Dylan hates Otto," Ellen said frowning, but she drifted toward the door with Connie.

"Have you eaten anything?" Connie asked Ellen but looked toward Otto.

He nodded. "Bar food."

"French fries, fried calamari. It was all fried, right Otto? I told him to quit ordering. It's why I'm so fat."

Connie leaned over Dylan who looked disoriented. In a better world, he would be spared them all, but if he had become their problem, they had also become his. Connie kissed him on the forehead, something she never would have done if he hadn't been lying in a hospital bed. She wondered if she was taking advantage. "Otto's going to tell you what he's been up to," Connie said, looking to Otto as she spoke. He ducked his head before he settled in the chair near Dylan. As he turned to the boy, he reached down and scratched the side of his calf and Connie remembered. She had not yet confessed to the poison oak in his sheets. They might still be on the bed. She hurried from the room, dragging Ellen behind, distracted by a miasma of guilt.

49

They wound their way out of the densely pillared parking lot, and Connie had to remind Ellen several times to buckle her seatbelt. Ellen snapped it loudly and turned toward the door.

"Every instinct I have is a hundred eighty degrees wrong when it comes to raising children. Every single one, completely wrong. First of all," Ellen said loudly to the cars crowded at the light, "he could have spent the summer with our sister Beth instead of me. She's a bitch, but she would be able to make vegetarian food. She'd simmer it up in resentment, but she'd fill that boy with calories, and she'd never have to listen to a lecture from a nutritionist about growing adolescent boys. Like I did," Ellen said, "and I listened, but I still don't know how to cook."

Ellen leaned her forehead against the window. The matching houses of a new development clicked past. Finite and organized, they were the sort of houses where projects got finished and the whole family gathered in the evening for dinner.

"Then," Ellen's voice rose to a declamatory pitch even though she kept her forehead pressed to the window, "I get the brilliant idea that he could work with you. You, the queen of depression. And the job? Counting condemned lifeforms. Of course, you put our little patch of loss into a broader context, because that's the kind of teacher you are. Yay! An inventory of loss leading to an understanding of the disintegration of the natural world in general."

Connie guided the car up the winding mountain road through the saturated light of dusk. The maple trees made a canopy that soaked the interior of the car in green. Every spring, the forest tried to swallow the world. Even now, with the glaciers melting and the oceans dying, grasses burst from the margins of the road and crowded the asphalt. Green things sprouted from the cracks in the pavement and a cloud of insects massed in the dying light over the pasture. Connie pulled into Ellen's driveway and parked the car, but Ellen didn't open the door.

"Here we are," Connie said.

Ellen slumped against the door, eyes closed.

"I don't want to go in." Ellen made her voice very small.

"Come on." Connie opened her own door and looked at Ellen expectantly.

"My house is full of reproach," Ellen said. "I can't throw things out like you do. I keep 'em, and they reproach me. The soy milk has blue-green mold around the spout, and I'm not supposed to wipe it off and use the milk anyway. The living room is cold, and I only have one comfortable chair. You know, I don't let Dylan sit there. It's my favorite chair. He stays upstairs, figuring out where I keep the pills. His mother hasn't phoned him once since he's been here, and I told him she was a selfish bitch who never wanted children and only gave birth to him because she hoped to lure his no-account father back into her life." Ellen opened the car door and half fell out. Connie waited as she gathered herself and stood. "I shouldn't have said that," Ellen admitted, "but I was a little drunk."

Ellen didn't notice that the house was clean. She closed the windows and went to the cupboard. "We need a gin and tonic."

"No, we don't."

"We can't have scotch. I'm all out, just like I promised." She took one glass, filled it with ice and half filled it with gin before topping it off with tonic water. She paused before she drank, eyeing Connie over the rim. "If I had a lime, it would seem more civilized." She flopped into the favorite chair. "I wish you'd have one."

Connie shook her head. "I have to go to Otto's."

"Why?"

Connie sat down at the kitchen table. "I was the one who vandalized the equipment. Not Dylan. Me."

Ellen looked at her with an expression of stupefaction. "But you're a solid citizen. Are you telling me the truth?"

Connie nodded. "Worse than that, Ellen, I rubbed poison oak into Otto's sheets."

Ellen looked confused for a moment, then her eyes widened. "That's diabolical."

Connie nodded again. "And I meant to tell him when I told him about the equipment, but with Dylan and all, I keep forgetting. So now I need to go over there and strip his bed before he sleeps on those sheets again."

"You scare me." Ellen peered at Connie, still trying to absorb the news. "Otto could end up in the hospital,"

"Some people aren't sensitive to it."

"He was scratching while we were in the bar." Ellen rubbed her finger over the condensation on the outside of the glass and then wiped the moisture on her forehead. "You've shaken my faith in humanity."

"I didn't know you had any," Connie said. "I cleaned your house up."

"That's not enough to expiate you," Ellen said. "Dylan's in the hospital. Otto might end up in the hospital. What do you have planned for me?"

Connie just returned the gaze, feeling sick.

"I've been calling his mother all day." Ellen rattled the ice in the almost empty glass. "I've got to send Dylan back. He's used to her. That's a form of stability."

"Not really." Connie could feel heat rise up her throat. She swallowed. "Dylan worries about his mother and tries to take care of her. It's not healthy."

"Maybe the responsibility is good for him. At least she isn't a criminal, Connie. Like you."

"I . . ."

"You're a criminal. The poison oak thing could qualify as assault." Ellen stared at Connie as though she was not only confused about *who* she was but about *what* she was. Then she swirled the last of the liquid around the ice cubes and tossed it all back. "I get irritable, and I drink too much." She rose to make another drink. "But poison oak? It's like you don't have any empathy at all. So I guess you didn't notice," she got fresh ice cubes and poured gin over them. "Dylan takes responsibility for us, too. And when he takes care of us, we pull the whole fucked-up world in. Lonely beavers and dead owls. Extinction. We broke him, Connie. You and me and our wholesome little neighborhood." She set her drink on the table before dropping herself back into the chair.

Dylan must have taken the camera at dawn. He had probably stayed awake all night, waiting for daylight while Connie soaked in her warm bath. How could she claim to know what was best for him? With all their resources, they gave Dylan his own bedroom and then opened his eyes. Habitats disappearing. Animals dying. They gave him a smartphone to keep track of it all, minute by minute.

Ellen took a long pull of gin. "Don't say anything," She looked sternly at Connie. "This is how I cope, and it's better than vandalizing the neighbors."

"I'll leave you to it." Connie pushed herself up from the table. She felt old and heavy.

"Connie." Ellen waited until Connie stopped, her hand on the door. "You told Dylan about the vandalism?"

Connie nodded.

"Jesus. Another disappointment for the kid. You know I held you up as a role model? Now he probably believes everyone's an asshole. Maybe they are." Ellen sighed and took a drink. "You'd better stay away for a while. Dylan will come back tomorrow or the next day. We've got a lot to figure out and I don't want him worrying about you or the forest or any of that. Just give us some space."

Connie nodded again.

Ellen raised her glass. "This is the last one." She held the sweating gin and tonic in front of her as though it were from a vanishing species. "I swear to God."

50

Connie stopped by her own house to pick up a set of clean sheets for Otto. She took her best set; they would be a parting gift, although not enough for reparations. Nothing was enough. Otto arrived as she was tucking them around his narrow camp bed.

"Room service?" he asked.

She looked up to meet his baffled expression.

"Otto, I've done a terrible thing."

"So you appear in my bedroom with new sheets? You people have funny customs up here."

"Don't joke."

"I'm sorry. It's been a hell of a day. Would you like a beer?" He pulled two bottles out of the mini fridge and handed one to Connie. "Please sit." He looked around and finally waved at the newly made bed as he perched on the nearby bureau. "I'm sorry I can't make you more comfortable. I don't do much entertaining here."

She sat where he had pointed, the beer untasted on the bedside table, her hands on her thighs. "I rubbed poison oak in your sheets when I came up to vandalize the equipment," she said all at once. "I hadn't planned to, but you were in the shed being mysterious. Maybe you won't get a rash."

He looked at her with disbelief. Then, shaking his head, he rolled up his pants leg to show her the spreading welts on the side of his calf.

"That's bad, Otto. I'm afraid it's going to be terrible for you." There was no point in explaining how the rash was a conflagration that would smolder slowly before bursting out in full fury and then fester for weeks. Theoretically, other outcomes were possible. "I'm throwing your old sheets away." She wadded them up and tossed them toward the tipi door.

"You must hate me." He half-leaned half-sat on the bureau, his shoulders slumped, his face tired and morose. "Really hate me." He took a long pull on the beer. "You don't have to drink your beer," he said. "You can go home. Thanks for the sheets."

Connie paused, uncertain. She couldn't imagine sitting on the bed, drinking beer with him in the darkening tipi like teens at summer camp.

"I don't hate you." Sorrow cut like a river. "I hate *me*."

"Moving here was the biggest mistake of my life," Otto said. "I may not know much about farming, but I really don't know anything about people."

"It's not your fault." Connie felt dreadfully sorry for him. "I've ruined everything." She was a contamination. She smoothed the bed and stood to leave. She rubbed new tears away and then remembered she had touched the poison-oaked sheets. She should wash her hands, but that simple act of self-care was impossible with Otto sitting there. Poison oak would serve her right.

"Drink your beer," he said.

Connie sat on the edge of the cot. The beer helped clear her throat.

"I don't mean to be callous." Otto was only dimly visible now. "But you're not in charge of the world. Forests have been razed for agriculture for millennia. And sometimes children die."

He was missing the point. "Forests are razed, Otto, but not my forest. And children may die, but not my children."

"I get it." He set his empty beer on the table with finality. "But my vineyard," his voice rose. "It's not an environmental disaster. That little patch of second growth timber wasn't worth all this trouble, Connie. You've lost more than a forest." He stood and took his empty bottle to a recycling bin by the door. He didn't sit back down. Connie rose and Otto led her out of the tipi. "And that was all your own doing."

51

Connie's car engine was a small violence in the night, but it couldn't be helped. She drove slowly at first, protective of her neighbors' peace. She didn't pick up speed until she was past Ellen's, where all the lights were still on. She avoided looking toward the house; she didn't want to see Ellen's slumped form still in her chair. Connie crested the hill and sped to her driveway, carried by urgency but knowing, of course, she was already too late.

She let herself in and dropped her purse on the counter. She didn't even turn on a light as she headed to the bathroom. The drawer was empty. Not only purged of excess, but the little bottle that she had saved, even treasured as a talisman, had disappeared. It wasn't in the cabinet or any of the other clean drawers. The family misery pills were gone.

Then there was nothing left to do. She closed the drawers and turned on the lights and took off her jacket. Then she washed the lunch dishes she'd left in the sink. As she was drying the soup bowl, it slipped from her hands, bouncing against the edge of the counter before shattering on the floor. She swept up carefully, shepherding the slivers of glass to a corner where she gathered them in the dustpan and tipped them into the garbage. Then, to be sure, she got down on her knees and used a damp rag to clean up the small pieces the broom left behind.

She had some remaining obligations. She would honor Ellen's request to stay away, but she needed to write Dylan a letter to share some things that were not destructive, starting with her admiration and hopes for him. Then she would share some simple resources—artists, books, websites. But when she turned the computer on, she was shocked to see an email from Dylan in her inbox.

Connie, it said, by the time you get this, I will be dead. I strapped Otto's camera to the fir tree just southeast of his shed. It will have recorded everything—the logging and my death (I erased you). It will record when they bulldoze my body into a pile with all the branches and other dead animals. Post it on YouTube. It might go viral and then people might want to do something about the disappearing forests. Some of them will be able to do more than I ever could have. Don't feel bad. I know Aunt Ellen and you tried to help, but I've been thinking about this for a long time. This way I can make a difference.

The thought of the video sickened her. Ellen was right, Dylan wasn't an activist. All he could do was lay his body down. But whatever theatrics Dylan planned for his suicide, Otto would have upstaged them, stepping in as the savior. CPR. EMTs.

She wrote back immediately: how glad she was that his plan failed, how much he could do alive, observing and drawing. She told him he should give the camera back to Otto. She promised she would do everything she could to help him.

Connie stepped out the back door, already regretting her email. She could have been more eloquent in praising him, but mostly she was appalled at how she'd promised Dylan she would help. Jesus! Her help had brought them to their current pass. Clumsy. Stupid. Blind. She closed her eyes a moment, flooded with shame. But the email was sent.

Her kitchen light spilled golden through the open door. Wind stirred the fir trees, and in the distance an engine whined as a car crested the hill. Behind her, the house was a gallery of small demands, while outside, the night yawned, immense. She turned out the light and took the old sleeping bag to make herself a bed beneath the big oak. Its stiff branches did not yield to the little breeze that toyed with the leaves and rattled the galls and gently cooled her brow and cheeks. She dozed and each time she woke it was to new territory—stillness, the constellations wheeling over her, an owl calling across the valley. Birds woke her before dawn, but Connie pulled a corner of the sleeping bag over her face and slept uncomfortably all through the morning. She got up to pee in the bushes and she thought she might go in, but she didn't, and although it seemed histrionic to lie there all day, true histrionics required an observer. At least she wasn't causing any trouble. By afternoon she felt settled and the evening passed. She had no obligations at all.

Now she knew the bumpy ground, the lump to curl around, the rock to avoid. In return for her efforts, the ground gave more support than a bed, more even than the floor of a house which rests hollowly on boards strung over air. In soil, nothing exists in isolation. Worms writhe in distress when suddenly exposed, the opposite of claustrophobic. There must be a word for that, but Connie didn't know it. She lay face down, splayed out. The thought of standing made her dizzy. When she rolled off the sleeping bag to squat at the edge of the lawn, she realized that rising further and remaining upright had become unthinkable, as though she would break some tether and be lost. Another day and night drifted past. Increasingly, dreams fogged her mind. She kept finding herself in a Lilliputian world where she had to be careful about moving. Like Gulliver, she was being bound by many tiny ropes. She drifted out of these dreams to bouts of such draining remorse she wondered if she could die of it and hoped it might be so. Some part of her recognized that food and water might help, but the recognition wasn't enough to make her stand.

Sometime later, a shadow crossed her tiny dream-world. She felt a warm weight on her shoulder. She thought the Lilliputians had finally succeeded in tying her down, and then the soil could take her in and close around her. She opened her eyes as Otto rolled her over.

"How long have you been here?"

His head eclipsed the sky. Connie admired the dark, bowed line where his lips met and the tracery of fine wrinkles in the tanned skin around his sad and bloodshot eyes. Then his head was gone, and her vision filled with sky, pale with clouds, and the snaking branches of the oak. She closed her eyes, and in the darkness, she fell deeper than the grass, even deeper than the soil. She fell to some layer underneath where time was unmeasured and endless. Nothing matters where nothing begins or ends. The Lilliputian ties melted away and Connie understood how hard it had been all along to hold herself together. Now that effort diffused, and she was filled with a serenity as chill and pure as a mountain stream. But the lovely fluidity froze into awkward chunks when Otto returned to sit her up. He supported her head and shoulders as he held a glass of water to her lips. Water poured into her mouth and down her throat. She pushed herself fully upright and took the glass from his hand and drank the water down.

"Let me take you in." He slipped one arm beneath her knees, the other behind her back.

"No." She braced against him. "Listen."

Robins and sparrows sang. Small birds chittered warnings from the bushes.

She cupped his cheek, her thumb rested near the sagging flesh at the corner of his mouth. The inner edge of his lip was as pink as a new petal and her finger strayed to touch the tender skin. He probably hated her, she remembered that much, but that had nothing to do with the warmth of his cheek beneath her cold palm. That warmth was a miracle, a lost piece of the sun sent wandering. How lonely they all were! She drew his head down and kissed him. He held very still. Connie strained toward him. Heat kindled at the base of her throat and between her legs. She pulled him to her and kissed him again hungrily, and the rising heat created a kind of light behind her eyes, deep in her head.

"Connie," he said. A warning. An objection.

"If you don't want me, go." Her voice was hoarse from disuse. "But if you do want me, even if it's only right now, stay." She ran her hand down his back. His thick muscles knotted with restraint. "Don't worry about before or after. Please." She clasped him with the little strength she had. He pried himself away. Air flowed between them, and Connie turned her face away, her cheek cold against the ground.

Then she felt his warmth again as he loomed above her and pressed his warm chest against her chest. He kissed her, pinning her between him and the ground. He was not tender. He pulled her pants off and held her shoulders to the earth as he entered her. Sex was like a storm, filled with fury, and Connie was so carried by the sensations of skin to skin and mouth to mouth that she was surprised when she came, and the fury ebbed. Otto slumped to her side with a sigh like he was about to speak. Connie laid her hand over his mouth, and leaned against him, spent. Above them, clouds folded in on themselves, their seams dark, their edges blossoming to white. Later, Otto carried her inside and fed her soup from her one remaining bowl. Then he took her to the hospital, and she did what they told her to do, and she let him leave her there.

Connie spent three nights at the hospital where she was given pills that left her feeling like she was wrapped in cotton wool. She won the weary gratitude of the staff and other patients by being polite and predictable. She didn't scream. She didn't cry. She met with a psychiatrist who encouraged her to make friends, and every day, as requested, she gathered with the others to listen to their stories. In turn, she recited the chain of events that brought her to them, but not the sex with Otto, which was discordant and inexplicable.

Other patients approached her sometimes. She tried to be friendly and remember their names, but they looked so much the same with their soft clothes and soft bodies. They talked about the food and the staff and their history of breakdowns, and Connie reciprocated as compliantly as she swallowed the pills every day. When she was almost ready to be released, she told the group about the sex. She had waited until she had enough authority to be plain; it wasn't Otto's fault. He had fucked her with something close to violence, but she had not been a victim. She had wanted to touch him and for him to touch her. She wanted the warmth of him but also the force and the struggle.

The day before she left, a patient named Maria approached after lunch. She had played violin in the symphony until she couldn't anymore, and her elegance was not hidden by the shapeless clothes. "There you are!" she said as though they were old friends. She settled in the opposite chair. She was crooked with arthritis and so thin she seemed almost weightless, but her strong hands gripped the padded chair as she leaned forward. "I only talk to the arsonists."

"Not arson," Connie corrected. "Vandalism."

Maria closed her eyes, their hooded lids papery over her eyeballs. She waved her hand with an irritated gesture of dismissal. "You're leaving us soon. And you won't be back." Her neck twisted permanently toward her missing instrument, so that she seemed always about to do something else, something beautiful. She crossed her legs. "I'll grace you with my wisdom." She paused and all her angles strung together for a moment, piercing and theatrical. "Don't go out there to be a good person, a giving person." Her glittering eyes fixed Connie with demented authority. "Only need is honest. Burning, holy need."

Connie stared back and felt a sudden rebellion. "And yet you give me advice."

Maria laughed. She was already turning to go. "Sometimes I need to be seen."

52

The first two mornings after Connie got home, she forgot to take the pills, and on the third day she threw them out. Even though she explained to her neighbors that she wasn't suicidal, someone came every day to check on her. They brought soups and cookies and neighborhood gossip, which they offered tentatively at first and then with bold enjoyment. That's how Connie learned that Otto's rash came on full-force while she was gone. Annabelle, looking for a riding companion, found him with his eyes swollen shut, the sides of his face blistered and oozing.

"I've never seen poison oak so bad," Annabelle said when it was her turn to visit Connie. She had brought peanut butter cookies, Otto's favorite. Half the batch had gone to him and half to Connie. "Both sides of his face are covered, but the center, his nose and chin and forehead, is completely clear. I told him he looked like a poison oak sandwich. Just a little slice of Otto in between."

Connie felt dreadfully sorry. "I should stop by with some of my extra soup."

"Give him another week. He doesn't want to see anyone. Well, he *can't* see anyone, but he doesn't want anyone to see him. He got some steroids, and I can bring him meals. He just needs time." Annabelle shook her head and her ponytail twitched like a horse's. "I'd be going crazy if I were him. I got him some audiobooks. We're listening to the whole Harry Potter series. Can you believe it? He hadn't read a single one."

Connie hadn't called Otto after she returned from the hospital. She was afraid he already felt responsible for her, and she didn't want him to think she had become his problem. Besides, she had been busy worrying about Dylan. Ellen had finally gotten ahold of his mother who, according to Ellen, raced down, maudlin and clingy. They were making arrangements to move Dylan back to Seattle where the only animals would be squirrels, gulls, and crows. Leashed dogs and lolling cats—none of them endangered at least. But what would become of him and his drawings? Connie wondered what he wanted. Had anyone asked?

"Dylan's still fragile," Ellen said on the phone. "Stay away for a while."

Connie didn't have the right to argue. She busied herself outside, hoping to see Dylan striding down the new road to the wetland, but he never came. In the late afternoons she visited the beaver lodge, but she never found him perched on top. She picked up the phone to call Ellen a dozen times, but each time she hung up before it rang. Ellen did not believe his suicide attempt was serious. More pointedly, she thought he had acted rashly out of solidarity with Connie, which was why Connie had not mentioned the video. Ascribing the incident to adolescent theatrics relieved the adults of some responsibility, but all Dylan's worries remained, and Connie woke at night panicked that he was dying somewhere all alone. The video was never posted on YouTube, and the camera might be strapped to the tree still. Had Dylan left some sort of manifesto there? Did he speak to the camera? Connie couldn't imagine a fiery protest; she imagined despair, rising like floodwater.

She put on jeans and a dark sweatshirt and took the dark colored daypack. A thrum of excitement carried her up the hill. It made her quick and alert, exactly the opposite of psychiatric medication, and she felt like an addict as she promised herself that she would give up sneaking forever once she knew Dylan was okay. The camera was easy to find still strapped to the trunk of one of the remaining fir trees. It angled toward the place where Dylan must have laid himself down. It was a little higher than she could reach. She would have to get a ladder from Otto's. Or leave the camera. She almost left then. She was deluded to think she could read Dylan's mood from a video when she hadn't been able to read his mood from his real-life flesh and blood. Her hands began to sweat, and she wiped her palms on her jeans.

But secrets are not stones you can keep in your pocket. They have their own life, more like seeds, and she realized the camera probably recorded her too, circling the tree like a hound. She was still in its sight. Now the video would show the browsing deer and curious raccoons. Dylan's suicide, dramatic or despairing. Then Otto's life-saving ministrations and the flurry of professionals. Then her. Skulking. Indecisive.

She skirted the camera's view as she crept back to the edge of the clearing. An aluminum ladder hung from the wall of Otto's neat workshop. Both Otto's cars were parked in the drive, Annabelle's too. Connie heard the drone of an audiobook coming from the tipi. She focused on that as she walked with authority to the ladder. If she was spotted, she would tell the truth, but she got the camera and returned the ladder without incident.

Back at home, she plugged the card into her computer. The motion-sensing camera recorded for ten seconds after it had been triggered and the resulting video was comically hectic. In hodgepodge succession, Connie saw the eyes of a deer reflecting strangely in the dark then the quick flight of a bird. Then Dylan arrived, shockingly pale in white painter's pants and a white thermal undershirt. For once, he'd dressed to be seen, but he didn't look at the camera as he stumbled over to sit on a felled log. He must have already taken the pills. He swayed, the sort of circular, stirring movement of a tree in wind. Then, he fell backward, melting to the soft soil in slow-motion release. His legs remained on the log, his big boots hanging in the air. Then the scene cut, followed immediately by the flight of another bird and a ten second shot of the glade, sunlight dappling the forest floor, the big boots still hanging there. By the time Otto triggered the video he had already spotted Dylan and was hurrying. Otto crouched over the boy, feeling for a pulse or breath, and then he began CPR. Repetitive, workman-like. He took a break to use his phone and started in again. Consistent. Monotonous. His face was periodically visible when he sat up to inhale before breathing into Dylan's lungs. Connie made herself watch the whole thing. It was a half hour before the EMTs arrived. Connie timed it. Otto never missed a beat.

The EMTs moved with the hustle of a silent movie. They flipped Dylan's feet off the log, slid him onto a stretcher and hurried away, moving jerkily among the fallen branches. Otto, spent and forgotten, trailed after. And the scene ended. Another bird flew through, and the camera showed the quiet spot for ten seconds. Then a coyote sniffing the artifacts of disaster. More deer. And then Connie marched up, clumsy and meddling. She turned the recording off before the scene had ended. She only meant to erase herself, but she made an error and cleared the whole thing.

53

She called Ellen the next morning. "Go for a walk?"

"*You* should go for a walk," Ellen said. Connie heard the voices of others in the background. Ellen took her mouth from the phone briefly and bellowed *No! There!* "But I can't come. I'm taking Dylan and my sister for a hike in the gorge." She didn't invite Connie.

Connie was persistent, but every time she called, Ellen and Dylan and Dylan's mom were busy hiking or shopping or online apartment viewing. "Dylan's fine," Ellen insisted. "He was depressed, but he's over it. I'm going to Seattle with them on Monday to rent the apartment. At least they'll have stable housing. His mom is doing better."

But Connie couldn't bear the thought of Dylan leaving without seeing him again. It was a physical ache, like a hole in her chest. She bypassed Ellen, who had not actually forbidden contact, and texted Dylan directly: *I know you're busy, but I'd like to see you before you leave. Join me in the wetland at one?* Her heart skipped a beat when she saw his one-word reply: *OK.*

Just before she left, she let Ellen know: Meeting Dylan for one last look at the wetland. I won't say anything depressing.

Connie arrived early. The margins of the marsh were dry and stiff now, and she spotted the first dragonfly of the season circling the beaver dam. That was the only movement. The sun was warm on her shoulders, and she took off her sweatshirt and tied it around her waist. Dylan came down Otto's new road like a big black bird.

His head moved, scanning to the right and left. He looked awkward, as though he were made for some other environment, but he had filled out some since he first came to the mountain, and he walked with a stronger, bolder stride. He stopped abruptly just in front of her.

"Hi," she said.

"Hi."

Then she didn't know what to say. The native flowers were mostly spent, and the birds were quiet at midday. No other animal stirred except for the dragonfly, busy in its own quadrant. She couldn't see anything to teach him. "Do you want to watch for a little while?"

Dylan set his bag on the ground and settled against the log where Connie sat. He pulled out pencils and paper and a stillness came over him as his hands busied over the page.

Connie slumped down off the log and let the knobby trunk cradle her neck. She looked up to the sky where bright cumulous clouds blossomed as steam rose from the warm earth.

"I've missed you," Connie said at last.

"We've been busy." Dylan didn't look up from his drawing.

"I know." She didn't want to seem critical. "But I got used to having you around." She closed her eyes and the sun poured onto her eyelids, her vision a field of red. "Are you eager to get back to Seattle?"

"Eager?" he asked pointedly.

She opened her eyes. Very high up, a raptor rested on a rising thermal. She thought it was a bald eagle, but it was too far away to tell for sure, so she didn't point it out to Dylan. "Are you looking forward to it?"

"Aunt Ellen's paying for the apartment until I'm done with high school. We won't have to keep moving."

"Did you go to that school before?"

"A little."

"You like it?"

"That doesn't matter. Everyone says you have to finish high school."

"There may be alternative schools that would work better for you."

Dylan shrugged.

She sat up and faced him. "Dylan, I owe you a million apologies."

He grimaced and shook his head.

"You almost got arrested," she said, "for something I did."

"No." He cut her off. "We did it. I was watching."

"So I owe you a million thanks. You looked out for me." It was a wonder when she thought about it, his generosity and how much she hadn't noticed. She sat back and covered her eyes with her hands. "At the restaurant, Ellen and I were joking like ghouls," she said from that cave of darkness. "We didn't consider how it would make you feel."

Dylan stopped drawing and looked directly at Connie. She could feel the force of his sonic gaze. She rubbed her face and brought her hands back to her lap.

"It was like you thought it was funny that everything is going extinct." His mouth made a thin, angry line, but his eyes were wide, and Connie thought he might cry.

"We must have sounded like we didn't care."

The emotion drained out of him, and he turned back to his drawing. "It's not like caring helps. If you can laugh, that's good." His pencil slid across the paper in sweeping arcs, deliberate and repetitive. "I can't laugh."

It was true; Connie had never seen him open his mouth and laugh out loud. Nothing close.

"Caring is the only thing that helps." When Connie quit caring, all she did was shrivel, and everything caved in around her.

He shook his head without looking up. She didn't know what her words meant to him. She probably sounded overwrought.

"Okay." Connie sat up and rummaged in her backpack. "I brought you the last of the energy bars." She pulled two cookies out and handed him the tin. "I included the recipe in case you want to make them at home. Or maybe your mom?"

Then he did laugh, a short bark. "Right."

Sesame seeds fell from Connie's lips as she bit into the brittle cookie. She pressed the fallen seeds onto her finger and licked them from her skin so as not to litter the wetland soil. It was a funny impulse; the seeds would never sprout from that cold ground. Besides, plants would have to migrate as the climate changed, and they would rely on the sloppiness of animals like her. She shook the cookie over the soil and contemplated the constellation of smooth seeds on the dark mud.

"It's so quiet," Dylan said. All they could hear was the distant static of the freeway six miles away.

"Will you miss that in Seattle?"

He bent his head close to the page as he drew. "It was pretty lonely here."

"I wasn't a very good teacher for you." Connie used the sole of her boot to press the sesame seeds into the mud.

"I learned a lot."

"You learned from spending time outdoors."

His pencil stopped, and he looked up from his drawing. "I wouldn't have listened to a lecture. Just sitting there, drawing, I got interested."

"I'm glad." She had wanted him out of her way, and yet he had lodged in her unlike any other student. "You have a gift for seeing. I know you have your Aunt Ellen and your mom, but I know a lot about schools. I'd like to help you."

He glanced at her before returning to his sketch. "Aunt Ellen thinks I should stay away from you."

Ellen was wrong. Connie had been careless and self-absorbed, but Ellen hadn't been any better.

"What do *you* think? Do you want me to stay away?" It was a simple question to ask, but asking it was one of the hardest things she'd ever done.

Dylan quit drawing and looked out over the pond. The water was hidden by lush growth, but you could tell it was a pond because it was so flat, the grass thick and even. "It's not your fault the world is so fucked up. And it wasn't your fault that I wanted to die." He looked at her frankly. He had never faced her like that before, eye to eye. "I'm not a very good student, and I don't know what Aunt Ellen would say," he told her. "But maybe you could help me."

"I'll talk to Ellen."

Dylan ripped the page from his notebook and handed it to Connie. He had drawn her with her head resting on the log and her eyes closed. Her neck arched back, her throat exposed. In a younger woman, the posture would be sensual and vulnerable, but here the crepe of her neck and the swell of jowl showed weary experience. It wasn't unlovely. Her brow drew down in a look of pain that surprised and saddened her. But he hadn't just drawn her portrait. He'd included himself: observed and observer. In his drawing he studied her intently. The dragonfly hovered between them.

54

Connie went right home and began researching Seattle schools. She was well-armed with useful information by the time she arrived on Ellen's doorstep the next morning. She called out as she let herself into the kitchen. A woman with dyed red hair who looked like a smaller version of Ellen was pulling clothes from a pile of laundry. She froze like a startled deer when she saw Connie. "Ellen," she called up the stairs, "someone's here."

Connie introduced herself, but Dylan's mom didn't stay to talk. She gathered the clothes and hurried upstairs.

"We're in the middle of packing," Ellen said as she came down from the bedroom.

"Can we take a walk?" Connie asked.

"We're really kind of busy." Ellen wore a stern and stubborn look. Connie ignored it.

"Just fifteen minutes."

They stepped outside. Wind stirred the fir trees above them, but across the lane they could see right over the cleared hill to the valley beyond. The scrubby forest surrounding Ellen's house seemed shabby and furtive now that it faced the open vista of Otto's vineyard.

Ellen scowled. "It's so clean over there it makes my place look messy." She waved her hand at the evening primrose that had seeded along the driveway and now towered above the grassy weeds. "The trellises will be so symmetrical they'll make my house look like it's falling down."

She was right, but her house *was* falling down. "When are you leaving for Seattle?"

"Day after tomorrow."

"Then you have time to take a walk."

Ellen planted her feet and shoved her hands in her pockets. Connie bumped her so that Ellen had to pull her hands out to keep her balance. Once they started moving, maybe they could start talking again. Connie craved it. "Come on."

"Short walk," Ellen barged forward suddenly, leaving Connie behind.

"I think you know how attached I've become to Dylan." Connie scurried to match Ellen's long strides.

"Oh, yeah. Like the albatross around the neck," Ellen said without turning around. "Where in the world did that expression come from?"

Connie stopped, suddenly overcome. "The Rime of the Ancient Mariner," she said with a shock of discovery. She knew the poem; her grandfather used to recite it after dinner, his wild eyebrows lifting and gathering, her family as captive as the wedding guest of the poem. She stood in the road, her hands in fists at her side. Ellen turned when she heard that Connie no longer followed. Remembering her grandfather's gruff and mournful voice, Connie lifted her chin. She spoke so the whole mountain might hear: "The many men, so beautiful! And they all dead did lie: And a thousand thousand slimy things Lived on, and so did I."

Ellen watched with narrowed eyes until Connie's fingers uncurled.

"I don't know what you're talking about." Ellen's expression was sour and ungenerous.

Connie wiped her sleeve across her face. "The guiltiest survives. But with a duty, Ellen." Connie caught up with Ellen so they could walk on together. "I know I can help Dylan."

Ellen shook her head. Her shoulders swayed with the negation. She stepped in front of Connie so that Connie was forced to stop. "You let me down." She stood close, challenging. "I was counting on your help, and then you went crazy. Crazy scares me."

"I need to help Dylan." Connie felt small and exposed and more confident than she had ever felt before. "I love him." She looked up to Ellen's stony face and told Ellen her ideas about the schools in Seattle. They continued up the lane as she described the options and the conversation she'd had with Dylan in the wetland.

"You wouldn't be seeing him that often," Ellen said.

Connie agreed.

"You wouldn't *have* to see him at all, you could still help with the school stuff and disabilities and all that shit."

Connie agreed. "I want to make sure he gets to college. That's all I need."

Ellen walked on. After several minutes she turned to Connie "You know, I'm sorry too. I shouldn't have said that about Cary and the weed spray."

Connie shrugged. It was just a fact.

"You were the best mother," Ellen said. They continued in silence. The rabbits that lived in the blackberries on the edge of the road waited, noses twitching, until they were very near before diving back into the bushes. By midsummer, less than half would remain. By the end of summer, you'd never see a rabbit.

"I'll talk to my sister about you helping. It's probably a good idea."

At Annabelle's, they turned back toward Ellen's house. Ellen slowed and kicked a rock into the bed of primroses. "As long as we're making things right, don't let Annabelle sink her talons into Otto." They had not spoken about him since all the trouble, and Connie felt a surge of shame. "You may not care, but consider Otto. He's gone through a lot because of you."

"Maybe he doesn't need to be saved." Connie hadn't told Ellen about the afternoon Otto found her. "Annabelle's lively and cheerful."

Ellen wrinkled her nose in distaste. "She's getting brighter."

Connie scoffed. "Annabelle's idea of culture is Harry Potter on audio."

"I don't mean smarter." Ellen rolled her eyes. "*Brighter*. Her hair got blonder, and her nails got pinker and everything she wears has sparkles on it. Where does she get sparkly socks?" Ellen demanded with deliciously familiar animus. "There must be some secret website. Even her panties are covered with rhinestones which must be uncomfortable."

"Imaginary rhinestones aren't uncomfortable."

"Imaginary rhinestones are the worst. When Otto's able to open his eyes again, she'll be so bright he can't see anything else. She'll marry him easy." Ellen stopped so suddenly that Connie almost bumped into her. "That will be on your conscience," Ellen said. "And you already have a lot on your conscience."

"I'm sorry for everything." They searched one another's faces, and it felt like standing naked before an audience, at their age. But they had been friends for decades, and as they looked into one another's eyes they decided to be friends for decades more.

"I'm sorry too." Ellen began walking again. "We fucked it all up, but it's okay now, right? We'll start doing things right, and after this walk," Ellen turned and looked at Connie sternly, "promise you'll visit Otto."

"He doesn't want company."

"He wants you. Go home, take a shower. Make yourself a little brighter, then go up to Otto's."

"Ellen." Once more Connie moved to pass, but Ellen blocked her again.

"It's the easiest thing in the world. Take him some calamine."

"Calamine," Connie said, walking on now.

"Take him some baking soda for a bath," Ellen said to her back.

"He doesn't have a bath."

"Oh!" Ellen hurried to catch up. "That's right! Take him to *your* bath. Make it all pretty. If you have any towels left, give him your best one." Ellen leaned in so her head almost touched Connie's head. "Make him a nice dinner. Comfort food. Dim lights. But no Harry Potter. The poor guy is infantilized enough. Talk to him about something adult." Ellen's forehead glistened redly as she squinted down the lane. "But you can't talk about nature without making him feel bad, so quit talking about nature." Ellen grasped Connie's shoulder. "Even if he brings it up. Promise?"

"I can't promise that," Connie said to her feet. Small clouds of dust rose from the gravel with every step. Her shoes were coated and her ankles greyly grimed. Ellen let her arm fall to her side.

55

Connie sat on the bench in her front hall and removed her shoes. Dust had worked its way through the fabric and her bare feet were also dirty. They had grown knobbier over the years, the boney toes beginning to jut in eccentric directions, and they looked strange and alien against the well-scrubbed floorboards. Connie showered and washed her hair and put on a clean cotton blouse. It wasn't the least bit sexy, but she had always loved its faded blue and she used to feel pretty wearing it. She even put on makeup. If Otto thought she was trying when he saw her, it would only be the truth. She would try. She called to warn him of her arrival, but the call went straight to voicemail. He might be out or resting, which might be best; she could leave her offerings at the tipi's little round entrance. She took him her best towel, wrapped around the calamine and the box of baking soda, because Ellen was right, it would be kind to offer a bath. She wrote a card. Not ardent, but an open door. At the last minute she grabbed the camera. She would return it to him, and she would tell him the whole, complete truth.

Connie clutched the towel and walked carefully toward Otto's tipi, trying not to raise too much dust around her newly clean ankles. As she neared, her heart began to flutter. She exhaled slowly, embarrassed at the betrayal of her body. She was so focused she didn't see Annabelle dart out of the tipi and only looked up at Annabelle's surprised "Oh!"

Annabelle wore a long shirt that covered her buttocks, but her legs were bare. "He doesn't have running water," she said, holding the empty glass for Connie's inspection. She shook her head as a mother might. "I have to run in and out for the simplest things." She hurried over to the spigot and filled the glass, and while her haste expressed some apologetic urgency, she paused in front of Connie. "It's not a good time for a visit. Sorry."

Annabelle's well-muscled legs were smooth and tanned all the way up to the swell of her butt beneath the creamy shirt. When she reached the tipi's opening, she turned and smiled. "I'll tell him you stopped by." Then Annabelle disappeared into the shadowed door like a doe into the woods.

Back at home, Connie put the soda away and restacked the towels. She left the camera on the counter, unsure what she would do with it. But it was the sight of her clean feet that made her call the realtor: those gnarled toes all scrubbed and hopeful. For a reduced fee, the realtor was happy to prepare a proposal for Otto to buy her house. Connie thought Otto might call her, but he did not. He accepted the proposal through the realtor and within the month, Connie purchased a condominium on the river in Portland. The glass cornered living room had water and city views, and it was a splurge, but freed of the farm's maintenance, her living expenses were modest. She could smell river mud from her narrow balcony and watch herons stalk small fish along the shoreline. To Connie, the move felt like a bold stroke, but neither Ellen nor the other neighbors were surprised. Poor folks. They were tired of her.

Connie's neighbor Fred hauled her sheep to the livestock auction, and that was that; she was no longer a farmer. She didn't have to advertise tools to her neighbors because Otto was glad to buy the hoes and rakes and shovels, and he paid well for the old tractor, although perhaps that was a kindness on his part. They managed the sales by email. Connie left the tools in the barn and Otto sent a check. She understood his need to avoid her. For her part, she stayed far away from his compound and never walked on the ridge, even though the oak grove remained, islanded in the newly voluminous field. She left him typed notes explaining the idiosyncrasies of the well and the furnace and the best ways to keep mice out of the garage.

She spent some of the proceeds from her sheep on a comics class for Dylan. When she visited Seattle about a month after he'd moved, he took Connie to the studio. Fierce presses and cutters loomed over the insubstantial young people as they curled around their computer keyboards in the stark industrial space. What those quiet kids created there was wild and funny and sly. Some of it could not be understood at all, not yet. They hardly spoke to one another as they worked side by side, and Dylan, as slim and dark as a parenthesis, fit right in. In fall, he'd begin classes at an alternative high school where he could get credit for the art classes.

As for Ellen, she was turning over a new leaf. She said she needed more money to keep up with Otto and the gentrifying neighborhood and in pursuit of that, she turned her attention to her insurance business, updating the website, joining the local Rotary Club. When Connie locked her front door for the last time, no one was around to say goodbye.

The August morning was bright and hot by ten. Sunlight spilled down the logged hillside leaving puddles of shade near the piles of debris that dotted the ground like grazing dinosaurs. Connie's little house looked vulnerable without the dark forest at its back. She allowed herself to really notice how decrepit it had become; the porch sagged and the exterior showed large, damp patches of mildew. She drove toward the condominium with a lightness and freedom that was similar to a sense of possibility. She didn't know who she was anymore. Not a teacher, not a farmer, not a wife, not a mother. In the end, it was a relief.

56

Connie brought very little with her. A bed. A reading chair. A couch. A table. She traded her car for a bicycle and took a job as office manager for a small organization that preserved and rehabilitated wetlands. She did everything from answering the phones to helping write grant proposals, and she began to facilitate educational outings for the local kids. Many of them had never left the confines of Portland. They had seen oceans and forests only in the same way they had seen outer space and apocalyptic futures—on a screen. She reveled in their wonder at the natural world, but she also enjoyed their umbrage. Yes, insects can be bothersome. It is sometimes too cold or too hot or too wet for comfort. No, the paths aren't safe if you're looking at your phone. But little by little, she thought they were learning: the world was not made for humans; humans were made for the world.

When Connie craved solitude, she slipped a nimble new kayak into the river where she skimmed the surface, small and light as a water bug. What she missed most were trees; visiting them was not the same as living with them, just as being in a crowd was not the same as having friends. She got a potted lemon tree and a hand truck and wheeled the tree between her living room and her four by eight balcony like a convalescent. She knew every leaf and used a watercolor brush to pollinate the blossoms.

Ellen refused to visit Connie's new condo until Connie had been there over a month. She wouldn't come, she said, until Connie was completely settled. Connie had finally called with a rather formal invitation and Ellen still resisted. "Are all the boxes unpacked?" she had asked. When Connie assured her they'd been unpacked for weeks, she asked about the kitchen and pictures on the walls. Finally, she asked if there were little piles of things in the corners. "You know," she had said with a tone of impatience, "things you've been meaning to finish but haven't."

But Connie didn't have those anymore so the morning of the visit, she left the dirty frying pan on the kitchen counter and an empty coffee cup on the table next to a used copy of *How to Win Friends and Influence People*. She wanted to understand what Otto had gotten from it, plus it would almost certainly needle Ellen. As Connie imagined her reaction, she realized how much she missed her old friend.

Ellen didn't ring from the lobby but came right up to Connie's door and knocked.

"Ellen!" Connie stood on tiptoe to give her a hug. "You didn't buzz."

Ellen handed Connie an orchid with flowers like little moons. "Your neighbor escorted me." She leaned out the door to wave, twiddling her big fingers ironically. Connie looked over her shoulder where one of the other tenants waited, arms crossed.

"Thanks!" Connie called and pulled Ellen inside.

"We came to the front door at the same time, and I came in with her." Ellen made a face. "I guess that's not allowed. You must have a real problem with people illegally dumping orchids around here because she wanted to arrest me. I wouldn't wait for the police, so she followed me up. I tried to make pleasant conversation, but she stayed a few feet behind to keep an eye on me. Do I look like a criminal?"

Ellen did not look like the other women who filled the building. Her hair was not a color you would pick on purpose and her nails were not only bare, they were ragged and a little dirty. Connie was so glad to see her.

"People are afraid of property crime."

Connie led Ellen into the living room, but Ellen crossed immediately to the balcony to look over the margin of shrubs and briars to the fat brown river. After some time, Ellen turned and surveyed the room. "You're not afraid of property crime," she finally said.

"No, not me."

"Because you have no property." Ellen nodded with approval. Here, in the polished building of wood and concrete, Connie's minimalism seemed subversive. Ellen crossed the room and sat at the table. She'd moved the chair so she could sit deep in the corner. She folded her arms over her chest and looked around. "It's pretty fancy here."

Connie joined her at the table and nodded.

"Your lobby looks like a bank building."

"I wanted a place on the river. They come fancy."

Ellen scowled. "You probably had to buy new clothes so your neighbors wouldn't think you were a homeless person sneaking in."

In fact, she had. "People really notice." Connie laughed. "One of my new neighbors took me to the Nike employee store. I think it was an intervention."

Ellen made a face and slid the coffee cup and *How to Win Friends* away so she could lean on her elbows. "That's the last straw!" She slapped her hand on the open book. "Are you going to become an influencer?"

Connie closed the book and set it aside. It was old and well-used, the glue brittle and the spine broken. "Maybe."

"That's disturbing." Ellen stood and began to pace. "You never used to worry about other people's opinions. God, Connie, I admired you so much." Ellen stopped for a moment and looked at Connie with something close to anguish. "I thought you and Dylan would be good for each other. He needed guidance and I thought you needed a kid. But Jesus! Your guidance . . ."

"Ellen."

"I know." Ellen leaned on the table, looming over Connie for a moment before dropping heavily back into the chair next to her. "Where was my guidance?" Ellen held her big empty hands in the air. "I knew I would fuck it up, so I put it all on you. Then you fucked it up, but I was the first fuck-up. First and last."

Connie leaned her head on Ellen's shoulder. "Shall we go for a walk?"

Ellen tipped her head to rest on Connie's. She waved her arm dismissively toward the window. "There's nothing out there but stores and traffic and people who care about the shoes you wear."

"Even here, we have a river and hills. We could go up to the park."

"All of it covered by people."

"The crowds are permeable. They'll let us pass."

Ellen sat up and looked at Connie with a doubtful expression. "Do I even know you? They're *people*, Connie, filled with ideas about everything, even the kind of jacket you wear." She went to lean against the window. "Think about all the folks we know on the mountain and how much trouble they are. They wouldn't even fill this building. And then there's that building," she pointed to a new apartment tower across the street, "and that building." Beyond, of course, building after building reared up, and beyond them, cranes constructed more. "If everyone wanted to leave at the same time, you'd have pandemonium."

"Where would we all want to go at once?" Connie asked, but honestly, the thought had occurred to her. She had a plan; she would get in the kayak.

"What about a power outage? One that lasted for a while." Ellen leaned out the balcony to see to the top of the neighboring building. "The elevators wouldn't work, and people would have to come down for water and food. Some of them wouldn't be able to walk back up. All the old and fat people would be homeless on the sidewalks, and they'd have to move into the homeless tents. The homeless people would probably be able to get up to the penthouses." Ellen clearly got some satisfaction from this idea. "That's why they invented Stairmasters," she said at last. "You can get exercise on any hill, but hills are not the problem. Stairs are what rich people need to master."

"A city is a fragile ecosystem." Connie lived on the fourth floor. She usually used the stairs, just to stay in practice. With care, her lemon tree might bear almost constantly, and she kept a small box of herbs and greens on the balcony. But until the apocalypse, she felt insulated by the people surrounding her. She was a drop in a strong current. In the mornings, people got up and filled the world with their business. In the evening they flowed back to their rooms. Connie waited at stoplights and surged with the others when the walk sign flashed.

"It's not so scary." Connie got her new shoes. They were bright white with silver and cushioning and a logo she could wear with confidence. She stuck her hands in the shoes and made them dance for Ellen's benefit. "Come on, I'll show you. You'll discover anonymity like you only dream about on the mountain."

57

Ellen came and walked with Connie most Saturday mornings, rain or shine. She grew bolder and more nimble as they threaded through the crowds along the river, so that even in the city Connie had to hustle to keep up, breathless as she told Ellen about the wetland work. The organization had focused on reclamation and advocacy, but with Connie there, education became increasingly important to their mission. Young people understood the urgency, and as bad as everyone felt about the whole situation, the problems would be their inheritance.

"How is the beaver at home?" From the center of the span of the Hawthorne Bridge, Connie watched the river sluice between its concrete banks. "What did the survey show?"

Ellen scowled. "I don't know. I never see Otto anymore. I don't think they did a survey this year."

The news did not particularly bother her. The surveys were for the children's benefit rather than the project's, and Connie had so many projects these days. She began to walk, looking down through the grating to the relentless water. "I thought Dolores would keep it going for sure. Is she okay? I could find volunteers if that's a problem."

Ellen scuffed her toe against the grating, as though looking for a rock to kick. "It's not that. Annabelle had some concerns."

"So what?" Annabelle had never been happy about the kids coming out. She accused them of feeding garbage to the horses through the fence when all they were doing was petting the horses' velvet noses and joking about the warm, grassy breath.

"I told you." Ellen scowled. "She moved Otto out of the tipi and into her house at the very first rain. The rest of us never see him anymore."

Connie told Ellen about the afternoon she stopped by with the calamine. She had never confessed to the afternoon under the oak.

"At least you tried." Ellen was mournful. "I guess it was inevitable. But don't worry." She poked Connie's shoulder. A little smile began to catch the corners of her mouth. "He's not even handsome anymore. You know how you used to overfeed the barn cats so they would be too lazy to catch birds? That's what Annabelle did to Otto." Ellen imitated by leaning back as she walked, pushing her gut ahead of her.

"Really?" Connie was never sure how much Ellen was embellishing.

"I'd tell you to come see for yourself, but he's never out. Annabelle has him working on bridle trails in between meals."

"No fair!" Connie objected. "He promised he'd make my house into an education center." But she was joking now. She knew it had been promised in jest.

"He still says he's going to. Then Annabelle starts to smile and nod and add, only add, mind you, that the house will be a tasting room, and it might not be good to mix the kids and alcohol. She thinks he should donate the money to some other educational endeavor." Ellen's eyes widened with an idea. "You should hit them up for money! Annabelle would pay a lot to buy her way out of that obligation."

It wasn't a bad idea. Connie's nonprofit had come up with a great curriculum for middle schoolers and had been talking about how to distribute it more broadly. Money would help.

"Want to get a crepe at the food cart?"

Ellen's face clouded. "It's too cold to stand in line to eat in a parking lot."

They had never done anything but come back to the apartment for grilled cheese sandwiches. From the condo, Ellen could contemplate the packed mass of humanity without having to rub shoulders.

58

One Sunday morning in November when the asphalt gleamed with a veneer of rain, Otto called and asked to visit. Connie hadn't seen him since he had taken her to the hospital, and his impending visit brought those confusing days back. She pushed the memory aside. He probably wanted to know more about the septic system or where the water lines were, and she focused on trying to remember the layout of the drainage field. She thought about his weight on top of her—his force, her desire—and she made herself recall the last time the septic tank was pumped instead. In the sheep barn, he had smelled of clean laundry and beer and another odor that was just him, an odor that she remembered acutely from when they lay together in the dirt beneath the oak. She could not describe the smell; the memory was visceral. And irrelevant. Perhaps he had questions about the well.

She snapped herself into rain gear and took the kayak out. Mist clung to the valley, and the glossy river dimpled as it received the rain. She drifted over dark water near the shore and rehearsed apologies for her inexplicable behavior. Their inadequacies begged elaboration and her imaginary conversations became increasingly complicated. When the harsh call of a heron ripped her from her reveries, she knew she was lost, but only for a moment. Upstream, downstream, east bank or west, this is the clarity of river life. She waited a moment, then nosed the kayak upstream. By the time she had put it away and shaken out her poncho, she simply hoped that time had faded the strangeness, and she and Otto could leave the past behind.

Parking was scarce in Connie's neighborhood. By the time she buzzed Otto in, he was thoroughly wet, an old felt hat squashed to his head.

"You look like a farmer!" She stepped aside to let him in the front hall.

"I feel like a farmer." He shook his legs and slipped out of his wet shoes. "There's something wrong with my back from sitting on the tractor, and a six by six fell against my shoulder yesterday. My arm is purple down to the elbow."

She didn't know how to talk to him. She hung his hat and coat on a peg where they dripped to the slate floor and led him into the dim living room. Even though a couple hours remained before sunset, passing headlights lit the puddles and the rain beaded a curtain around the balcony. Connie had turned on the gas fire, and the toothed flames glowed blue along the red and grey fake log.

"Remind me why I wanted to be a farmer." He sat heavily in a chair near the fire, a damp paper bag seeping onto his lap. He pulled a bottle out and brushed at the wet spot on his pants. Wadding the paper, he leaned forward to throw it in the fire, then realizing his mistake, set it on the table. He picked it up again and wiped the moisture from the wood with his sleeve.

"Otto." Connie extended her hand. He smiled up at her, chagrined, and gave her the bag. She threw it in the kitchen trash.

"You did good." He tipped his head to the room. "You've got the river right there." He spoke as though she had conjured the place herself out of nothing.

Connie felt a flash of irritation at his congratulatory tone. "Life is smaller and simpler here. It's easier to get things right."

He held the bottle out so she could see the label. "I brought you my favorite scotch. I've made a study of scotch," he laughed. "Still studying. I bring it as a housewarming and an apology."

She sat down and for a moment hid her face in her hands. "You're not the one who needs to apologize, Otto. I can't tell you how sorry I am."

He waited until she took the bottle. "I understand."

Connie set the scotch on the table. "I don't think I do."

"That little forest really mattered to you." He scratched his chin, watching her.

Again, irritation; that little forest had been big enough for rare flowers and an ancient yew.

Otto leaned forward, elbows on his knees. He looked older than when he'd first arrived on the mountain, his face tanned, his broad belly resting on his lap. "What you did was crazy-wrong."

"Nothing but trouble," Connie agreed.

Otto shook his head. "Not nothing." He held her gaze to make her listen. "You saved the oak grove and you probably added three days of life to the forest."

Connie laughed. "That's about it."

"It isn't nothing. Dylan tells me there are insects that only live for a day. You might have saved three generations."

It didn't really work like that, and his generosity made her uncomfortable. "You've seen Dylan?"

"I went up to Seattle last week and took him out to lunch. He told me about his comics class. That was nice of you."

"Let me show you." Connie took a small, framed poster from the wall. "He earned a commission." She handed the print to Otto. "A poster for my wetland organization. Look how professional it is!"

Dylan had drawn the scene with the detail characteristic of all his pictures; it was wild with life. Birds and bugs and bushes and beavers challenged the margins of the page. Hidden here and there, as though they were somehow underneath the action, children planted trees and pulled ivy and spied on pollywogs. Otto studied the poster, then he leaned it carefully against the wall and smiled at Connie. Connie told him how conscientiously Dylan had worked with the organization, minding specifications and meeting deadlines. Otto didn't respond, he kept smiling until Connie grew fidgety. She stood.

"I have a gift for you, too." She pulled the camera from the closet and set it in his lap "Your lost wildlife camera."

"I thought Dylan took it. It disappeared right after he'd been lurking around."

She told Otto about Dylan's video. "I thought I could have a secret look, but I was such a clod I ended up taking the camera. I'm sorry," she said formally. "It wasn't mine and I had no right."

Otto turned it over in his lap. "It's all erased?"

"It's all erased."

"We're starting over." He set the camera on the floor by his feet. The fire didn't crackle or shift. They watched the little flames rise steadily from the perforated pipe.

"After you moved, my life got very easy." He patted his belly and laughed. "I got the land cleared without any delays. Ended up moving in with Annabelle. You probably heard?"

"Ellen told me."

"Annabelle keeps a very comfortable home, but I don't know. Now she's organizing monthly cocktail parties to seed a committee to build trails all over the mountain. Not one person is talking about invasive species. We miss you."

"I'm pretty good here." Connie looked out the window to the weaving traffic and she realized she meant it. "I ride my bike and recycle. I do good work. I've made a few friends." She was growing new roots. She had thought it was too late. "You'll be happy; I'm getting better at being harmless in the world."

"Harmless." Otto wrinkled his brow and rubbed the skin between his eyes. "I'm not buying it. Harm. Benefit." He waved his arm, sweeping things away. "I've been thinking about Dylan and the forest. He wasn't suicidal until he started surveying."

"That wasn't the forest; that was our fault."

"You're wrong." Otto braced his hands on his knees and faced her squarely. "There's no real distinction. That forest lived and died only in the context of us."

Technically, he was correct. They were certainly responsible for its death. And its old-growth splendors survived as long as they did because Connie pulled the English ivy before it swallowed the calypso orchid. She rooted out the laurel and holly that would have choked the snowberries a decade ago. Should she have bothered? Would it have been better if there had been nothing left to grieve?

"So if Dylan had remained in the city, his heart wouldn't have been broken?" This question haunted Connie.

"Maybe. But if the forest broke Dylan's heart, it also woke him up. He has a future now, though it's a hard future." Otto studied his hands and rubbed one thumbnail, blackened from some accident. "I don't think it's possible to do things right. When we blast to break up the rocks for the vineyard, the whole mountain trembles. Each time I give thanks that you're not there to see it."

"What you're doing, it's not wrong." Connie spoke slowly, hoping he could hear her reassurance. It's like this: in a plague of locusts, we don't blame an individual bug. But she didn't tell him that. "Under the circumstances, that land was bound to sprout a vineyard."

Otto stretched his legs before the regulated fire. He was outsized in the small living room. Connie used to feel that way indoors. Now, her feet were always clean, always in shoes, walking smooth level pavement. "I know it's not wrong," he said, "but it's not right, either." He squeezed his eyes closed a moment before looking back to Connie. "You know, Dylan feels responsible for you."

Shame once more contracted within her. "He takes things on." She didn't know how to untie that knot. "Maybe I should stay away. Be a little more hands-off . . ."

"No." Otto leaned forward on his knees. He brought his face near hers and looked up from beneath his brows. "You're absolutely wrong. I think he's still pretty depressed."

Connie nodded. It worried her every day.

"But he won't hurt himself again because he doesn't want to hurt you. He thinks you need him."

"I do." Connie could feel tears start in her eyes, and she swallowed hard to keep them from spilling. "That's a big burden for a child."

"He's a young man," Otto said. "And burdens make us strong. He told me all about you, so I wouldn't be mad. He says you were not desperate because you were crazy; you went crazy because you were desperate. He says you're right to be desperate."

Desperation was exactly what Connie had tried to avoid. Every lesson plan she'd ever made, the neighborhood pamphlets, gardening, and husbandry, were walls constructed to keep desperation out.

"Pour us some of that scotch," Otto said. "If you don't mind."

She brought two glasses back from the kitchen and poured them each a couple fingers. He raised his glass toward the fire to look through the amber liquid. He took a mouthful and held it a moment before swallowing. "Honestly, I brought the scotch for me. Liquid courage. I was afraid you hated me. After I took you to the hospital, you never spoke to me again. Not one word."

"I never hated you." Connie had smelled of soap as she walked toward Otto's tipi bearing gifts. She flushed with embarrassment, so relieved that Annabelle had spared her the humiliation of offering her best towels, her calamine, and her sorry self.

"You made it plain you didn't want anything to do with me," Otto said. "You sent that text that you were going to stop by, but you didn't. You didn't even call me. You had that realtor call."

"Otto, I did stop by, but Annabelle popped out just then to get you a glass of water. I didn't want to disturb you two."

"You should have come in. She would have had to turn off Harry Potter." He groaned and closed his eyes a moment. "God, you must think I'm an opportunist. When I found you, I should have taken you straight to the hospital."

"I stopped you."

"You were delirious. Actually delirious." He turned his hands and let his empty palms rest on his thighs. "At the time, it seemed like some kind of weird dream. But later . . . it was just wrong."

Remorse rose again, but Connie swallowed it. She spoke as simply and honestly as she could manage. "I think I would have died if you had denied me." She didn't have the words to explain the heat and weight of his body over hers. The ferocity of desire, the anger even, reached something in her that kindness never could have reached. "Afterwards, I didn't call because I didn't want to impose. Being crazy and all. Please forgive me."

Otto reached out and took both her hands. Outside, the rain came down harder. "I thought you would never speak to me again. Then Annabelle showed up with her dinners and her steroid cream. I followed her like some kind of sleepwalker. But I woke up.

Probably we should all be desperate. I left Annabelle's and I live alone again. I've been so sorry."

Connie twisted her fingers free. "There's nothing to blame you for. I know you felt isolated."

He laughed. "Not as isolated as I am now. Annabelle doesn't even invite me to the cocktail parties. I miss you."

"What do you miss most? My neighborly warmth or the vandalism?"

"Yep," Otto nodded. "The whole package."

The silent flames burned along the log that never crumbled or cracked. A rime of crusty grey overlaid the glowing embers, but the ash never grew. It never mounted and spilled.

"You really forgive me, Otto?" A part of Connie cringed at the supplication, but she needed to know. To think that others might rise from the messes she made and take her hands was more than she had ever hoped for.

"We're all complicit." Otto looked at her with kindness. "I forgive you, Connie. I'm hoping you will forgive me."

She reached out and squeezed his hand briefly. Outside the window, traffic flowed over the bridge like illuminated circulation. A stream of white flowed toward them; a stream of red, away. When night came, the city closed around the condo, and her little suite of rooms became her whole world. But from the outside, Connie's apartment was only one light among thousands of lights.

"So we're starting fresh." Otto leaned toward her. "I'm afraid you're going to say no, so just listen. You remember I said if I won the bet, I would make the Sweet Farm for Sustainable Ag? Well, I lost my bet, but Dylan got me thinking about education. I've been talking to Dolores from Soil and Water about coordinating nature classes. Day camps for urban kids like Dylan. Like I was too. I went to Seattle to talk to Dylan about hiring him this summer for the project. He's interested. We all think you'd be the best person to direct this." Otto placed his fingers lightly over her lips. "Don't answer yet." He held her gaze, then lowered his hand to rest on her thigh. He squeezed briefly. His grip was strong, almost painful. Then he stood. "It's time for me to go."

Connie, flustered, stood too. She followed him to the door and waited as he put on his coat and squashed the still damp hat to his head.

"I should make you dinner." She was suddenly aware that she had offered him nothing. "But I don't really have anything," she said with confusion. "I could take you out? There's a Thai place on the corner?"

Otto turned. A big smile brightened his face. "Next Thursday?" he said. "Only it's my treat, for the bet, since you didn't want my tipi."

Connie followed him out the door. "I'll walk you to your car."

"It's raining!"

But it wasn't raining hard. Cars amplified the sound of water as they cut through the streets, displacing and rearranging the currents that gathered toward the storm drains and rushed to the river to flow to the ocean. A warm wind blew from the south. Connie didn't even bother zipping her jacket. From the condo, the night had seemed inhospitable, but it was a gentle rain, and the sidewalks were soft with fallen leaves.

END

ABOUT THE AUTHOR

Jane Carlsen lives with her husband among the trees in Portland, Oregon.

ABOUT THE PRESS

Unsolicited Press is based out of Portland, Oregon and focuses on the works of the unsung and underrepresented. As a womxn–owned, all–volunteer small publisher that doesn't worry about profits as much as championing exceptional literature, we have the privilege of partnering with authors skirting the fringes of the lit world. We've worked with emerging and award–winning authors such as Amy Shimshon-Santo, Elisa Carlsen, Sommer Schafer, and Laura Gaddis/

Learn more at Unsolicitedpress.com. Find us on Twitter and Instagram @UnsolicitedP.

www.ingramcontent.com/pod-product-compliance
Lightning Source LLC
Chambersburg PA
CBHW061119310726
48974CB00002B/606